EACH
OUR OWN
DEVIL

Cover designed by Vanessa Mendozzi Design © 2017

Book interior designed by Q Book Editing Services © 2017

Edited by Q Book Editing Services.

Printed and Bound by Createspace, Inc.

ISBN 978-0-9812429-4-1

Printed in the United States of America.

EACH OUR OWN DEVIL

By

JOEL BAIN

DUMPLE MEADOWS PUBLISHING
VANCOUVER, CANADA

"WE ARE EACH OUR OWN DEVIL,
AND WE MAKE THIS WORLD OUR HELL."
- OSCAR WILDE

CUBA

I

Never had a couple looked so out of place. Blonde hair and blue eyes were rare in Havana as was the tongue of Swedes. The hot Caribbean sun scorched their pale skin, but they were too enthused to complain. The island nation of Cuba welcomed them with a greeting sign in English, but they didn't know it. They spoke only a few words of English, and even less of Spanish. They looked as lost as could be. If it were not for their enthusiasm, they might have looked isolated waiting for a taxicab by the airport roadside curb. The woman glowed in her loose-fitting bright blue sundress, disguising her pregnant belly.

Her partner hailed a cab to take them to their resort hotel. He stood lanky but had soft and charming features, which played a role in drawing her to him. He tried his best to appear confident in front of his wife.

As the cab approached, he grasped her hand and

gave it a weak squeeze. The cab driver jumped out and scooped their luggage, placing it in the rear trunk. The husband helped his expectant wife into the back seat and followed her in.

When the driver returned, he attempted to communicate with them, but it was a fruitless effort. The husband flashed a hopeful grin and gave a hand-written note with their destination. The driver recognized the address and did his best to convey his understanding to the couple. They were on their way, much to their relief.

Later that evening within a gated seaside resort, the couple sat down for dinner. They shared a brief kiss just before beginning their meal. Within minutes, the woman's water broke. A flash of embarrassment came over her, but she became much more concerned about another fact: their child had chosen that moment to be born. Her husband shouted in broken English for a medic. He comforted his hysterical wife.

An ambulance shuttled them to a hospital outside the resort. The ride was rough, but the husband and wife clung each other's hands. When they arrived, the paramedics ushered the parents into the delivery ward. Again, they ran into the language barrier, as the doctors spoke frantically in Spanish. The couple's inability to communicate traumatized them, but after a hard, quick labor that involved many attempts at conveying instructions through body language, a child was born.

The mother spent several days in the hospital recovering from the premature delivery as did the newborn boy. Complications from the premature birth required him to stay beyond the mother's discharge from the hospital. The couple's romantic getaway to Cuba became consumed with visits to the hospital, as their appetite for anything else had dissipated.

After a week, the couple took the child and the birth certificate produced for them back to the resort. The young couple embraced their new roles as mother and father. The rest of their vacation passed almost exclusively within their hotel room. The mother nursed her son as her husband gazed upon the child. They named him Heinrich in honor of his mother's father, who had died in the Second World War.

Once their ten-day vacation ran its course, they checked out of the resort and caught a cab to the airport to return home with their newborn son. They checked their bags and passed security, but customs stopped them. The officials demanded papers for the infant. The couple had none but the Cuban birth certificate provided to them.

Communication was difficult due to the language barrier again, but the officials clarified that the child couldn't leave the country. The child was born on sovereign Cuban soil and he was a Cuban national without the proper paperwork to leave the island nation. Neither did the parents have any documentation of the child's Swedish citizenship.

The parents returned to the resort and sought guidance from their national embassy in Havana. Little was accomplished though, as the father lacked the necessary documentation to register the child's foreign birth.

Several days later, the Cuban authorities came knocking on their door. Their tourist visas had expired. Escorting them to the airport again, the authorities checked the parents into their flight and ushered them through security. When it came to the customs officials, against the parents' will, the child was taken from them. The officials re-iterated that the child didn't have the proper permission to leave the country. The parents were required to leave due to their expired visas. The father attempted to bribe the officials. He offered their wallets, their wedding rings, and any jewelry they had on them, but the officials were unswayed and shuffled the child away.

The mother became so hysterical in seeing her son taken away from her that it required four male officials to restrain her. With their hands on her, the father responded with violent force. An official knocked him unconscious in response. They carried the father onto the plane. The officials dragged the mother to her seat and waited with her until the plane took flight. Her husband slumped unconscious beside her and bore a bandage applied to his head.

When the time came to shut the plane door, a customs official helped a medic from the airport administer a sedative to the mother; they gagged the woman to not disturb the other air travelers. The door was shut, and the plane took off for Sweden, leaving the child in the care of the Cuban customs officials.

II

An orphanage just outside Havana received custody of the boy. Two single women, who had never married or had children of their own, ran the care facility. The government gave them the job through which they earned their weekly allotment.

The orphanage operated in a poor state of disrepair with pipes leaking and insects making homes in the warm, damp wall linings. Food was sparse for the twenty orphans living there, but the women did their best to scrounge more food. Most of the orphans were between the ages of three and five.

Despite being an infant, the boy was passed over quite a few times whenever potential parents came to the orphanage. While Heinrich wasn't an outright ugly child, his appearance left much to be desired. His feedings lacked nutrition as he no longer received his mother's breast milk. He lay in his crib and competed for attention from the women caring for the many children. His cries went unanswered, and he only ate when the women had time to tend to him. The overworked women couldn't care for all the children, so most nights the young boy cried himself to sleep and without a feeding.

Months went by with twenty-six sets of would-be parents passing him over with no intention of adopting him. And while he may not have been of the age to comprehend what occurred, being overlooked and neglected affected the young infant.

When he neared his first birthday, a family came into the orphanage. They brought with them a four-year-old son, Jose. The family scanned the children with no age in mind. They discovered Heinrich. He looked pleasant enough to the mother with his dark blue eyes nestled in his pale face and a tuft of blonde hair on his scalp.

The parents talked it over while their child seemed indifferent about their discussion and looked bored. They spoke with the caretakers and asked questions about Heinrich. The women shared the nature of the boy's arrival to the orphanage, but regardless the parents agreed to adopt the child. They filled out the proper paperwork and within an hour, they left with Heinrich in their possession. The family gave him their surname, Juarez. Heinrich Juarez.

Heinrich found the sunlight uncomfortable as he rarely went outside the orphanage in his first year. They carried him through the streets, bundled in cloth, and while Heinrich wasn't cognizant of what he saw, the entire world around him made the boy curious, yet unsettled.

When they arrived at home, they set up a crib in Jose's room. The house stood in better shape than the orphanage he had called home; not as many insects, but rodents were visible from time to time. The parents fed him powdered milk formula as much as they could afford, but this was limited as the father earned little money. Their stipend from the government would increase by adopting Heinrich as the mother was the primary caregiver to the children and stayed at home.

The first months traumatized Heinrich. Resettling from his earlier bed required an adjustment. Many unfamiliar sounds accompanied his first nights in his new room, which terrified the boy and induced him to tears. Jose resented Heinrich for preventing him from finding sleep. He complained to his mother about how Heinrich cried until all hours of the night. The parents had little they could do as their apartment only had two bedrooms, and they couldn't afford to alter the boys' arrangements.

III

As the years passed, Jose grew to hate his younger adopted brother. The boys never played together, or if they did, it resulted in a physical altercation in which the older and much larger boy dominated his puny younger brother. Jose was malicious toward Heinrich and cared little for the nuisance that had invaded his home.

The parents intervened from time to time in the spats between their boys, but they had adopted the mindset that the children ought to work out their differences on their own. They didn't think it was the parents' responsibility to police the children. The boys needed to learn how to deal with conflict.

As the boys grew, Jose picked on Heinrich more, whether it be tripping him or causing mischief against him. He was an outright naughty boy toward Heinrich, but always convinced his parents it was the younger's fault. Heinrich avoided any interaction with Jose for fear of being bullied or receiving the blame.

When Heinrich started school, the other children intimidated him. He was different from them; they made that clear to him. He struggled to make friends and often played on the field's edge alone. He amused himself with the dirt while other boys played soccer or baseball.

Jose became a talented ballplayer while Heinrich was anything but since he wasn't athletically inclined. His small stature didn't bode well for such physical activities. Him tiring whenever he played with the other boys made it worse for him. The kids picked him last whenever divvying up their sports team, so he gave up bothering to be a part of the other boys' sporting matches.

In his classes, Heinrich wasn't gifted academically either. He struggled with mathematics and he had poor penmanship. His teacher stopped calling on him. He was too shy to produce an answer. He feared being incorrect and being made fun of further by his classmates. By his second year in school, the other children bullied him at least twice daily, if not more. He secluded himself, seeking to be alone in his imagination.

He failed his second year of school and stayed back another year. The children in the school decided Heinrich was stupid. Jose meanwhile earned praise as a child prodigy in baseball despite still being yet a young boy. As the years passed, Jose's celebrity grew, while Heinrich struggled with each year of school. The administration held Heinrich back more until he was much older than any of his other classmates.

When boys Heinrich's age became interested in girls,

he attempted to get the attention of his female class-mates. The girls fled from him and his schoolboy advances as he was much older than them. He hadn't mentally developed as fast as his peers, which only reinforced to them that he was witless. His father gave him stern lectures for being such a poor student and for embarrassing the family by his inability to pass his courses.

One day on his way to school, several bigger boys, one of which was Jose, confronted him. They picked on him and teased him for being a moron, for being terrible at sports, and for not having a girlfriend. They pushed and kicked him, hoping to egg him on to respond. He only accepted their abuse, which led to them getting more violent as they grew frustrated with his apathy. Jose instigated the others to beat Heinrich and teach him a lesson for not standing up for himself. They kicked him to the ground, giving him a significant number of bruises and cuts. When older men across the street shouted at the boys, the bullies left Heinrich alone.

Before the men could tend to him, Heinrich ran off sobbing from the beating he had received. As he stumbled toward home, he ended up before the footsteps of a Catholic parish. He spotted a cross atop the roof. Tears welled up in his eyes again, as he cast himself on the steps, praying to Jesus that the bullying stop. His sobs grew in strength and passersby overheard him shouting by the name of Jesus.

When he had caused a disturbance, a priest chased him away from the church footsteps, scolding Heinrich for losing control of himself. The priest threatened

Heinrich with a licking if he didn't quiet down. He fled the priest's hands and ran back to his home.

When he arrived, nobody else was home. Heinrich tended to his wounds, washed himself, and splashed cool water on the bruises throughout his body. He retreated to his room and lay in his bed. He cried until he fell asleep.

As the years passed, Heinrich became more withdrawn, even distancing himself from his parents, who were busy providing a life for their sons. He struggled with each assignment given to him in school, leading the school administration to expel him. His teacher had held him back so many times that the administration didn't think Heinrich merited the financial cost to continue educating him. Other boys and girls put the minimal funds to better use. It drew his humiliated father's ire that his son, albeit adopted, had flunked out of school. His father told Heinrich that if he was at least expelled because he got into trouble that might be one thing, but as he wasn't, it was unfathomable. Heinrich remembered these words.

His parents sent him to scrounge around the city for items they might re-sell at the neighborhood flea market. He stole nothing, but perused through the things of which others had disposed. His fellow Cubans had little to spare, so he gathered only a few items, which made him feel like all the more a failure.

Jose enjoyed local fame due to his growth as a ballplayer. He developed a respectable arm and made waves as Cuba's next great hope in baseball as a pitcher. Jose dreamed of one day becoming a professional baseball player in America; the allure of wealth and fame appealed to him. Both Jose and Heinrich were exposed to the covert propaganda dropped from America, showing the promise of the American Dream.

Heinrich measured himself as nothing but a failure compared to his praised brother, who received their parents' worship. Heinrich experienced little adoration. He knew that he didn't make his parents proud.

Joy and happiness filled only one day of the year for Heinrich, his birthday. When his eighteenth birthday neared, he dreamed of the big day. His mother promised to make him his favorite cake while his father pledged to bring him home a present. Even Jose laid off of picking on Heinrich around his birthday. In the days that led up, Heinrich fantasized over what gift his father might bring for him. Thinking about the tantalizing cake made him even more excited. He spent most of the days before his birthday inside as the weather didn't cooperate.

When the day came, the weather became more unsettled, and the government declared a storm warning. The winds overpowered, and many people stayed inside rather than working; Heinrich's father spent the day at home. Weather postponed Jose's ball game, so he stayed home too.

The weather grew worse. Heinrich, Jose, and their father worked together to ensure that they readied their house for the coming storm. They boarded up the windows and brought in everything that might fall victim to the wind. The evening of his birthday, they hunkered down inside and waited out the storm. The winds grew in fierceness and battered the sides of their home. Rain poured down, causing leaks to develop within the roof. They placed pots, cups, and bowls under each of them, but as the storm worsened, they soon ran out of containers, and rainwater dribbled everywhere. The howling winds were unnerving, and the weather became even more haunting when the electricity cut out and sent them into darkness. The rain beat down on their home, sounding like hail on the rooftop while the wind eliminated almost every other sound.

A snapping noise came from the ceiling. Water gushed through the roof, flooding their home. The family scrambled in a panic to protect their belongings. Heinrich opened the front door, judging it beneficial to let the water escape, but as he did, powerful winds overcame him. The wind threw Heinrich outside and to the ground. Jose shouted at him to shut the door, but Heinrich struggled to stand. Seconds later, such a powerful gust of wind battered the home that it knocked down their flimsy house.

In terror, Heinrich found the strength to pick himself up. He ran toward the collapsed home, seeking to save his family members trapped inside. He shoved aside the crumpled roof. He detected no screams, but neither was he able to stand for long as objects flew and smacked into him. He shielded his face with one hand, while with the other, he lifted away the pieces.

The rain pounded on his skin and drenched him with the precipitation. The winds knocked him to the ground, but he picked himself right back up. This pattern repeated and exhausted Heinrich. He retreated from the beating he received from the flying debris.

Across the street, he found a nook of shelter under a neighbor's archway. He clung to the doorpost. The rain caused him to shiver while he contemplated the wreckage that was his home. The storm pounded on for hours, but Heinrich sat there waiting it out. He could do little in the midst of the storm's fury.

The next morning came after Heinrich had passed out against the door frame. The clouds above were still ominous when he awoke, but the rain had stopped. He looked first to his collapsed home. Mud and broken brush covered the house. When he rose, pain covered his entire body. He had received cuts and scrapes the night beforehand, most of which had scabbed up. He restarted his excavation effort. Heinrich shouted his family members' names hoping to alert them.

Jose called out to him. They called back and forth to each other many times until Heinrich was better able to locate his sibling. He threw debris aside until he uncovered Jose, whose shoulder looked displaced. Heinrich tried to pull his adopted brother out, but he drew pained screams from the elder sibling. Jose instructed him what to move so he might get out. He drew Jose out of the rubble, and beyond his shoulder and a few cuts and bruises, Jose looked okay.

The two brothers called to their parents. They heard nothing. They moved debris for a sign of them. Their voices both became hoarse from shouting their parents' names. Jose found the first sign of their mother, drawing Heinrich over to help. They threw the pieces of their home aside though Heinrich's brother struggled with his mangled shoulder. Their mother was unresponsive and did not move. They checked her throat for a pulse, but sensed none. They checked for breathing, but no respiration.

Jose collapsed to the ground and teared up at the realization that his mother was dead. Heinrich struggled to come to grips with reality, so he kept searching for even the slimmest hope she was alive. Jose shouted at him that he was wasting his time. But as Heinrich kept trying, he noticed their father under her in the rubble. Jose was too distraught to help, but Heinrich reached down and called to his father. He too was unresponsive. Heinrich shouted for help from his brother, but no aid came. He reached down to confirm if their father was alive, but just like their mother, no pulse.

Heinrich fell to the ground next to his sibling, realizing like Jose that their mother and father were, in fact, dead. Tears welled up in Heinrich's eyes as he placed his head in his hands. Jose stopped sobbing. He stared at his dead mother.

Heinrich reached out to his brother to console him, but Jose rebuffed him. He shouted at him how it was Heinrich's fault, and that if he didn't open the front door, maybe their home wouldn't have been knocked down.

Heinrich didn't know what to say. Jose blamed him and cast judgment for how he had killed their parents. He didn't stop there. Jose wanted nothing to do with him. He said that if he ever saw Heinrich again, he would kill him. He beat on Heinrich with a thick wooden shaft. Heinrich curled in defense while Jose shouted at him to leave and never come back.

Heinrich begged his brother to stop, but Jose kicked

him all the harder. Jose clubbed Heinrich one last time across the cheek, drawing blood. He relented and spun away from his brother. Heinrich clutched his face in pain. His hand was covered in blood. Jose declared that he would never see Heinrich again as he was leaving Cuba for America. He didn't know how, but he was finished with the island nation. Nothing kept him in Cuba.

Heinrich peered at Jose in fear. His elder brother, while clutching his shoulder, repeated that he would kill Heinrich if he tried to find him. If Heinrich knew what was best for him, he ought to act as if he never knew Jose. The older brother turned his back on Heinrich and left the site of their parents' death. Once Jose was out of sight, hatred replaced the fear of Jose in Heinrich's heart. While Heinrich was still yet grieving, he had been abandoned yet again. He made a promise to himself: if ever he saw his adopted brother again, it would be Jose who would wish he had never known Heinrich. He would kill Jose without hesitation.

IV

In the days following what the government later declared was a hurricane, Jose lived up to his promise, and Heinrich never saw him again. Heinrich received seventeen stitches on his cheek, creating a hideous, unfortunate scar from Jose's beating.

The government allotted Heinrich a new home since it was his eighteenth birthday and that earned him the right to have a place of his own. He took possession of a shoddy shack in the slums outside Havana. And since he was no longer a student but an adult, he received a job. The government assigned him to work in an anvil factory to perform menial cleaning tasks that demanded little of him.

His boss, a foreman named Juan, was an unpleasant fellow. He drew pleasure in humiliating Heinrich in front of the other co-workers. Juan gave him the most horrid work to do and berated Heinrich for his inability to accomplish the most basic of tasks. The foreman told Heinrich with great frequency how lazy and wimpy he was. What made matters worse was that his co-workers were not fond of him, and they blamed him for their shortcomings. For Heinrich, it differed little from his school experience, since his co-workers picked on him and bullied him into doing their jobs.

One day after returning home from work, Heinrich was busy opening a can of tuna for dinner. His meals were about as extravagant; only a marginal step down from what he ate with his adopted family. As he ate away at the can, a stray dog let itself into his shack. He assumed that it was wild, but the dog struck him as pleasant enough. Heinrich offered it his tuna since it was a thin, mangy mutt. It ate the tuna and wandered back out of the shack. He smiled and wished other humans might be as pleasant as the dog.

The next day at work, Heinrich's foreman lectured him again, though this time for having left the factory floor dirty and unswept. Heinrich promised to not let it happen again, but his foreman doubted his ability to keep his word. The foreman pointed out the previous times that Heinrich had failed to live up to the minimal job expectations. In Heinrich's mind, he tried hard at work, but it was never good enough for his foreman. He left work humiliated.

The one positive that day: it was payday, so he received his allotment. To cheer himself up, he stopped by a food cart to buy a few fruits to eat at home. A lovely young lady watched over the fruit wagon. Heinrich found her easy on the eyes. He asked for an apple and two bananas. She smiled and handed them over to him, cringing at the sight of his facial scar. She asked for the corresponding money. He gave it to her, but stared at her, unsure of how to ask a girl out, as he didn't have a track record of success. She felt uncomfortable and asked if he needed anything else. He blurted something about how much her company would be, which offended the young lady.

Heinrich came to realize the manner in which he had misspoke. He apologized that he didn't mean to proposition her as a prostitute but wanted to ask her out. She refused and asked him to leave. Heinrich apologized again, but she only repeated her request that he leave.

Heinrich returned to his shack dejected, and yet again, humiliated by his gaffe. He sat down on his shack's dirt floor and contemplated his rather sparse home. He sighed and nabbed a bite from his apple, bringing him comfort.

Without Heinrich noticing, the stray dog had let itself into Heinrich's shack again. The dog gazed at him, as if requesting a piece of the apple. He smiled and took a bite of the apple, handing it to the dog. It ate the apple and asked for another piece. Heinrich obliged and flicked it over to the dog who ate it and left on its way.

Weeks later after work one day, Heinrich wandered the streets of Havana after being humiliated yet again by his foreman, though this time for being two minutes late for work. Heinrich paid no attention to where he went, but meandered around not wanting to return to his depressing shack. Heinrich passed through the alleyways and streets to the point that he no longer remembered where he was.

A luminous gate drew him to the end of one street. He had never been there before. He marched down to see why such a radiant gate existed there.

As he approached, he picked up the sound of the ocean. When he reached the gate, he found before him a luxurious resort with a beautiful, clean pool, overlooking the sea. The sun shone down upon him and those within the resort. Little did he know it was the same seaside resort at which his parents had vacationed.

Poolside, the most beautiful woman lay on a beach chair in a bikini that showed off her generous curves. Heinrich dreamed of being in the company of such a gorgeous woman, let alone having her attention. He envied other men for being able to talk to women. He reconsidered all the little girls in elementary school who had run whenever he talked to them. But as an adult male, he wasn't only interested in the company of a woman. He wanted to kiss one.

Heinrich knew little about sexuality, even if his adopted father had spoken to him about it and how it was natural for a man to one day desire a woman. Heinrich, recalling those conversations with his father, finally understood what he had meant. He lusted after the woman by the pool. A server approached her, carrying a drink for her. He studied every move of her body as she sat up. He pressed his face closer toward the gate.

He smelled the scents of the kitchen pouring out from within the resort. Guests enjoyed finer food than he had ever eaten in his entire life. They all dressed better than he could fathom for himself. He examined his tattered clothing. He felt less of a man.

A woman as beautiful as the one poolside would pay no attention to him. Heinrich didn't have the wealth to afford such a lifestyle. He had no hope of ever advancing in his work at the anvil factory. He even inspected his shoes and noticed how scuffed they were with the holes in them exposing his feet. Heinrich went to turn and leave, but snatched one last glance at the stunning woman.

As he pressed his face against the gate, a security guard at the resort noticed him and shouted at him to get back. Heinrich backed away from the fence as the guard ran toward the gate. The guard blew his whistle, alerting the other compound guards. Before Heinrich could even think of running away, guards outside the resort apprehended him. The guards called the police, and the authorities seized Heinrich. They gave him a stern lecture and told him never to return. If he did, he would be charged with trespassing. As it was, they would keep their eye on him to make sure he never made such a mistake again.

Heinrich returned to his shack more depressed. He flopped onto his uncomfortable bed. He had no appetite to eat the food he had since it didn't compare to that which he saw at the resort. His food dissuaded him from eating altogether, thus he went to sleep on an empty stomach.

The next morning, Heinrich awoke and lay in his bed for hours. He wasn't motivated to start his day; let alone go to work. He rose and opened another can of tuna. Heinrich ate half of it but he wasn't hungry for the rest, even if his stomach growled at him. He got dressed for work; he was oblivious about the time.

He strolled to work noticing nothing about those he passed in the streets. Heinrich had no purpose or happiness in his life. When he arrived at his workplace, the other co-workers were hard at work. When they recognized him, they shot him dirty glares. Heinrich checked the clock. He was two hours late for work.

His foreman approached him with a face of fury when Heinrich realized his tardiness. The foreman screamed and shoved him to the ground. He shouted that he didn't take well to being disrespected. He grabbed hold of Heinrich's shirt collar and pulled him from the ground. His foreman dragged him to the factory entrance as the other workers watched. He threw Heinrich off the property and told him never to come back again unless he wanted a worse licking. The foreman said he was firing him once and for all for being late two days in a row.

Covered in dust, Heinrich stared in shock as his foreman stood over him. He was more afraid what the foreman might do next. The foreman spat on him, turned his back and stomped away. He commanded the others to get back to work, otherwise they would be without a job too.

Heinrich rose and didn't even bother dusting off. He teared up at being rejected yet again. He ended up at his shack and threw himself onto his bed. Heinrich pictured his deceased parents and how ashamed they would have been if they saw him. His heart broke as he pondered his birth parents who abandoned him. Why didn't they want him?

Heinrich never amounted to anything, and he could

only ever dream of the luxuries of the resort he had discovered. He fantasized about the loving embrace of a woman, but he didn't believe he would ever experience such a luxury. He scowled at his shack. He was too embarrassed to ever show a woman his home. Heinrich sobbed at the hopelessness of his life.

When he finished sobbing, he opened another can of tuna to eat. He hadn't disposed of his earlier half-eaten can, but by that point in time, flies had made the old can their new home. The tuna lacked flavor and tasted bland. He ate it as he had nothing else.

After a few bites, a rustle came at the door. The stray dog let itself inside. It drew a smile from Heinrich, having never been happier to see the dog. He threw the dog some tuna, which it accepted. The dog asked for more, so Heinrich handed it over. He reached out to pet the dog, but the stray mutt growled, taking a defensive posture toward Heinrich. He tried to reassure the dog and gave it a chance to sniff him by reaching out his hand. The dog instead bit Heinrich's hand, causing him to recoil and drop the tuna. The dog barked at him, grabbed the remaining can of tuna on the floor, and stormed out of the shack.

Heinrich felt such intense pain in his chest, drawing out the heaviest of sobs he had ever experienced. He didn't even sense the pain from the dog bite. He dwelled on the emotional trauma of what transpired. He extracted what little money he had in his coin collection and left his shack.

The evening set in and dark clouds formed above. Heinrich headed to the seediest part of town he knew, and there, he searched for a woman. He passed several, standing on the street corners in varying states of undress. He found a woman that pleased his eye. Heinrich approached her and handed her the money while attempting to thrust himself upon her. She rebuffed his advances and pushed him away, so she could first look at how much money he gave her. She threw the money to the ground and told him it wasn't enough.

Heinrich begged, saying he had never experienced a woman's affection and that he was desperate. He got on his knees and pleaded with her to have pity on him. He cried again, taking her hand with his, but the woman kicked at him to let go. She screamed and drew other women's attention, and perhaps her pimp nearby.

Heinrich checked to see if anyone came, but while he wasn't looking at her, the woman delivered a swift kick to his face, knocking him to the ground. He clutched his jaw in pain as the woman ran away. The facial pain reminded him of Jose's rejection.

Heinrich chased and screamed at her to stop. He caught up to the prostitute. He tackled her and flipped her over on the ground. He tried to kiss and grope her, but she smacked his face, causing him to recoil. When he looked at her again, she spat in his face. Her saliva landed in his eye, obscuring his vision. He drew his hand to his eyes, and she planted her knee to his groin. The kick knocked him off the woman. He curled into a ball and gasped in pain while the prostitute scampered off and screamed for help.

Heinrich crawled onto his knees, though he struggled to breathe. He panicked for fear that the girl's pimp might find him, but then realized he didn't care. Heinrich had received a beating before, and it didn't matter if someone else beat his face in, since no woman had ever found him attractive. He already had a hideous scar. Instead of running, Heinrich lodged himself against the side of the building next to him until he regained his strength. No pimp came by, nor did anyone cause him any trouble. The other prostitutes moved away from him.

Heinrich slumped there sensing his life had little value as no one scolded him for what he had done. He knew it was wrong to attack a woman. If she hadn't beaten him off, he would have regretted what he had intended to do. Heinrich felt even more pathetic knowing a helpless, drug-addicted woman had beaten him.

When he could stand, he rose. As he hustled toward his home, he cried, but he didn't even care if anyone saw him. He passed several streets but didn't feel he came any closer to his destination.

A man approached him and asked him if he had any interest in his product. Heinrich glanced up at him, trying to suggest that he wasn't interested. The man offered marijuana.

A thought came to Heinrich's mind. He asked the drug dealer if he had any poison. The dealer was surprised but he knew someone. He told Heinrich to wait and that he would return. The dealer came back with a small clear vial. Heinrich asked the price and the dealer told him. Heinrich led the dealer back to where the prostitute had thrown his money, and he collected the coins left undisturbed. The dealer counted the coins and despite them being short, he agreed to sell the vial to Heinrich.

Heinrich grabbed the bottle without saying thank

you or goodbye. He went on his way. The dealer inspected the money in his hand and examined Heinrich before going about his business patrols for more potential customers.

Heinrich arrived home at his shack. He looked absent of any emotion but was determined to do what he had set his mind to completing. He flopped onto a rickety chair in his shack. Heinrich eyeballed the vial of poison in his hand. A crudely drawn skull and crossbones sticker covered the exterior. He stared at it before unscrewing the lid. He held the opened bottle and lifted it to his mouth, but not quite to his lips.

Heinrich took a deep breath and consumed the contents of the vial in its entirety. Its taste was wretched and almost induced him to vomit, but he forced himself to swallow it. He sank into his chair and waited for something to happen. He expected something immediate but felt nothing.

Heinrich wondered if the drug dealer had cheated him, but a sharp pain started to grow in his stomach. His breathing became labored as he gasped for air. Hot sweats covered his body as he became warm and cold at the same time. A heaviness came over his chest. He grabbed at his torso, but it did nothing to bring relief. He wheezed for air as his throat closed up on him.

Heinrich tried to scream for help, but no sound came from his lips. A hideous and disturbing choke came from his throat. He panicked and leaned farther back, causing his chair to fall backward and take him with it. He bumped his head on the ground, but it didn't cause him to pass out. His lungs stopped functioning and his vision went blurry. The last sight he saw was the bare light bulb hanging from the ceiling of his shack. It flickered, and it all went black for him.

INFERNO

V

Heinrich awoke marching in a single-file line shrouded in darkness. When he had started marching, let alone standing, he had no idea. In front of him rose a fortress of blazing light, shining brighter than the sun at its highest point. He shielded his eyes while trying to better decipher what stood before him. Multiple marching lines all proceeded toward the fortress's almost hidden entrance. As they got closer, a few in the lineup offered up their positions for others to go ahead of them. These individuals stood rigid while shaking with utter fear and trembling.

All around the marching masses were towering beings, whose figures were difficult to discern due to the same blistering light that shone from them. They supervised the lines to ensure order. The towering figures stomped their ground-shaking feet to silence the panic of those who came closer. Something about them demanded respect, though they showed no demonstration of violence, nor did they need to make an example of any who dared to forgo orderliness.

Heinrich tapped the shoulder of the individual in front of him. "Where am I?" he asked.

"Hell if I know," replied the person.

The mass marched forward. Another towering figure directed different lines to pass through the entrance to the fortress one at a time. The figure stopped the line and let another line go in its place. Above the main gate, a sign read in several tongues, "Ye Who Shall Pass Beyond These Gates Shall Find No Return From The Great Abyss."

The figure guided the flow. The pace slowed down as Heinrich approached nearer to the fortress. With time, his lineup got through. He entered, revealing a radiant city. It looked spotless despite the crowds. More beings stood guarding the streets of the town as the orderly crowd pressed forward.

The lineup came to a stop in front of a foreboding courthouse. It took its place in the midst of a city square though the streets were vacant except for the figures and those being instructed to wait. No life lived in this city. No one entered through the courthouse's grand entrance. Instead, instructions came for the crowd to enter a holding space to the right of the courthouse. A wooden gate with a small opening allowed a single-file line through it. Guards stood stationed by the door and on top of the wooden gate. They held no weapons in their hands, but Heinrich knew better than to try anything silly.

The guards directed Heinrich's line through the

imposing wooden gate. He studied the guards above. They showed no emotion, neither anger nor joy.

Once inside the cordoned off area, all sat on benches or wherever they could until receiving further instructions. Under no circumstances were they to leave the holding space. Heinrich surveyed for a place to sit, but everyone else had claimed the seats, so he stood.

A few souls quivered in fear as they reclined while others shed tears due to the uncertainty before them. Older individuals with grayed hair and aged skin were at complete peace with what was before them. They showed no fear or despair but looked ready for this moment. Heinrich didn't know what to feel, but he didn't seem concerned about what may befall him wherever he went next.

A man approached Heinrich. "Good sir," he said. "Take my place in the lineup. If they ask for your name, tell them you are Joseph."

"Why?" Heinrich replied.

"Please!" he insisted. "I beg of you."

From behind, a figure approached and grabbed the shoulder of the begging individual. "Take your place! Do not disturb the other souls," said the towering figure, twice the size of Heinrich. The pleading soul left Heinrich alone and found a place against a white tree.

After several hours, Heinrich and the others received instructions to press forward. They funneled to a processing area where they said their names and accepted a stone token with a number engraved on it.

Once they moved, souls bargained to exchange their stone tokens, but again, the towering figures stopped each one of them. The beings made no threats or intimidation upon the offending souls, yet all complied when demanded. They entered a wide corridor with doors to separate holding areas. Heinrich's group went into one marked by the number 27. The other holding areas bore numbers with at least one 7, though they counted in no particular order. Their final holding area was much dimmer than anywhere else in the shining city. As they entered, a medium-sized figure stood guard by a door. While the rest of Heinrich's group came in, they took seats on the floor.

The figure guarding the door spoke, "When your number is called, you are to present your stone token to be collected. You will then enter the courtroom to be judged." It surveyed its audience as it bellowed. "When you enter the courtroom, you are not to speak until spoken to, nor are you to make any gestures of any kind. When the Almighty One enters the room, you will stay standing the entire time; you are not to take a seat. Do not look at Him; you cannot see His face. It is covered, and it will remain as such."

The instructions finished, and the figure resumed guarding the door. After a few minutes, the figure called a number. The soul with the corresponding number approached the guard and handed it the stone token. The guard opened the door, ushered the soul through, and closed the door behind them. A moment later, a bright light shone through the tiny crack beneath the door and went dark again.

The figure called another number in random order. Soul after soul passed through, never to be seen again. Heinrich kept waiting to be called. After what seemed like an eternity, his number was summoned. He approached the figure who collected his stone token and opened the door for him.

Through the doorway, three other figures waited for him. They shut the door behind him, and as soon as it was closed, the figures stripped him of his clothing. Heinrich tried to cover his nakedness in front of them, but they scrubbed him clean with water and a soapy substance. They placed sackcloth on him. It all happened in a matter of seconds, and they motioned without speaking for him to proceed forward. They opened the doorway, but Heinrich paused before passing through. He took a deep breath and stepped forward.

VI

Through the door, two angelic guards grabbed hold of Heinrich. They guarded the exit from the corridor on the exterior and linked arms with him after bonding his hands together. The angels drew him past rows of pews reserved for witnesses. The seating remained sparsely filled. Heinrich recognized no one sitting in viewing area, but as they marched forward, they passed through a small gate. The angels seated him at a table and stood guard behind him.

Heinrich examined the room. A bench sat lining his left. Several men reclined, who he assumed were wise, holy men. The closest to him was a man of sun-drenched skin, wearing a white turban on his head. It bore a symbol of a crescent moon above his forehead. He wore white linen cloths wrapped around his torso. A dark colored, groomed beard covered most of his face.

Next to him sat a man with skin tones no different from his neighbor. He also wore white linens wrapped around his body, but he was a man of humble means. He smiled kindly toward Heinrich. Beside him farther was a large male, wearing a yellow sash over one shoulder as his covering. He was rotund with bright lips while he lounged with his legs crossed and his eyes closed. He paid no attention to Heinrich.

Beside him farther was an individual with blue skin, wearing a golden turban on its head. It possessed two sets of arms, and it wore a pinkish-purple robe, covering itself like a vest. On it rested fine gold and jewelry, and on its ears, golden rings hung. Its expression seemed pleasant enough as it stood next to its companions.

Next, an elderly man squatted with grayed hair and a full gray beard. He wore a red tunic while over his arms and shoulders draped a red robe. In his hands, he held two large stone tablets with a language that Heinrich couldn't discern. A wooden staff with growing live buds rested upon his arm.

Even farther down the bench reclined another elderly fellow with no hair on his scalp, though he had a thin, yet long beard dropping from his chin. He had a fuller mustache. His eyes were narrow, but his nose rounded. He wore more clothing than any of the others as his robes appeared heavy. Beside him was a fellow who looked similar, but he didn't wear the thick clothes. He possessed a white robe and tunic, and had receded gray hair. He had a long, but thin white beard.

At the bench's end remained another male dressed in all white except for a golden cloth tied around his waist. He held an intricate wooden rod on his arm. On his head perched a white headdress while on his face hung a thick brown beard that reached down to his collarbone.

To Heinrich's right, a lone individual reclined behind another table. It peered at Heinrich with perverse delight. The being looked shifty and untrustworthy, yet it tried to convince Heinrich that it was truthful. Heinrich cast his attention away and took stock of the bare table before him. An angel, who Heinrich assumed represented a bailiff, called out to Heinrich, "Who do you take as your council?"

The individuals on the bench all gave their attention to Heinrich and waited for his response. After a moment, the kind man stood to approach him, but Heinrich rebuffed him, "I'm representing myself, and myself alone."

The man stopped. Heinrich's words shocked him. The man fixed his gaze upon Heinrich and examined his eyes, "But I have not forgotten the faith you once placed in me as a child," he said.

Heinrich dismissed the man with his hand, "I will stand before god on my own."

The man returned to his seat among the others on the bench, looking despondent and heartbroken by Heinrich's refusal. The angel instructed all to rise for the Almighty One's entrance. All rose, including those on the bench, except the being behind the table who remained seated. Heinrich followed its lead and stayed in his seat.

At the front of the room, a raised bench sat with a gavel on top of it. A large, thick veil draped all over the raised bench, making it difficult to see through. Just to the right stood a doorway. It opened and a great light shone through as the Almighty One entered. Heinrich shielded his eyes from the brightness. To say it was overwhelming was an understatement in Heinrich's eyes. The glory of the Almighty One made it difficult to perceive anything. As He approached His bench of judgment, a legion of angelic guards took their place in front of the bench to defend Him. Seven stood with intentionality to Heinrich's right in front of the mysterious individual's table.

"You may be seated," said the Almighty One. Silence followed His speaking as He scanned the documents. After more silence, He spoke again, "Heinrich Juarez?"

Heinrich rose to his feet and appeared as confident as he could, though he felt overwhelmed.

The Almighty One cast a glance at him. "I see you are representing yourself as your advocate," He said. "Do you understand where you are?"

"I think so," replied Heinrich in his most confident tone. "I've been putting the pieces of the puzzle together as I go, but I think I do, yes."

The Almighty One shifted to the individual behind the table, "What are the charges you bring against the defendant?"

Remaining seated, the individual scanned the document before speaking. "This soul is guilty of the most grievous sin. If you look upon his dossier, you will see an extensive list of grievances committed against you. The worst of all is that he violated your sovereignty by murdering his own life with his own hands. His pathetic tale begins with hatred of those who cared for him and those within his community. He desired revenge on the justification of hatred and stigmatization, but as you know in your eyes, these are not justified causes of revenge, let alone self-inflicted murder. From that point, he solicited a woman for relations that are not honorable in your eyes, but selfish and unloving. And while he was unable to follow through with these desires, his heart lusted after such things. In your judgment, so the heart wishes, so the soul is. When all this failure overwhelmed his entire being, he committed the most grievous sin of all by taking his life to end his own suffering. And you know the penalty mandated for this wrongdoing."

The Almighty One peered at Heinrich and examined him before speaking. "How do you respond to these charges?"

"I don't deny what has been spoken about me," replied Heinrich.

"How then do you plead?" asked the Almighty One.

"Not guilty," replied Heinrich.

The Almighty One looked suspicious of Heinrich's words.

"Yes, these charges being brought against me are true," said Heinrich, "but I do not plead guilty."

The individual behind the table spoke, "There is a punishment more fitting for this soul than an eternity in Hell—"

"Shut your mouth," barked Heinrich, surprising himself with his confidence. "I have something to say..."

The bailiff motioned as if it were about to intervene against Heinrich, but the Almighty One gave him permission to speak.

"I don't accept the legitimacy of this court," said Heinrich. Gasps filled the courtroom. The bailiff again cast a glance to the Almighty One, but it was ordered to stand down. "I will not be judged by any who stand before me ready to condemn me, especially you who hold the gavel in your hand. I can only assume that you are the one that many around the world call upon as god, but I reject your authority and your judgment. As far as I can see it, you've done nothing for me, but caused utter misery, suffering, and pain in my life. Thus, it is I, who has been wronged, not you who calls himself god. Therefore, I refuse to accept any judgment placed upon me as being legitimate or having any relevance."

The man who earlier wanted to speak on Heinrich's behalf stood to interrupt Heinrich, but he received a disapproving glance from Heinrich, telling him not to dare. "I want nothing to do with you either," shouted Heinrich. "I renounce any prayer or show of faith I uttered as a child."

The individual behind the other desk sat pleased with this outburst, thinking how easy it made its job.

"I hate you, who claim to be Almighty," said Heinrich, appearing more flustered and enraged as he spoke. "And I can think of nothing worse than spending an eternity with a divine being who did nothing to intervene among his own creation's suffering, but worse, then stood to judge him. When my parents were forced to abandon me, you did nothing but allowed it to happen. When my brother made me the object of his violence, you didn't take up my cause. When my adopted parents had their lives threatened by a hurricane, you did nothing but consume their lives. When I sought affection and acceptance, you didn't permit me anything but abuse and rejection. You did nothing. You just...sat there in Heaven and did nothing."

The courtroom went silent. No one dared speak, let alone cough. The sparse audience gazed back and forth between the Almighty One and Heinrich to determine who would say the next word.

"I would rather spend eternity in Hell than spend one day in the presence of you in Heaven," said Heinrich in closing. The audience gasped at Heinrich's declaration. The individual behind the other table cast a surprised glance to Heinrich. As the Almighty One scrutinized Heinrich, the tension built as everyone waited on what response the Almighty One might have for this bold soul.

"Do you realize the significance of what you are saying?" asked the Almighty One.

"I do."

"Forgive him, Father," pleaded Heinrich's would-be defendant from the side bench, "for he does not know what he is doing."

The Almighty One inspected the prosecutor, "Lucifer, do you raise any objection to this soul's expressed request?"

"I do not," it said with a glistening of joy in its eye.

"Then I see no reason not to oblige your request, Heinrich Juarez," said the Almighty One, "but know that this is your expressed desire and yours alone."

Heinrich nodded. The Almighty One motioned to the bailiff, and the bailiff seized Heinrich's arm. A guard of angels fell behind to protect the Almighty One from any attempt by Heinrich to reach through the barrier. Heinrich glanced ahead, and the bailiff directed him toward a double door labeled as "The Way to Hell."

The bailiff stopped Heinrich before reaching the door. "You must open the door yourself," it instructed him. "And when you pass through, you will lose consciousness, but you shall come to, and you will know where you are."

Heinrich glanced at the sign and the door handle. He took one last glance at the courtroom and placed his hand on the handle. He opened it and vanished through it into utter darkness.

VII

The Gates of Hell stood before Heinrich. An intense heat emanated from them. The groans of Hell were loud and obnoxious. Two demons stood before the gate ready to receive Heinrich. As they led him through the gates, souls attempted to flee through the opening, but an invisible force held them back. When he and the demons passed through the invisible barrier, a way parted for them between the moaning inhabitants of Hell.

Above him, he perceived a sign bearing the description: "None shall leave who pass through these gates." It was translated into many languages. He and the demons continued through the crowds. The souls were in terrible, humiliating pain, though from where in their bodies, Heinrich couldn't tell. Once Heinrich passed through the crowd, he came to a lake of burning sulfur and lava. In the distance, he couldn't make out much, but he perceived that an active volcano supplied the lake. Souls swam in the lake, screaming in agony, while pleading for someone to come to their rescue. Along the lake's perimeter, lifeless bodies rested, having escaped the torment of the Lake of Fire, only to collapse on its shores. They whimpered in pain amidst tears. The demons waited for him as he surveyed what was to become his new eternal home.

"Why do these souls suffer so, while I experience nothing but the immense heat of Hell?" he asked one of the accompanying demons. He received no response.

The demons ushered him to follow them. As he did, lifeless souls ran to and fro without purpose or direction. They sought distraction from the suffering they had endured for centuries in Hell. One soul threw itself at Heinrich, but the demons diverted it. They didn't even touch the soul, but held out their arms. The soul tried harder to break through whatever power they wielded against him. The demons uttered a ghoulish incantation. The soul went hurling into the Lake of Fire where its screams filled the ears of all around the lake.

Without taking even a moment's notice of the fate given to the castaway soul, the demons continued forward and led the way to a holding area. A spiked fence encircled it with a gate guarded by armed demons to ensure that none entered or exited without their permission. The transporting demons signaled to the armed demons, who opened the gate.

The demons nudged Heinrich forward. He took a step and examined the other inhabitants. Most of them looked as he did, unharmed and untouched. Others looked sinister and untrustworthy. He kept his guard up. He felt uncertain about the crowd with which he made himself a part.

"What's your name?" asked one missing his left eye.

"Who are you?" he responded.

"Zigmund," was the reply. "Now tell me your name."

"Heinrich."

"What are you in for?"

"I'm here by my own choice."

"Right…" said the one-eyed man. "Everybody is here for a reason."

Heinrich stared before turning away.

"Me, I'm here for being a thieving fool," said the man. "I snatched a few purses from grannies, but I was just trying to survive."

Another soul stepped forward, a woman, though it was hard to tell by her haggard appearance. "Who's your friend?" she asked Zigmund.

"Don't know," he replied, waving his hand as if to dismiss Heinrich away. "Won't say much."

"My name's Heinrich," he blurted out.

"Heinrich?" said the female.

"That's all I got out of him," said Zigmund.

"I'm here because of suicide," he confessed.

"Me, it's swindling," admitted the woman. "The name's Patty."

Heinrich extended his hand to her, but she looked down at it and back up to him. "There's no need for pleasantries here, my boy. This is Hell."

He withdrew his hand and tried his best not to feel spurned. "Who are those guys staring at us?" he asked.

"That's Coltor and Thomas," said Zigmund, giving a sign to them to say things were okay. "They're with us."

"What'd they do?" asked Heinrich.

"Coltor is a rapist. Thomas, he murdered someone."

"You hang out with people like that?" asked Heinrich.

"Why not?" asked the woman.

"They're bad people!" protested Heinrich.

"And what are you?" asked Zigmund.

"I'm not a bad person," he defended.

"I'm sure you're not," said Patty. "The fact of the matter is that you're in Hell just like the lot of us."

"But I didn't kill anybody!" he said.

"You killed yourself," countered Patty, "and according to some people's beliefs, that's just as bad."

"I'm not bad," he reiterated, crossing his arms as he stood up straight.

"You can believe what you want about yourself, but it doesn't change that you're one with the rest of us in Hell," said Zigmund. He glanced at Patty and motioned for them to return to their friends.

Heinrich looked around. He had no other friends with whom to associate. He caught up to them and tugged on Patty's elbow, "Wait up!"

"What is it?" she replied.

"So maybe I'm not a good person..." he said, avoiding eye contact with her, "but could somebody just tell me how this works?"

"How what works?" asked Zigmund.

"How Hell works."

"We're just as new to this as you, my boy," said Patty. "We're in the same position as you. We just arrived here ourselves."

A massive, hideous demon swung open the gate to the holding area; its eyes red with fire and with horns for a beard. In its mouth appeared snakes for a tongue, while in its hand, it held a staff with the dead head of a rhinoceros. When it spoke, it did so with a horrid, yet deep slow hiss. "Get up. You're all coming with me," it bellowed, motioning them forward with its staff. "I will show you to your place in Hell."

They marched out in a disjointed mass, a few souls pushing others to get farther away from the demon. No one wanted to be near it. Heinrich and his companions linked arms to stay together as others tried to break their grip. "Stay with us, kid," said Patty, as she drew his arm closer to her.

Desperate souls fled from the crowd, and the hideous demon called for ghastly demons to cut them off. They met them head on and thrust their sharp staffs through the souls' torsos. The souls went flying into the Lake of Fire.

"Let that be a warning to any of you," said the horned beast leading them beyond the Lake of Fire. They again picked up the groans from those suffering in the lake. Even as they trampled farther from the lake, the heat never lessened. It was intense wherever they went. They came to a dark forest, whose branches grew so wild it inhibited entrance into it. On each side of the forest stood steep cliffs. The beast uttered an incomprehensible command which drew the forest branches back, and led to an open path.

"Behold, the nine circles of Hell," shouted the demon as it elevated its hands. "You will be left where you belong. Do not try to escape. Your sins will bind you."

As the mass moved together toward the forest's entrance, a coldness came over Heinrich. He anticipated what evil might be within. The pathway declined downward. In the upper branches of the forest, winged creatures swooped around, though with the darkness of the tress, he couldn't discern their appearance. He gripped closer the arm of Patty, "What is this madness?" he asked.

She shrugged as she gazed into the upper reaches. They apprehended a scream. A flying beast snatched one from their group in its claws. The demon rotated, acknowledging what the crowd had seen. "She is being taken back to Limbo. She isn't ready for her final resting place. She will suffer yet still."

"Look!" said Zigmund, pointing forward. The forest broke into a shrouded clearing. "This must be the first circle of Hell."

In the clearing ahead, a cliff with a jagged fence dropped on the right. On the left, another cliff bore down. As they proceeded, they came upon more agonizing souls of Hell. They were naked, but no one could differentiate between their sexes. Their bodies bore no genitals or sexual organs. No breasts were visible on the souls, but neither were buttocks; only sealed orifices all around, even their mouths. Their bodies were frail and thin, lacking strength, definition or muscle tone. The massive demon guiding the group stopped and called out the names of those who were to reside at this stage. Heinrich paid little attention until Coltor's name was summoned. Coltor looked at his companions with fearful eyes. His eyes focused on the horned demon staring at him. It knew who he was and summoned him forth with its piercing red eyes. Coltor clung closer to Thomas with whom his arm linked. The demon gave a signal, and three demons appeared on the exterior of the crowd and propelled their way toward Coltor. The screams that came from him weakened Heinrich's grip on Patty's arm.

"Hold tightly!" she commanded Heinrich, so he did, but it was pointless. Thomas gripped both Coltor and Heinrich's arms, but the demons grabbed hold of Coltor and dragged him away. He screamed for his friends, who stood there in defeat as one demon stood between them and Coltor. The demon dragged him away from the crowd and threw him into a pit unceremoniously.

"Any others who might consider resisting?" demanded the massive demon. Other souls volunteered to emerge from the mass. The demons directed them elsewhere down a mysterious path.

"Where are they going, Ziggy?" Patty asked.

"This is the first circle of Hell," he replied, seeming to understand what they witnessed. "Coltor will stay here because of his sins of Lust."

"Onward!" shouted the massive demon. They marched forward and passed an uncountable number of sexless souls left unable to please themselves. Pain didn't fill their eyes so much as sadness. An eternal loneliness weighed on them; each isolated with no grouping together. Their punishment was being alone for the rest of eternity. They received no sexual pleasure of any kind in return for the sins they indulged upon during their lives on Earth.

As the group arrived at the end of the first circle, they lumbered down a swirling decline. They couldn't perceive anything in the distance beyond the cliff's edge. A desolate wasteland spread forth in front of them. No sign of plant life or vegetation was present. It was barren beyond the gate that separated the first and second circles of Hell.

The inhabitants of the second circle were either far frailer or more massively obese than those in the first circle. Heinrich struggled to understand why this was the case. On the side of the pathway, one soul wheezed in pain as he had cut open his own stomach. Blood covered his hands as he fumbled with his exposed intestines for all those passing by to see. His stomach was empty, even if the soul was a rather large being.

As the crowd moved forward, fruit trees stood high on the left embankment. A small gathering of souls clamored to climb the embankment. Laid in a crumpled heap were the mangled bodies of the souls who had tried to reach the fruits only to fall to the ground far below. Others waited below the trees for fruit to fall. As Heinrich's group marched past, twice a winged creature swooped in and prevented falling fruit from reaching the souls below.

The massive demon led the group forward until they reached another empty clearing with no life visible, not even famished souls. It bellowed more names, though this time, none of Heinrich's friends detected their names called.

"Zigmund, what is this place?" asked Heinrich.

"Can you not tell?" he replied. "This is the circle of

gluttons, whose appetite will never be quenched."

The group moved forward again, passing from the second circle of Hell.

"My friends," said Zigmund, "I shall not stay with you much longer."

"What are you talking about?" demanded Patty.

"He knows his place is coming in the next circle," said Heinrich.

"It is true."

"How do you know that?" said Thomas.

"The next circle is for those who spent their lives chasing money and wealth," said Zigmund. "The thieves, the stockbrokers, the businessmen who took advantage of others, we are all going to be there."

"Can you be certain?" asked Patty.

Zigmund nodded. Patty linked her arm closer to Zigmund. He rotated his head and shook it in disapproval. She knew that she must not.

They marched forward through another gate and beyond it, they found a crowd of demons. They looked cultured in a bizarrely human manner. Below them, souls took the place of servants to the demons. One polished the shoes of one demon while another fed the demon with a fork. The horned demon led the crowd forward through other souls subjected to servitude. Zigmund's heart beat quicker with each step they took, as he foresaw the fate that was before him.

"Be strong," said Patty, gripping her friend's hand.

Zigmund nodded and tried his best to put on a good face. The massive demon halted the group and called out names. Zigmund's was the second to be called. The demon leered straight at him. Zigmund noticed another supporting demon had spotted him. "I'm coming," he volunteered as he let go of Patty's hand.

"Be strong, Ziggy!" she shouted through the crowd.

"Silence her!" bellowed the massive demon. Patty yielded to its request, showing she wouldn't resist. Zigmund weaved his way through the crowd to its periphery. There, a demon pointed the direction for him to go. Their demonic guide ushered the group forward again, passing more indentured souls. The agony witnessed before didn't seem as evident as in the circle of Gluttons. The front of the crowd tried to look away, but couldn't.

As they marched forward, they arrived at the circle's end and entered the fourth circle's entrance. Beyond the divide between the third and fourth circle, massive piles of rubbish were scattered, swarming with what looked like demonic flies. Throughout the mountains of garbage were the souls of those who were lazy or slothful. They were implanted in the ground without the ability to move. Flies perched themselves on the souls and thrusted something painful upon the sinners. Still other flies, they brought food close to the trapped souls, but just out of their reach. The souls pleaded for help from someone to bring the food closer to them.

The fourth circle carried a stench that smelled horrendous and overwhelming. A few in the crowd stumbled from being overcome and fell to the ground, but no one helped them up. The crowd trampled them without mercy, and it wasn't until the crowd left the battered souls behind that the demons swooped in. They whipped them until the souls rose and limped their way back into the rear of the crowd.

Names were called yet again, and several departed from the crowd with faces of terror at their new reality. The crowd continued from there and passed more disturbing sights of despair, though each did their best to ignore the agony. Most were more concerned about what foul fate might befall them in their own corresponding circle of Hell.

They came to the end of the fourth circle and entered the fifth circle of Hell. They found the most bizarre form of torture in Hell. The suffering didn't appear to be physical, per se, but instead a perverse reconstruction of religion, except those being worshipped, were demons. Cathedrals stood upside down or on their sides with stairways reaching the entrances. Though the souls couldn't see what happened inside of them, outside were massive idols of satanic figures. Before them were souls who had their bodies pierced and slashed, and each bowed down before the statues.

Farther ahead, a small marching crowd appeared as if in a procession. Each of them was covered except for their exposed genitals. On their heads were coverings bearing pentagrams. They shouted chants of praise honoring the Master of Hell, Lucifer.

Behind them stood a three-headed demon with a cat-o'-nine-tails, though on the ends were the heads of red bears, eager to devour whenever given a chance. Farther, there rose a hill with three crosses, each upside down, though the one in the middle was minuscule. Three souls hung inverted on the crosses and begged for mercy from those passing by to relieve them of their suffering.

Such great fear consumed Heinrich. He almost faint-ed from the sickness he experienced within. Patty gripped his arm and yanked him closer, giving him a re-assuring nod.

Once they passed through the fifth circle, they came to the sixth circle's entrance, which appeared like that of a prison with bars preventing any from entering or leaving. This circle of Hell had demons guarding the entrance on both sides of the bars.

On the inside, demons fought to keep the souls back. The souls' eyes raged with violence. It wasn't until the massive horned demon leading Heinrich's group uttered a vile command that at once, the souls fell to the ground and parted. They bowed down to the demon. The gate opened, and the crowd squeezed to fit in through the small entrance.

Once the gate closed, the rabid souls became consumed by the violence in their minds. Those on the periphery of the crowd found themselves under assault from the violent souls filled with spirits of anger, vengeance and revenge. The demons kept the crowd moving, uncaring of whatever abuse the unassigned souls received.

As they progressed forward, the angered souls dispersed, as most of them remained concentrated around the entrance. Farther ahead, a raving madman lunged at a soul in the crowd. A demon fought off the violent soul.

The group stopped, and the demon called out names again. Thomas heard his name called, so he let go of Heinrich's arm and exited out of the group.

"Which circle is this?" Heinrich asked Patty.

"This must be the circle of murderers and those

who commit violence against others," she replied, "but I really don't know. It is only my best guess."

Then Heinrich overheard his name called. He eyed the demon who called his name. Heinrich gave Patty a surprised look. "I don't understand. I'm not a murderer," he said.

"You murdered yourself," she said with concern. "You said you were here because you killed yourself, did you not? This must be the ring reserved for those who have taken their own lives."

"It can't be!" pleaded Heinrich. "It can't be!"

A demon shoved its way through the crowd to reach Heinrich. Patty let go of his arm, "It's no use," she said. "This is the fate given to you!"

"It mustn't be!" shouted Heinrich again. The massive demon in front shouted commands to the other demons to silence him.

"Heinrich! Stop protesting!" she called to him. "It will only make it worse! Remember Coltor!"

Heinrich stopped shouting, and stuck his hands up, "I'm here! I'm coming."

The escorting demon propelled its way forward while Heinrich pushed harder through the crowd to meet it. When they crossed paths, he reached his hand out to the demon who looked surprised by the gesture. "Lead me," said Heinrich. "I'm ready to go."

The demon inspected him and pointed him toward the other souls who had departed from the crowd. He ran to catch up with the others and passed a few souls, who flinched as he approached, taking defensive stances against him. Heinrich lifted his arms to show his non-aggressiveness. He headed forward until he found Thomas and called his name when he saw him.

"Let's stick together," suggested Thomas, looking over his shoulder. Heinrich agreed. As they followed the others assigned to this circle of Hell, their former group marched away from them. Heinrich attempted to catch a glimpse of Patty as if to say goodbye, but he couldn't see her.

Once the crowd left that circle of Hell, demons led Heinrich and Thomas into the forest farther beyond. Like the earlier forest, it was dark and foreboding. Along the forest's floor were near-lifeless corpses of souls so beaten and bruised that they could no longer stand. They couldn't even move out of the marching crowd's way. Several cried out in pain from being trampled upon, but their cries were so weak that they were almost unnoticeable.

Inside the forest, the other souls disappeared and took cover from whatever beasts may have inhabited the forest. Thomas and Heinrich trudged side by side and kept their eyes open for whatever danger may befall them. Between the trees, lurking souls focused their sights on Heinrich and Thomas. Heinrich drew his companion's attention. The souls were stalking them. More souls crept in the shadows with crafty intent in their eyes.

While the stalkers distracted Thomas and Heinrich, a larger, murderous soul sprang out of the shadows. He tackled Heinrich, bowling over Thomas en route. Heinrich's companion lunged onto the attacker's back, beating him with his hands while Heinrich defended himself in vain. The murderer released Heinrich to focus on bashing Thomas. Heinrich pounced at the murderer and kicked at his knees, but this only caused the predator to respond by pushing Heinrich to the ground. While the murderer focused on Heinrich, Thomas took a massive swing to the fiend's jaw, knocking him to the ground.

Heinrich and Thomas discovered a great crowd of souls surrounded them, looking upon them as a hungry man does on a meal just before he consumes it. The two friends retreated to defensive positions; their backs to each other. They held their fists up, ready for whatever attack might be intended for them.

One from the crowd leaped forward and offered himself as a challenger while his colleagues cheered him on. He went for Thomas first and landed several blows before another from the crowd came out to attack Heinrich. Blows flew on both ends, but only a few connected. Before they knew it, Heinrich and Thomas were on the ground battling their competitors, and soon, more from the crowd joined in on the beating.

"Help us! Somebody help us!" screamed Heinrich in between receiving kicks and punches to his midsection. Thomas pushed off his attackers and helped Heinrich up, allowing them to regain a defensive stance.

"Who do you think will listen to your cries here?" shouted one from the crowd. "Hell is a place of anarchy where the strongest brute survives. The only intervention you will find from the demons is when a revolt comes against the natural order of Hell."

Soon more combatants came at Thomas and Heinrich. The two new arrivals held their own because of

the strength and ability of Thomas. The attackers went
after Thomas, realizing for them to win, they had to
overwhelm him. Heinrich responded by taking a stand
against them. He shielded his friend, but it wasn't long
before they knocked Heinrich to the ground. The two
deflected the crowd's attacks. The crowd had enough
and swarmed. Heinrich looked to his friend between
blows to his whole body, thinking that this must be the
end, but then he remembered that he was in Hell.

A loud shout came from the crowd, causing the mob
to stop their beating. They backed away. One emerged
from the crowd taller than the rest. "Enough!" said the
towering person. "These souls have endured enough,
and yet, they didn't plead for mercy."

Heinrich and Thomas tried to sit upright, but it was
painful to do so. Heinrich's vision blurred from the
beating he had received, thus making out the face of
him who spoke was a challenge.

"These two are worthy enough to join us," said the
man, speaking to his crowd who Heinrich realized were
his followers. "They are good enough if we are good
enough for them?"

The man waited for a response. Thomas spoke first,
"We will go with you." He rose and searched Heinrich
for his agreement. He nodded, and Thomas helped
him up.

"Good," said the towering man. "Follow us, and we
will lead you into safety within the Forest of Sheol."

VIII

"There's been a disturbance," said Lucifer. Residing in an upper courtyard of Pandemonium alone, the devil sensed something amiss in Inferno. Lucifer marched to an exterior open archway and surveyed the burning landscape of its kingdom. The souls suffered in agony as they should. The demons tortured the sinners as they ought. No open rebellion was discerned, nor was any mutiny visible. Lucifer turned from the archway and paced within the expansive courtyard. Lucifer considered the kingdom for which it was responsible and fear crept into the devil's mind. Though Lucifer couldn't perceive what was causing the disturbance, it knew something threatened the whole order of chaos in Hell.

Lucifer called upon Luvart, a lesser demon serving within Pandemonium. The devil commanded the demon to send out a call for a report about the physical conditions of Hell. Lucifer sought an in-depth study of the lower realm. After a while, Luvart returned with the reports that Lucifer had ordered, and while it confirmed something was awry, the reports were void of any specific cause. Demons throughout Hell had perceived an unbalancing or a disturbance. But all investigations yielded little more than that. Frustrated with the lack of detail, Lucifer expelled Luvart from the courtyard, but demanded Apollyon report to Lucifer.

Apollyon arrived with haste and paid honor by kneeling to Lucifer, its master and chief.

"Something is happening in Hell, Apollyon," said Lucifer.

"So you sensed it as well, my lord?" replied Apollyon.

"And you said nothing about it?" said Lucifer, looking upon Apollyon in anger.

"I have been investigating," said Apollyon, pushing back against Lucifer's condemnation.

"Oh? And what have you found?" asked Lucifer.

"Nothing as of yet—"

"Why do you waste my time?—"

"My lord!" barked Apollyon, standing in defiance. "You are not the only one whose fate is at risk in this situation. Resolving this is my highest priority; I interrupted my investigation to answer your call."

"Apollyon, search this out!" commanded Lucifer. "I want to find out what is going on, and I must know in short order."

"My lord, you have my word," replied Apollyon.

"Find out who is at fault and bring them to me."

"Assuredly," said Apollyon.

"Something is about to happen," replied Lucifer. "It must be stopped."

IX

Among the brood of murderers, Heinrich and Thomas marched through the Forest of Sheol with an uncertain sense of security by being in the horde that had accepted them. Other roaming souls in the forest stayed away from them, perhaps out of respect, or fear. The two companions stayed close.

After covering a distance through the forest, they arrived at a small encampment. No tents had been pitched, but it was sheltered. Branches lay on the ground in a circle, serving as bedding on the perimeter for the community. In the middle, fallen trees were carved into a table while stumps stood beside as makeshift chairs.

On the table sat the most revolting food imaginable. No plates or utensils of any kind; just food slopped onto the table. Thomas and Heinrich hunkered down in front of what was a serving. Others in the horde took seats and feasted. The two friends, who despite experiencing hunger, took longer to warm up to the food in front of them. Something moved inside the burnt chunk of bread before Heinrich, but he didn't recognize the insect. Thomas took the first bite and almost vomited, but to be polite, he swallowed. Heinrich took a bite. He tried his best to look grateful for the nourishment, but as the two kept eating, they realized the food provided no satisfaction to their hungry stomachs. The food left them as famished as before.

"What is this food?" asked Heinrich.

"Does it not please you?" asked the leader of the horde.

"No, I feel just as hungry as I was before I ate," commented Heinrich. "And I should have eaten my fill by now."

"Alas you have learned, there is no pleasure to be experienced in Hell. The food has no taste, nor does it satisfy."

"Then why eat at all?" asked Thomas.

Another spoke up at the table, "We do in hope that maybe one day, we will be satisfied."

"Yet we know we never will," inserted another. Heinrich scowled at what remained of his food. He resigned to the senselessness of eating more while also realizing that it didn't harm him either. When the brood finished feasting, the leader drew Thomas's attention by raising a hand to catch his eye.

"Tell us," he said. "What is your name?"

"Thomas," he replied, as he wiped crumbs from his lips.

"Speak a little about yourself," he instructed him.

"What do you want to know?"

"Begin with why you are in Hell."

"I'm a murderer," he said, drawing the laughter of the table.

"We all are."

Thomas paused before continuing. "I killed my brother," he said. "I killed him because he stole from me. He stole everything that ever meant something to me, so he could feed his gambling addiction."

Thomas explained how his brother went into massive debt and borrowed money from Thomas to create a temporary buffer between him and the loan sharks on his back. Things went sour when the loan sharks pursued Thomas and threatened his life if he didn't give them the money that his brother owed. They harassed him so much that it filled Thomas with hatred for his addicted brother. His sibling had made a mockery of his family. When the mob threatened to kill his brother as leverage to make Thomas pay, he one-upped them by killing his brother and fleeing the state. After escaping across three states, he had the misfortune of being rammed by a train when he had ignored an unmarked railway crossing.

"I wish I could change what I have done," concluded Thomas. "But what's done is done. I am guilty as charged, and I accept my punishment from the Almighty One."

Heinrich cast no judgment in his heart toward Thomas. Instead, he experienced a sense of understanding for what drove him to do what he did, nor did the table cast judgment upon Thomas.

Others at the table shared what they did to merit an

eternity in Hell. The first spoke up and suggested he went above and beyond Thomas by murdering his whole family in a murder-suicide. He couldn't imagine killing himself and leaving his family behind.

The next shared that she murdered her abusive husband, but it didn't stop there, as she also killed their two children. She was convicted of the crime and suffered the death penalty. Another soul at the table spoke and said that he murdered far more people than he could count, all while following the orders of his government leaders. He commented that he didn't imagine that he would ever be held to account for obeying. In hindsight, he committed a grievous sin and believed he deserved to be in Hell.

And yet another soul shared that she killed a teenage girl while driving drunk. She collided with the girl who was walking home on the side of the road. She said that even still, she struggled to come to terms with the consequences of her actions, but she accepted that she deserved the ghastly eternity dealt to her.

The table gazed at Heinrich. They sought to learn what sinful crime he had committed against the Almighty One to deliver himself to Hell. He deflected the attention, but his audience demanded a monolog. With coaxing, they got him to explain his life story.

He spoke about his experiences on Earth back on the island nation of Cuba, and how his birth parents abandoned him. He told the group about how he was forced to live a miserable existence with no form of love, affection, or joy. His audience experienced a sorrow they had yet to endure even in the pit of Hell. When he concluded with his suicide, a solemn silence hung over the group. No one knew what to say, no words of comfort or cheer, nor any suggestion that he could take relief from it all being over.

"Unlike Thomas here," said Heinrich, turning to him, "I don't accept my punishment, nor do I recognize the judgment of him whom Thomas calls the Almighty One. It was my choice to spend eternity in Hell and my choice alone."

The leader of the group replied with his eyes watering ever so slightly, "I speak for all of us when I offer you our condolences for such a pitiful and dreadful life. No man should suffer such a fate. Truth be known, I have never been so moved by the testimony of another soul's life."

"I've never heard such a sad tale of one's life before," spoke another from the group. "What you experienced is profoundly disturbing…"

Heinrich was uncomfortable with the response, having never known compassion or pity.

"You have the respect of the horde," said the leader. "We are proud to count you as one of our own, even if the only murder you committed was upon yourself."

Heinrich nodded. Neither had he ever been counted as one with anyone before. It led him to believe for the first time, he might experience a level of companionship and acceptance.

X

Months later in eternity, Apollyon stormed Pandemonium with haste. The demon requested an audience with Lucifer and the demon was ushered into the devil's presence in the same courtyard as earlier. Upon seeing Lucifer, Apollyon saw weariness overtaking the devil.

The unknown was taking its toll. All investigations revealed little information, but Lucifer was aware something had to be stopped. The devil did not fear losing its position as Master of Hell, but the very existence of Hell remained at stake. Hatred of Inferno was weak among the souls. The suffering failed to linger in the atmosphere. Whenever Lucifer toured the underworld, the souls didn't cry out to the devil for mercy as they always had before. An indifference spread over the souls' faces, and while no joy appeared in their eyes, Lucifer feared that its domain was crumbling.

"Apollyon, my most faithful servant," said Lucifer cryptically. "What news do you bring your master, or do you only show yourself to ask for more time when there is none to be given?"

"My lord, I have discovered the root of this disturbance we have both sensed," said Apollyon. Fear resonated in Apollyon's face over what it had learned.

"Speak with haste!" Lucifer beckoned the demon.

"A cancer has spread within the sixth circle of Hell," said Apollyon. "One of the condemned souls is the sole cause for the disturbance."

"Who? Who is this defiler of my infernal justice?"

"You ought to remember him, my lord," replied Apollyon. "Were you not there to accept his arrival into our kingdom?"

"Don't be trite with me," shouted Lucifer. "There are far more souls here than I can individually remember. It is not my task to keep a record of every soul in Hades. Is this not the work of lesser demons? To ensure torture and affliction upon the souls, and render them defeated?"

"Then allow me to refresh my lord's memory of this soul's judgment day."

"Yes," replied Lucifer. "Please do."

Apollyon recalled to Lucifer the moment that Heinrich had made it his request to be delivered to Hell. Apollyon reminded Lucifer of Heinrich's sad excuse of a life back in Cuba and what led to his eventual suicide.

"Do you not remember this soul?" asked Apollyon. "I can see in your eyes that you do."

"Yes…yes, I do," replied Lucifer, as the devil turned to gaze over Hell. Heinrich hadn't struck Lucifer as memorable at the time. Lucifer struggled to believe this soul could be the cause.

"Dealing with him has not been so simple."

"No...no, I don't expect that it has."

"We cannot send him away," replied Apollyon. "Not even to roam purgatory in perpetuity. He came here by his own volition."

"Yes, I understand that—"

"Not even the Almighty One would take him back."

"As I am aware—"

"How could you have agreed to—"

"Cease your interrogations, Apollyon," shouted Lucifer, turning from Apollyon's face. "You know your role; you have a job. Worsen the torture on this man. See that he suffers and endures more punishment—"

"Don't you think I have tried, my lord?" defended Apollyon. The demon's exasperation was evident to Lucifer. "I would not bring you this problem without having tried to deal with it myself, but it is beyond my grasp as chief torturer. The soul has nothing to lose. He has endured the very worst one can endure as a human, but here, he has found friendship—"

"Then isolate him from his companions!"

"We have tried, but he merely makes more comrades wherever he goes."

"Then feed him to the Lake of Fire—"

"As he already has."

"And still nothing?" said Lucifer with disbelief in its eyes.

"Nothing, my lord."

Lucifer's mind recalled Heinrich as a soul of little strength, character, or will. Believing that this soul could endure such torture and not be broken perplexed the devil. Lucifer's mind swirled, trying to figure out what to do about Heinrich.

"It seems as though whatever we do to this soul," said Apollyon, "it only worsens the disturbance. You must deal with this, my lord."

"So it may seem."

"What would you have me do?" asked Apollyon.

"Put together a guard. I want an intimidating force. I want him to know that this ends this very moment. Hell will not fall to one human soul. Our mastery shall be preserved, and this disturbance will be ended. I shall resolve this matter once and for all."

"How?"

XI

Heinrich minded his own business and passed his time in Hell. Despite Apollyon's efforts, Heinrich re-embraced his place in the company of his violent horde. Heinrich hadn't realized Apollyon singled him out for torture, but when it was finished, he returned to the sixth circle, pairing up again with Thomas. Heinrich wasn't much for combat despite his proven ability to defend himself. He went along with the horde as a spectator when they roamed through Hell. He tended to his new friends whenever they didn't fare so well in combat.

His newfound camaraderie was a treasure to him and wherever he went, all the other souls knew who he was. They had heard his stories, whether directly from him or by means of another tortured soul. Heinrich couldn't recount a moment on Earth equaled to the contentment experienced with his new friends in Hell.

Sure, the demons came by from time to time to ensure the inhabitants of Hell remembered who was in charge. The demons subjected them to degradation and punishment whether it be hard manual labor or being forced to suffer. The food still tasted awful, and no pleasure of any kind was experienced. But for the first time in Heinrich's existence, he embraced what acceptance felt like through his connection to the horde.

Lucifer wandered through the bowels of Hell with Apollyon and a legion of demons. They passed through the many circles, surveying the operations en route to seeing Heinrich. The measures of pain and suffering wielded against the inhabitants of Hell didn't appear to be working. The souls weren't in agony as much as they had been. Again, the souls didn't cry out for mercy from Lucifer when the Master of Hell passed through their respective circles.

Lucifer marched with the horde of demons to the sixth circle, Apollyon still by its side. They passed into the dark Forest of Sheol and the relative calm there surprised them. The devil and its horde looked silly stomping in with such a great company when it looked unnecessary. After marching, they discovered Heinrich's location.

Heinrich was splitting rocks with others in his horde under the demons' supervision; their daily punishment. No purpose came from their work. The demons forced them to do hard work with no meaning. Among the rock fields, Heinrich and his friends shared jokes and laughed with each other as they slaved away.

Apollyon called upon the supervising demon and

demanded to understand why these souls weren't suffering. The demon had no defense. It claimed that it couldn't break the spirits of the souls ever since Heinrich arrived, confirming Apollyon's investigation. Lucifer sent the demon away, but not before making the demon call upon Heinrich for an audience with the devil. Heinrich obliged and presented himself before Lucifer and Apollyon.

"Are you the one called Heinrich?" asked the devil, looking at his pathetic appearance. Lucifer re-examined Heinrich, having long since forgotten him until Apollyon refreshed Lucifer's memory. The devil sought to see what was so powerful about this impish soul that looked unimpressive.

"I am," he replied.

"There is a problem," stated Lucifer with eyes revealing frustration.

"What is it?" asked Heinrich.

"It is simple," said Lucifer, turning away from Heinrich. "My demons tell me that ever since you came to Hell, you have disturbed the balance and order of this place as one of eternal shame and humiliation."

Heinrich peered at the devil and felt surprised. He was flattered. "How is that?" he asked.

"Because, as I have learned, you have done nothing but tell everyone about your pathetic excuse of a life back on Earth," barked Lucifer.

"I don't understand," he said. "Why is that a problem?"

"As you may or may not be aware, Hell is a place of eternal suffering, torment, and damnation. No soul wants to be here, and I am to ensure that those sent here suffer for their sins on Earth. This isn't a happy place, but one of pain and agony. No pleasures are experienced here. No joyful thoughts are had by any soul spending its eternity here."

"I'm not sure what this has to do with me."

"You, infantile filth," the devil shouted, "are killing the atmosphere."

Heinrich almost laughed, but controlled himself.

Lucifer said, "You've made many of the prisoners of Hell feel like they do not have it so bad here; that it is bearable and that they could get used to it because of hearing about your experience on Earth. Your story has gotten around, I'm afraid, spreading like wildfire and easing the suffering of the souls of Hell. They believe they do not have it so bad compared to what you experienced on Earth as a human. To sum it up for you, as you are of a simple mind, you are putting everything that I have created at risk."

"I still do not see why this is my problem," said Heinrich with bemusement in his tone.

"I wouldn't expect for you to understand," Lucifer replied, "but understand this, I will not tolerate you jeopardizing everything I created here in Hell. This will stop."

"You cannot send me to Heaven—" said Heinrich before being interrupted by the devil.

"I will not send you to Heaven," said Lucifer. "I will send you back to Earth to re-live your life."

Heinrich gave the devil a blank stare. "I have no interest in doing that," Heinrich protested, refusing such an idea.

Lucifer was unprepared for such a response. "How

dare you tell me what I can or cannot do!"

"You aren't sending me back to Earth," shouted Heinrich. "I'm staying right here."

"And why is that, son of Adam?"

"Because..." said Heinrich. "For the first time in my existence, I have friends."

"Meaning?" asked the devil.

"I like living in Hell."

Lucifer was furious, but the Master of Hell tried to control its response. It wasn't getting anywhere with Heinrich. "We can make you see things our way," said Lucifer.

"You can't change my mind," he said. "I asked to come here. I came here by my own choice."

"We have demons trained in torture."

"No offense to you, Lucifer, Master of Hades," retorted Heinrich, "but I'm in Hell, and that is already a part of the deal. What further torture could you wield against me that would make me relent? You may make me suffer, but I won't fear death. You cannot kill me. I am already dead."

Lucifer studied Heinrich before motioning for the guards to give space. "Come for a stroll with me," the devil requested. Heinrich agreed, and the two went off alone into the forests of the sixth circle. The devil explained how Lucifer came to be the Master of Hell. It spoke about the mutiny in Heaven when the Almighty One made His Son, Jesus Christ, His second in command instead of Lucifer.

The devil wasn't the only one surprised by this decision of the Almighty One. Lucifer was God's most trusted angel in Heaven, even more than the angels

Gabriel and Michael. Other angels in Heaven believed that an injustice had been committed against Lucifer. If the devil was overlooked for exemplary service to God, it was detrimental to the hope they had in elevating themselves in the Kingdom of Heaven. They felt as though pleasing God was impossible if He favored His own kin over the accomplishments and achievements of His servants, the angels.

A war took place in Heaven, which Lucifer and its supporters lost, leading to the banishment of the devil and its cohort to the bowels of Hell. No souls accompanied them or tended to their needs. The angels, now being called demons, sought revenge for their humiliating defeat. Lucifer recalled that for a great long time, the Almighty One had spoken of creating a being which He looked after and called His creation.

Lucifer shared with Heinrich how it convinced its allies in Hell that if they forged a way into the created world of these beings that the Almighty One called His own, they might have their revenge by driving a wedge between God and His creation. In doing so, perhaps they might become the Masters of Hell. They would bring the souls of human beings who rejected the Almighty One to Hell, and those souls would become the slaves of demons and worship them instead of the Almighty One.

The devil explained that it all began with Adam and Eve, which in its mind was a simple act of deception. Throughout the ages, the demons' challenges of polluting the minds of humans evolved. Demons had to adapt in finding the weaknesses in the hearts of men to sway them from the bosom of the Almighty One.

After the enticement of Adam and Eve, though, the Almighty One met with Lucifer through an intermediary. The devil argued for taking possession of those souls who had rejected God in favor of worshiping themselves; Lucifer had learned that these souls couldn't spend eternity with the Almighty One.

When the devil promised to punish the souls under his domain, God asked what punishment Lucifer had in mind. The devil's response was that it would give them what they wanted and chosen as the masters' of their souls, nothing more and nothing less. When the Almighty One saw this as being appropriate, He agreed to Lucifer's proposal but stated that there were ramifications that even the devil could never comprehend.

Lucifer shared with Heinrich that as the Master of Hades, it had an obligation to keep its part of the agreement with God. If things continued in the current direction since Heinrich arrived, it undermined the arrangement with the Almighty One. Hell wasn't a place of contentment and satisfaction for the damned souls inhabiting it, but rather one of suffering and torment. Lucifer and its demon horde were to be in authority over the souls, and they were entrusted with making them suffer.

"There is a certain reputation I am expected to maintain," said Lucifer, "and this story of your miserable existence on Earth is threatening the order of chaos. If I fail to ensure these conditions persist, Hell will close in on itself and no longer exist; you will have none of the companionship you cherish. It will implode, and all will be abolished. You and all your friends. For reasons such as these, it is imperative you accept my offer so that everything can go back to normal."

Heinrich was still insistent that he had no interest going back to re-live his life. He didn't have regrets about his life, rather his whole life was altogether terrible. The devil pressed him further to accept its offer, but Heinrich had his own reply. "I'll only go back to Earth if you will meet several of my conditions."

"I'm listening," said Lucifer. "Offer your terms and I'll see what I can do."

Heinrich began with a sigh, "I won't go back to Cuba. I want no memory of Cuba in my new life. No communism or any authoritarian regimes. Send me to America."

The devil considered it before nodding in agreement, "We can pull a few strings."

"I want to live in a city of prosperity and freedom," said Heinrich.

"Is there anything else?"

"I want a life of wealth," replied Heinrich. "I never want to work again."

"That can be arranged."

"I want to be liked. I want friends like I have here."

Lucifer wasn't so warm with this request. "Certain things we can and cannot do," it said. "We cannot make humans do anything; free will and all. We can make the conditions right for this to happen though."

"That's fine," conceded Heinrich. "I also want a beautiful girlfriend."

Lucifer was about to speak before Heinrich interrupted, "Scratch that, I want three beautiful girlfriends."

The devil smiled with an impressed grin. "You are ambitious, but again, free will and all, it cannot be guaranteed; plus most women possess the wisdom not to lend themselves to a male of many tastes."

"Can you set it up or not?" demanded Heinrich.

"We may have a solution."

"No tricks or anything."

"No tricks."

"I also have business I'd like to finish up on Earth," said Heinrich.

"What unfinished business were you thinking?"

"I want revenge," he said. "Against my brother."

"What kind?"

"I want him dead."

"That could be tricky," replied the devil.

"Those are my terms," said Heinrich. "Take them or leave them."

Lucifer studied Heinrich and deliberated his requests, putting its arm around Heinrich. "We have a few of our own terms and conditions. If you go back, you will do something for us."

Heinrich hesitated but still gave his attention to the devil. "I'm listening."

"Just a few tasks, nothing too challenging," said Lucifer. "But more importantly, if you want us to help bring everything about that you desire and have set out as your conditions, you will agree to having a demon indwell within you."

"I will do no such thing!" shouted Heinrich.

"I'm afraid you have little choice," replied the devil. "In fact, maybe I misspoke a little. This is the case not only because of your desires, but the manner in which you killed yourself. It is the only way. I am not the Almighty One. I cannot create new life, but I only can tinker with that which I have been given. Your suicide so damaged your heart that it will not work on its own. We cannot resuscitate you naturally. The demon, however, can get your heart beating again and operating."

"How can I trust you?"

"How can you not?" replied Lucifer. "The demon will help you achieve all your conditions, whether it is friends or girlfriends. It will help you meet women and make friends. We have a considerable amount of experience watching how you humans operate. We see your patterns, and we are familiar with how you work. We have you figured out. It is the only way possible."

Heinrich considered Lucifer's words and weighed whether they were trustworthy. "Is there anything else?"

"There is one more thing. You must swear your soul in an eternal oath that you will return when you are finished re-living your life," said Lucifer.

"I don't understand why that is an issue."

"You must swear and make an eternal oath which can never be broken," said the devil. "Eternal oaths are ones that even the Almighty One will respect and will not come between. Any attempt to break it will be dealt with by swift and eternal consequences. The one who tries to break it will serve out eternity in utter isolation in the lowest ring of Hell."

"Okay. It won't be an issue," conceded Heinrich. "Are there any more conditions?"

The devil scrutinized Heinrich with hesitation and suspected Heinrich's commitment to the terms. "No, that is all," it replied. "I will call upon you when the time comes to make your oath, and we will proceed with the indwelling of the demon within you."

"You know where to find me."

XII

A legion of demons led Heinrich, drawing an attentive crowd through each circle of Hell that he and the demons passed. A great confusion spread regarding what was happening with him. Heinrich didn't tell a soul about his deal with the devil. Neither did he even get to say goodbye to his new friends since Lucifer wanted no one to dissuade him from the agreement they came upon together. Nor did the devil want others to get any ideas about the potential to leave Hell.

The demons took him toward the abode of Lucifer, Pandaemonium. Heinrich learned that several of the other chief demons took up residence with the devil. The residence was palatial, though constructed with the bones of every living creature imaginable.

They marched through a large gateway guarded by two of the most hideous demons that Heinrich had ever seen; each with five identical heads on their bodies, resembling the monsters from the fairytales that Heinrich had read to him as a child. One was that of a wolf's head, though its hair was red and white with teeth oversized for its jaw. Next to it was the head of a rhinoceros, and its tusks looked sharpened for increased violence. Beside it was the head of an eel-like creature, whose jaw extended forward, revealing hundreds of piercing incisors. Beside those heads, he recognized an ant-eater and a dragon head. Both demons looked upon Heinrich without suspicion, knowing who he was and what his purpose was within Pandaemonium.

They passed through many courtyards and hallways, each decorated documenting the sinful arts of the devil and its company. On the walls, blood-soaked paintings revealed the bloodiest of battles in human history, though brought to life with varying shades of blood. Down another hall was a corridor marked Heroes of Hell, honoring the greatest servants of Lucifer and its legions. Each face was so satirized in portrait, it was difficult to determine who these mortal souls were. As Heinrich strode by each passageway, he sensed the absolute hatred of the Almighty One and His creation by Lucifer and its horde.

Heinrich entered a high-ceilinged audience room, where he found Lucifer waiting for him. A pentagram was engraved upon the center of the floor. Beside the devil stood a naked androgynous demon, resembling a jungle witch doctor. Heinrich assumed it was a priest-like being for whatever rite Heinrich had agreed to undertake. Also in the room was an operating table constructed with the bones of creatures long since passed away. Lucifer greeted Heinrich with a nod as the demons ushered him forward into the devil's presence.

"Are you ready?" asked Lucifer.

"I am."

The naked demon stepped forward, "To begin the ritual, we must first start by marking your soul," it said.

Heinrich gave the devil a startled look as he didn't remember this as a part of the terms.

"It is a part of the process," Lucifer reminded him. Another demon handed the priest a red-hot rod drawn from the fire. It bore a pentagram, and as the priest approached with it, demons grabbed hold of Heinrich's arms to prevent him from moving. They tore his shirt off to reveal his bare chest, and at once, the priest branded Heinrich with the pentagram in the middle of his torso just above his sternum. He screamed and writhed in pain. He begged the priest to stop, but the priest maintained the pressure without letting up until Heinrich had the mark burned onto him.

The naked priest demon threw the branding rod to the ground and began a grotesque dance. It bent itself in such fashions that looked unnatural. It bowed down to Lucifer and worshipped by praising its evilness and promising to bring about its dominion over the entire universe, both temporal and eternal.

The demon picked itself back up and muttered phrases like incantations. The whole room shook and made the noise of an amplifier reverberating before giving hideous squeals of feedback, piercing Heinrich's eardrums. Lucifer and the demons didn't even react to the painful sounds. Heinrich writhed and attempted to cover his ears, but the demons holding Heinrich prevented him from protecting his hearing.

The demon turned to Heinrich, putting its face in front of his. "Do you swear that Lucifer is the master of your soul, holds rights to your eternity, and that you are the servant of its every wish and command?" it asked.

Heinrich took a glance at Lucifer, who nodded to him. "I do," he said.

"Do you swear to return to Hades when your service to Lucifer is rendered complete?" it asked.

"I do."

"Do you swear to praise the majesty and wonder of Lucifer, also known as Satan, for now, and eternity ever more, bringing the power of Lucifer's name to all corners of the human world, and of the world of angels and demons?" it asked.

"I do."

Lucifer looked upon Heinrich with approval and motioned for the boned bed to be brought forth by the other demons. The demons holding Heinrich placed him on the bed and tied his wrists and feet to it to restrain him. The priest shuffled beside Heinrich's head and spoke at him. "You must lay as still as possible, human. This is the rite of indwelling. We begin by cutting your chest open."

Heinrich interrupted the demon, "Lucifer, I don't remember this as a part of the deal either!"

"It is the only way to do it," it replied. "And I suspect it will be painful, also vitally necessary, if you want all your conditions and requests met."

Heinrich scanned the priestly demon, "How painful will it be?"

"You will know no greater pain in life either in the natural or supernatural realm," it replied. "But you will survive, and it may make everything else pale in comparison."

Heinrich braced himself by holding rigid before nodding to concede that he was ready.

"Very well," said the priestly demon. It reached its hand out, and another demon placed a jagged knife in its hand. It muttered words, while looking down to the ground. With no warning, it thrust the knife into Heinrich's chest in a stabbing motion through the middle of the branded pentagram. Heinrich writhed in pain, but the demons restrained him. They struggled to keep him down, let alone still. The priest withdrew the knife and blood pumped out of Heinrich's torso. The witch doctor dressed the wound to keep it from getting too messy while still allowing the blood to flow. The demon invoked an incantation, and the entire room shook with a great wind.

The floor itself rattled, and even Lucifer struggled to keep its balance. A black mist entered the room from the ceiling, and it spread about the room before coming together. The mysterious cloud distracted Heinrich from the excruciating pain in his chest, but only for a moment, as the mist replaced his pain with overwhelming pressure all over his body. The mist lingered above Heinrich before channeling itself into his chest cavity through the wound, causing him to shriek in pain again. Heinrich's writhing knocked one demon to the ground, but it picked itself back up and held him down.

The priest finished the operation by stitching Heinrich's torso shut, but it was difficult as he couldn't hold still. The two demons holding him down got control of Heinrich and held him still, allowing the witch doctor to get his chest cavity stitched. When it finished, Heinrich's arms were released, and he clutched his chest, though it brought no relief or comfort.

Lucifer approached Heinrich and put its hand on his shoulder. "Congratulations," it said. "You fared much better than I expected. Follow me."

Heinrich climbed off the bed with the help of the demons. They led him behind the devil, who meandered to a full-length mirror. Heinrich stood next to Lucifer and withdrew his hands from his torso to examine the branding and the stitches on his chest.

"Was that necessary?" he asked.

"It was," replied Lucifer. "We had to mark you as the property of the devil."

Heinrich recoiled, "I don't remember agreeing to that either."

"I needed some guarantee you will return here when your second life is finished," said the devil. "You have seen Hell. I cannot have you warning others about the misery that is to be wrought here. This seals the contract."

Heinrich scanned his chest once more and touched the mark. He endured a shooting sensation of pain as he grazed it.

"It is time for you to go," said Lucifer, ushering Heinrich toward another door in the room.

"There's a passageway from Hell to Earth?"

"How do you think demons roam Earth?" replied the devil. "One last thing must be done."

Lucifer motioned for the priest to return. The demon placed its hands on Heinrich's body and patted him over as it chanted evil utterances and moans. The demon led Heinrich toward the passageway and it opened the doorway itself. It backed away and banged on the floor behind Heinrich.

"The way is open," said the devil, directing Heinrich to proceed forward.

"Won't people wonder about my chest? The stitches and the pentagram?" asked Heinrich.

"Heart surgery," said Lucifer without a thought. "And besides, tattoos are popular with humans these days, I hear."

Heinrich turned toward the open passageway. Nothing stood beyond the doors except darkness. No light entered it, and no light returned from it. He ventured toward it until he perceived a misty, yet flat barrier between the room and the passageway. He hesitated and glanced back at Lucifer, who again motioned for him to proceed.

"This is what you wanted," said the devil. "Take it and fulfill the contract."

Heinrich took a breath and stepped through the barrier. As soon as his toe passed through it, a faint vacuum sucked him in and drew him away from the room. He perceived a circular nature to the wind based on how the rounded sides of the vacuum battered against him. With each hit, his chest hurt all the more. His consciousness waned as he sought to make sense of what he saw: a strange manifestation of a visual battle between light and darkness to overcome each other; each holding the other from coming any further.

Heinrich rushed toward something. All went black, and he passed out.

UNITED STATES OF AMERICA

XIII

A chilly breeze passed over Heinrich's face, but it wasn't until the blast of a horn that he startled. A heavy rumble below him carried a quiet drone throughout his body. Opening his eyes and seeing the sky above, he sat up. A breeze flowed over his bare chest while a burlap sack covered the torn linen pants on his legs. His hands clutched at the scar on his torso though no pain came from touching it. Coldness enveloping his body drew his attention from the scar. He discovered an empty lifeboat was his place of rest. It looked as though it had been undisturbed for some time; the life vests showed aging and weathering. He found a tattered t-shirt and put it on.

He climbed out and discovered behind him the tall tower of a freighter. The horn blasted, causing Heinrich to startle again. He traversed over toward the freighter's edge. He viewed the familiar sight he had seen in forbidden materials back in Cuba: the Statue of Liberty, the symbol of New York City. Lucifer had been faithful to the deal, far away from the memories of Heinrich's former life.

The skyline of New York fascinated Heinrich. As he reached the ship's edge, he took in the massive buildings. Never had he seen anything like it in Cuba. He viewed propaganda showing the glory of American capitalism, but seeing the buildings in front of him, he struggled to believe his eyes.

The marvels of mankind, came a voice that rang loud in Heinrich's ears. He searched to determine who stood near him and had spoken, but no one was there. His eyes scanned the ship, looking for a prankster. "Who spoke?" he asked.

It is I, said the voice as clear as before. *Your assigned spirit guide as instructed by Lucifer.*

"Where are you?"

I am within you, it spoke. *Do you not remember the ceremony?*

"I do," replied Heinrich, his hands returning to his chest yet again. "What am I to call you?"

Mephistopheles, the voice said.

Heinrich hesitated to say more. He was unsure about this arrangement, though he didn't doubt his reasons for agreeing to it.

Take cover. A sailor is headed in your direction!

Heinrich discovered an individual coming toward him, though it didn't appear as if Heinrich was seen. "Where should I hide?"

Whence you first came, instructed Mephistopheles. Heinrich did as directed and found his original hiding place. He leaped in and lay against the edge of the lifeboat. Minutes passed with no activity; he detected nothing but stayed still. The ship's horn sounded again. Another sailor called out to someone in a language Heinrich didn't understand. The intensity of the shouts increased, making Heinrich wonder if something was amiss.

"How do I get off this ship?" Heinrich asked the spirit aloud.

Quiet, said the spirit. *You must be silent. The time is yet to come.*

The ship's engine softened; it didn't steam the ship forward any longer. Heinrich grew uncomfortable in his position and lifted his head above the lifeboat's edge. He couldn't see anyone, but something was going on. His curiosity made him eager to identify what was happening. He took in the New York City skyline from the security of the lifeboat; they arrived closer to port.

"Is the time now?"

Get out of the lifeboat and stay low.

Heinrich climbed over the edge with a stealth approach. No sailor was visible. Near the ship's ledge in the distance sat a rolled up rope ladder. He trotted toward it.

Not there! instructed Mephistopheles. *It is too obvious; you'd be seen within a second. Run to the forward bow of the ship, but not to the front entirely. You must leap from the starboard side of the ship.*

"Are you mad?" asked Heinrich. He was tempted to return to the lifeboat and take his chances.

The ship is turning to starboard, which will leave you safe from being drawn into the wake of the ship. Even still, the propeller is stationary. The ship is being led by harbor tugboats. You will be safe. You must trust me.

Trusting a demonic spirit seemed questionable to Heinrich, but after everything he had witnessed since Cuba, he had little choice. He navigated his way forward on the ship, being careful to stay out of the sight of any of the sailors on the ship's deck. He was mindful of anyone who might discover him from above on the ship's bridge. Heinrich grew nervous the closer he approached the ship's bow. The sailors were working and observing the ship's connection to the tugboats.

Gliding along unseen appears to come naturally to you, the spirit said to Heinrich.

"I've gone most of my life being invisible to others," said Heinrich.

The sailors in front of Heinrich kept watch of anything that might cause alarm or peril to the ship and its connection to the tugboats. Heinrich studied them for his moment to follow Mephistopheles's instructions. The ship moved slower, judging by the scenery passing gently.

The man on the right, slowly advance until you are within arm's reach. Then club him over the head.

Heinrich surveyed the much larger man. The confidence Heinrich gained in Hell did little to convince him that this was a good idea. He inspected his open fists. He clenched them and made a puny fist.

Not with your hands, you fool, said Mephistopheles. *Find something blunt. You would not stand a chance against that hardened beast of a man.*

Heinrich didn't like being dismissed. An errant rock lay among the debris ahead of him. He gazed back to his hands and the rock. Heinrich began his approach toward the stone. Once he neared the rock, though, he discovered that his nerves had calmed. He was confident about himself. He didn't fear death. He experienced it before, and he had returned.

Heinrich acquired the rock in his hand and moved closer still to the intended victim. He was within a tackling reach of the man when the sailor shouted to the tugboat below. The man was the most vulnerable he had been, and Heinrich leaped to strike, but against Mephistopheles's advice, he dropped the rock to the ground. He sucker-punched the sailor from behind, which didn't render him unconscious but only dazed. The man spun to face the direction he had received the blow. In a hazy blur, Heinrich stood before him, but before the man could defend himself, Heinrich landed another blow to the man's chin. Heinrich's victim dropped to the deck and Heinrich rendered him defenseless and unaware.

Heinrich tried to determine if the other sailor had been alerted, but the sailor's eyes still looked overboard.

Jump now! ordered Mephistopheles. Heinrich approached the edge, and while he may have been fearless about attacking his now unconscious victim, the drop to the water below eroded his confidence. *Jump, you fool!*

Heinrich's hands gripped the railing. The water didn't look freezing or even choppy. It was so far down. He cast a glance toward the bridge; no one had discovered him yet. His eyes went upward to the skyline, and he reminded himself why he stood there. He leapt to the harbor below. The fall lasted far longer than he had hoped as he anticipated the crash into the water below. *Straighten your legs!*

He sank deep beneath the waterline by following Mephistopheles's instructions. Heinrich wasn't the most gifted swimmer, but he managed well enough. He swam forward and away from the ship, hearing the muffled drone of the ship's engine in the water all around him.

The water was too filthy to see anything, and when he tried, his eyes stung. It was the first time he preferred anything from Cuba, like the clear ocean water. He kicked and brought himself to the surface. No one had noticed him. No call for man overboard, nor did anyone try to rescue him. He was used to that.

Heinrich's next concern was to avoid the path of the rear harbor tugboat maneuvering the freighter's stern. When he was safe from it, he swam harder toward the water's edge. He was exhausted and took breaks to regain his strength. The water was colder than he had wished and his clothes weighed upon him in the New York harbor. The freighter steamed away, passing alongside what Heinrich later learned was Governor's Island. Other boats passed by, though to Heinrich's relief, far enough away that he was still undiscovered.

Heinrich grew bored with swimming in the unappetizing waters of New York City, which furthered his determination all the more to make land. The closer he came to the shore's edge, the smaller he felt compared to the buildings he gawked at earlier.

Heinrich grazed the harbor's bottom below him. His feet sensed both silt and small pebbles, the former of which made it difficult to step forward. Heinrich's whole body felt spent, but he continued until he collapsed on the beach. His feet lay still in the water, but mostly, he was on dry land. Heinrich told himself that he had made it. He embraced a self-congratulatory sense of approval. After he caught his breath, he climbed farther up the beach and sat to take in the view of the opposite New Jersey shoreline.

Impressive, said the spirit, interrupting Heinrich's peaceful thought. *You are not finished yet.*

Heinrich exhaled and lifted himself from the beach. He found concrete stairs that took him from the shore and onto a busy boardwalk alongside the traffic of New York City. He paused. He hadn't seen cars as modern as these before. Heinrich had been transported to another world. The sight of the famed yellow cabs darting in and out of traffic and honking their horns as they forced their way forward; he had arrived in America.

Happiness became real for the Cuban castaway. Heinrich advanced down the boardwalk to take in the sights before deciding to cross the street. He followed along with a few other pedestrians and took their cue when it was safe to cross. New Yorkers didn't follow the signs.

Heinrich scampered over to a large storefront with a glass window display, showing off an arrangement of purses and female mannequins in fine clothing. He examined his still wet clothes. His eyes went back to the display when he noticed his reflection. He stumbled backward in shock. He palmed his face in horror, but he realized that was a mistake; his face was handsome. The facial scar was nowhere to be seen.

"What has happened to my face?" asked Heinrich aloud. He stepped closer to the glass to study his visage.

We had some resources do a little work on you, said the spirit. *If you were going to have everything you desired, we needed to update what we were working with.*

"Is this still my same body?" said Heinrich, while pulling his shirt up to check out his stomach; the same stomach he knew. "You couldn't have made me a little more fit?"

Sadly, human advancements have yet to arrive to sculpt bodies with muscle tissue. Maybe one day.

Heinrich warmed to his new face the more he examined it. He looked like an attractive man. His face had sharp features. His eyes were more prominent than before, drawing attention to their blue color. He liked his smile too, and his teeth looked clean and straight. His hair, though wet, looked trimmed and ready for styling. He didn't look out of place in New York City besides the river-soaked clothes that still clung to his body.

Call a cab, instructed Mephistopheles, drawing Heinrich's attention back to the traffic.

"I have no money," he replied.

Check your pockets. Heinrich discovered something was there that he hadn't yet noticed; two crumpled and soaked American dollar bills. He had $30. Heinrich approached the sidewalk's edge and glanced over the passing taxi cabs. He tried signaling one, but it drove on without stopping. He noticed that a few had lights on while others did not. He attempted again with an illuminated one and it drew itself alongside Heinrich. He opened the door and climbed in.

"Where to?" asked the cabbie.

The Shaughnessy. You have someone to meet. Heinrich repeated Mephistopheles's instructions and the cab driver took him on his way. Heinrich almost asked Mephistopheles a question aloud before realizing that it would look like he was talking to himself. He decided if he thought about it, Mephistopheles would answer him but he got no response in his thoughts. He tried thinking harder about his question, but still no response. Heinrich was confused.

XIV

The taxi pulled in front of a long maroon awning, where a bellboy opened the car door for Heinrich. A finely dressed doorman opened the front entrance and nodded respectfully to Heinrich. As he stepped into the foyer of the Shaughnessy, he discovered the finest restaurant he had ever set foot. Typically in Cuba, such a place was rare, but one existed for the political elites. He once snuck in for a glimpse as a young boy but was shooed away.

"Sir, may I help you?" asked a male host behind the table. The man leered down his nose upon Heinrich in a contemptuous manner. Heinrich's clothing had only half-dried, and his hair still looked wet and unkempt. Worst of all, his smell was breathtaking, but not in the good way. He brought with him the scent of the ocean and seagulls.

Tell him you have a reservation with Mr. Dante Condannato, instructed Mephistopheles. Heinrich did as told and the host showed an immediate sense of deference. The host promised to take him to his table. Heinrich glanced behind himself to make sure that it was him that the host displayed such reverence. Heinrich followed the host into the restaurant's dining area, which had more chandeliers than one could imagine a single restaurant ever having. The light that shone fascinated Heinrich.

The restaurant maintained an air of elegance among what was the midday mealtime. He noted the clothing of the other guests; people far more influential than he had ever associated with. They made no notice of him until the smell of the ocean hit them.

The host led him to a table at the rear of the restaurant, which looked like a place of honor. It was plainly visible to all in the restaurant, and above it was the grandest of all the restaurant's chandeliers.

A man was seated facing Heinrich. He took notice of Heinrich about the same time Heinrich did of him, though the man showed little emotion or joy upon seeing him coming. The host directed Heinrich to the chair opposite of the man with Heinrich's back to the rest of the restaurant. He sat, and waited for Mephistopheles to tell him what to do or say, but no instructions came.

The man studied Heinrich but cast no judgment upon him. He dressed in an elegant navy blue suit with a darker blue dress shirt beneath but no tie. Heinrich paid attention to the man's features. He had blue eyes, matching Heinrich's, and a head of elegantly manicured blonde hair. The more Heinrich studied the man, the more he realized how much they looked alike.

"So you are the one that I was told to anticipate?" asked the man. Heinrich nodded as told to do so by Mephistopheles. "I always knew this day would come; I just didn't know how soon."

The man cast his eyes to the tableware in front of him. He tapped the fingers of his right hand on the table. "What did Lucifer promise you for your soul?" asked the man.

Heinrich said nothing but again waited for instructions from Mephistopheles. Before any answer came, two large men appeared. He assumed they were the man's bodyguards, as they circled behind him, but Mephistopheles's instructions came for what to say.

"It matters not what my arrangement is," said Heinrich, as he motioned with his right hand to the two men. "Your time has come. Lucifer has completed the deal made with you. You have met your service, and you are finished, Mr. Condannato."

"I know," said the man, as he cast his sight away from Heinrich and back toward the table. "I know this much indeed."

The two large men ushered the fellow to rise from his chair. He did as guided, and the men took a gentle grip on the man's arms and led him forward. Heinrich followed behind the two men, as Mephistopheles told him to do.

As the men neared the foyer of the restaurant, they strayed to the right where an elevator waited with the door open. An elevator operator exited the elevator and made himself disappear. Heinrich followed in after the other men. The elevator sprang upward, and the men stood in silence. It headed to the roof, which Heinrich judged was forty-five floors above. It made no stops on any of the floors until it reached its peak. At such a height, a noticeable breeze blew when they exited the elevator. Thick, dark clouds formed in the distance, casting a mighty shadow on them. He followed the two large men leading Mr. Condannato, and they brought him near the roof's edge facing the street below. One of the men grabbed a firm grip of both Mr. Condannato's arms while the other approached Heinrich and handed him a crumpled shut paper bag.

You must kill this man, said Mephistopheles to Heinrich. He opened the bag and withdrew a 9mm handgun inside. Heinrich looked up at the man, who appeared resigned to such a fate; that this was what he knew was to become of him. The bodyguard withdrew from Heinrich to the intended victim and assisted the other in taking a firm grip on Mr. Condannato's arm.

"Why must I do this?" Heinrich asked quietly of Mephistopheles. His hushed tones were masked by the breeze picking up. It drew a chill inside of Heinrich.

It is the way that things must happen; you will understand. But you must do this now.

"Just shoot me," urged Mr. Condannato. "But you should know that you will be standing here yourself one day when Lucifer deems you as having rendered your service complete."

Heinrich sized up the handgun and took a grip of it. As he looked upon it in his hands, he felt strength he had never experienced. He fixed his gaze upon the man, and defeat filled Mr. Condannato's eyes. Heinrich had the power to end a person's life, and that made him feel more of a man than ever before. Why should he care about Mr. Condannato's well-being? He had lived well and made his fantasies come true.

Shoot him.

Heinrich lifted the gun to Mr. Condannato and pointed it toward his chest, his finger on the trigger. *Not in the chest, you must shoot him in the face.* Heinrich paused, but staggered closer to the man and directed the gun's chamber to Mr. Condannato's forehead. The man closed his eyes in anticipation of his doom. *Not the forehead, put the gun in his mouth and point upwards.* Heinrich did as he was told, which appeared uncomfortable for the victim.

Heinrich looked at the man but glanced away before pulling the trigger and releasing the explosion in the chamber of the handgun. Mr. Condannato fell to the ground, his fall caught by the bodyguards. Heinrich struggled to bring himself to look at the man for fear of what he might see. When he did, Mr. Condannato's body had twisted and fallen on its chest.

"Hand me his belongings," Heinrich instructed the men, who emptied Mr. Condannato's pockets and produced a wallet, a set of keys, a cellphone, and a building FOB. They also removed a signet ring from the dead man's hand, which bore the symbol of a pentagram with a goat's face on it. Heinrich placed it on his right index finger, while the other belongings he stuffed in his pockets.

Heinrich turned the gun on one of the bodyguards, who looked surprised. Heinrich shot him in the head before firing the gun on the other man, and causing him also to drop to the ground.

Heinrich grabbed hold of the larger man, and tugged him toward the roof's edge and shot the man in the stomach, though he was already dead. He shoved the dead bodyguard off the roof. He went to work disposing of the other bodyguard. As he lugged the second man over to the edge, he picked up screams from the street below as the first man's body thudded. Shortly afterward, he sent the second man down.

Mephistopheles told him that Mr. Condannato must follow them, but Heinrich struggled with handling him for fear of seeing the gruesome sight that was once the dead man's face. He succeeded in bringing the man to the roof's edge. Time was of the essence, Mephistopheles told Heinrich, and before casting the dead man to the street below, he placed the gun in deceased's hand and fired it into the air. Heinrich propelled the dead body overboard and sent it crashing to the street below. Heinrich didn't wait to see the man fall, but departed from the roof and into the elevator. The ride down seemed like it took far longer than the ride up. Heinrich fidgeted with his fingers. He was surprised with himself for having been able to do as instructed.

"Where do I go from here?" Heinrich asked Mephistopheles aloud.

Check your pockets and take the dead man's identification. That is where you are headed. There is a cab waiting out back of the restaurant; it will take you there. The address didn't mean anything to Heinrich. He knew nothing of New York City's geography, but he was pleased that it was anywhere but there.

XV

The taxi dropped Heinrich off outside the front entrance to a tower near Central Park. Heinrich looked up and struggled to make out its top; its height so immense. The glass-covered sides gave a providential view of Central Park to the north.

He pranced into the lobby of the tower as guided by Mephistopheles. He entered the elevator and used the FOB he had removed from Mr. Condannato. Mephistopheles told him to select the 81st floor, and the elevator began its ascension. A peaceful jingle played as Heinrich embraced the luxury of the elevator. He sighted the floor reading on the elevator, and the numbers slowed as it neared the floor of his choosing. The door opened, leading Heinrich to a dark corridor. It lacked generous lighting and created an eerie aura.

Heinrich stepped forward. On the corridor's walls were many classical paintings featuring human encounters of the supernatural. One featured a hideous demon delivering a victim to an unpleasant death of being buried alive. Another painting showed a goat-headed humanoid figure who oversaw the torture of human souls in Hell. Heinrich believed the depiction inaccurate since Hell appeared static and far too much like Earth in the painting.

At the corridor's end, a man of impressive stature stood by a door. Heinrich approached him, and the man cast Heinrich an intimidating glance. *Show him the ring*, said Mephistopheles.

Heinrich complied. The man backed away from the door while opening it. "Welcome, Mr. Condannato."

Heinrich passed into an apartment with a dimly lit lobby, much like the corridor preceding it. What hit Heinrich was its stillness. Having just ventured through the busyness and chaos of New York City a thousand feet below, Heinrich experienced a sense of calm he didn't expect.

The apartment had an open concept, its essential feature being the view of Central Park, though the glass windows dimmed to offer privacy. The lobby had steps below to an expansive living room. Couches of dark, natural colors surrounded a rich mahogany coffee table. It looked sufficient to entertain large parties while to the right of the living room was the master bedroom. It must have been dozens of times the size of his residence in Cuba.

Heinrich threw himself onto the couch and enjoyed the cushioning embrace of the pillows. He considered it heavenly but stopped short of finishing that thought.

"Mr. Condannato, at your service," said a feminine

voice, drawing Heinrich's attention. A plainly, though professionally dressed woman had entered the room with her head bowed. She stood with a gracious, yet fearful expression. Heinrich rose from the couch and looked her over.

"If there is anything you need, I would be most happy to assist you," she spoke again, hoping to garner a response.

"A change of clothes?" said Heinrich. He tried to determine whether she was trustworthy.

"Of course, my lord," she said, as she hurried off to the bedroom. "If you will follow me, I would be happy to help you find an appropriate outfit in your closet."

Heinrich followed, and once they stepped into the bedroom, he was where he wanted to be. The curtains were drawn back, casting generous light into the room. The bed was far grander than he had ever imagined. It ought to accommodate at least eight people. The linens were of dark satins; they looked unused while the furnishings were of the finest carpentry.

The woman led Heinrich to a walk-in closet that also served as a dressing room. The closet had more colors and clothes than Heinrich knew existed. He didn't believe it was possible to wear such combinations or styles.

She produced a fine silk shirt, a pair of slacks, socks, and polished leather shoes. She showed him to his underwear cabinet and told him to choose whichever style he preferred. He considered changing but asked her to take his clothes to the washroom so he could shower. After, he sent her away and requested that she wait on him outside as he cleaned up.

When Heinrich finished, he called out to her for assistance as he was unaware of how to dress in such clothes. Instead of her came a middle-aged Arab man. He bowed before Heinrich, appearing as his personal butler. He said he would be happy to assist him with dressing. Heinrich felt comfortable around him, as the man was skilled at his craft. He blended a personality that was both focused, yet charming. When they completed Heinrich's dressing, the butler led him over to a tall mirror on the wall to admire his outfit. Heinrich marveled at how clean and polished he looked.

"You are an excellent specimen, sir, if I may say so myself," said the man. The man led Heinrich out and they met the woman again.

She led them to another door out of the bedroom. The door opened to a modestly sized office space with a dramatic curtain hanging from the ceiling that was ever so transparent. Behind it was a carved desk and a sitting chair. Looking forward from the desk and through the curtain stood a set of immense double doors. A candle flickered on either side. The office too seemed silent other than the sound of their steps on the wooden floor. A seating area sat in front of the desk for more informal meetings while the chairs could also face to the desk for more professional contexts. On the desk were files laid out in intricate order, and beside them rested a day planner.

The woman encouraged Heinrich to take a seat behind the desk. She excused the butler, who left.

"That will be everything," said Heinrich to the woman. She nodded her head and departed through the door back to Heinrich's bedroom and into the apartment. Heinrich slouched in the chair and sought a comfortable position. He scanned the room and ascertained an immense power within the chamber. Besides his flattering outfit, the room made him understand what it meant to be a confident man.

He inspected the day planner in front of him and found the names of guests listed. On one column, a caption of VIP stood atop, while another column was captioned with VETTED. None of the names carried any significance to Heinrich.

"What is this place?" Heinrich asked Mephistopheles. "And why do they call me Mr. Condannato? I have so many questions."

It would be natural for you to feel that way, said Mephistopheles. *You are Mr. Condannato to the staff of the house; you wear the ring of Mr. Condannato, therefore, you are.*

"Do they not remember what he looked like?" asked Heinrich.

They do, and you were made to look like him. You noted this yourself, did you not?

"I did."

You must know this, Heinrich. To much of the world that knows of Mr. Condannato, he is suspected to be immortal. You are not the first Mr. Condannato. You are just one in the long line of Mr. Condannatos. The person of Mr. Condannato has a rich history in New York City as a broker of power, a harbinger of wealth, and a picture of fame. He is everything you were not in your former life.

Heinrich marveled at such a reality. "But who were the two I met?"

The man, his name is Yousef. He is to be your personal butler. He will ask few questions of you; he knows better. He does his job well, and he is a faithful servant. You can trust him.

"I felt that."

The woman, you can call her Bianca. It is not her name, but it is the name she has chosen. It matters not why to Lucifer or the horde of Hell. She is your personal assistant. She will aid you in managing your affairs, arranging meetings, executing your plans, and introducing you to your long list of friends.

"I thought you couldn't make people like me or be my friend?" asked Heinrich.

We cannot, but if they believe you are Mr. Condannato, they will resume their friendship as they did with your predecessor. What you do with these relationships is your choice, for better or for worse. You possess the ring; you are Mr. Condannato.

"What about this list of names?" asked Heinrich. "Who are they?"

They are also unimportant, but you must know that people do not simply come to see you in this very office; they must be selected. You will entertain many famous individuals from the seat you sit, but outside those double doors, you will see your empire: Babel.

"Babel?"

It is the most sought after nightclub in New York City.

"A nightclub?"

No one pays to come to this nightclub. It is by invitation only, and these invitations are highly sought after. Outside those doors, you will find the VIP area, where many spend evenings hoping for the chance to see you, let alone catch your attention. If you venture a little farther, you will find a balcony that will allow you to survey the small crowd that gathers each night Babel is open.

"I'm to be a nightclub manager?" said Heinrich. "I don't know the first thing about management."

Worry not, Heinrich. There is a skilled staff who are com-

mitted to serving Lucifer and operating the club. Consider it this way: you are merely a figurehead of the operation. They know it not, but I guide you. Bianca will assist you. You will find her a tremendous, if not invaluable, help.

"I have another question. Why can't you hear my thoughts? Earlier I asked you several questions but got no response," said Heinrich.

We demons do not have the power to read humans' thoughts.

"How is it I can hear you in my head then?"

It is how the one in Heaven created you, humans, with free will and all. You are free from spiritual beings entering your mind and reading your thoughts, but we have the capacity to insert thoughts into your mind. There is only one who can listen to the thoughts of mortal humans, and it is the one who resides in Heaven. Not even angels can listen to the thoughts of humans. But we have watched you, humans, long enough that we can sometimes predict what you humans are thinking.

"How will I ask for your help when I'm with other people?" asked Heinrich.

Worry not about that. You must trust me, Heinrich. I have done this a long time. Lucifer has had me aid many a soul before, and I am good at this devilry. Ever since the war in Hell, I have served Lucifer in this way, leading many a fool astray. Others I have helped receive what was promised to them by the lord of Hell. I have been a faithful servant of Lucifer, and I know what I am doing.

"Okay."

Any other questions?

"Yes," said Heinrich with an evil grin. "When will I be introduced to some women?"

XVI

After a later evening nap, Heinrich enjoyed his first meal at the apartment. It was an exquisitely prepared dinner, possessing more flavor than he had ever experienced in Cuba. Mephistopheles cautioned him from overeating as he could have eaten more than his fill. Much needed to be done that evening, and Heinrich couldn't be bloated.

Heinrich made his first pass through the double doors that led into the nightclub from his office. Mephistopheles told him that for many of the guests of Babel that evening, Heinrich wasn't recognizable. He passed into the VIP area and cast a glance toward the bartender who gave him a muted, but respectful nod. The employees recognized Mr. Condannato as they couldn't determine a difference between the two; they looked so similar.

It was also imperative that Heinrich kept the hand

with the signet ring in his pocket. Rumors spread that the ring was the only true way to know who Mr. Condannato was unless one had met him in the past.

The VIP area remained sparsely filled; the way it was intended to be. Those individuals brought upstairs were few, and even earning access wasn't a guarantee that one gained an audience with the master of the house. Mephistopheles explained that strict rules were in place that no one approach Mr. Condannato, even if they had met him before; nor was anyone to speak with him unless Mr. Condannato spoke first.

Heinrich journeyed over to the balcony overlooking the club. A dance floor was the centerpiece below, but few occupied it. Most of the guests enjoyed themselves in the lounge that surrounded the dance floor.

Mephistopheles explained that this wasn't a club that one came to dance. It was a place to network and mingle with the most elite in New York City, and maybe even get invited to the VIP area.

Mephistopheles explained further that gaining access to Babel was almost impossible. One was chosen. It wasn't something for which you applied. The spirit explained that admission was based on the recommendation of others in the inner counsel of Mr. Condannato. Still, one might be noticed or come across by another spirit, at which point the individual received a recommendation for an invitation to the club.

Many famous souls passed through, and while they might never have imagined being invited, the fact that they were, had a substantial influence on their future careers.

Mr. Condannato was in the business of making

connections and granting favors, but one condition of this service was repaying favors or service at a later time. One such man was Tony Saunders, little more than a failed television producer, struggling to get any of his productions picked up by the networks. But after gaining an audience with Mr. Condannato, not only did he land a services agreement with one of the Big Five television networks, his first series became a smash hit and earned him critical acclaim. He won several awards, making him the most sought after producer in New York City.

Another beneficiary of Mr. Condannato's service was none other than Alessandra Dolcini, a Broadway actress who struggled to make the leap from the background to the center stage. With Mr. Condannato's assistance, Miss Dolcini received the lead role in one of the largest Broadway productions ever made, and her performance earned critical acclaim. When she failed to return the favor to Mr. Condannato, her body was found drugged and maimed in the trunk of a car underneath one of the many bridges leading into New York City. She was framed as a drug addict who got mixed up with the wrong crowd; yet another cautionary tale for the masses. As in the case of Miss Dolcini, explained Mephistopheles, failure to return the favor to Mr. Condannato wasn't met with restraint but with the most extreme justice.

"How does all this connect with me and my revenge?" asked Heinrich.

Against your brother—

"*Adopted* brother," stressed Heinrich.

This has everything to do with this end. You told Lucifer that not only did you want revenge, but you wanted friends and influence. It all just so happens to be that your adopted brother needs your help.

Mephistopheles explained that Heinrich's sibling suffered in his attempted escape from Cuba. The man with whom he bartered for his safe passage to America was an inexperienced sailor. Their ship went off course and caught a drift out toward the Atlantic rather than landing at Key West, Florida as planned. This miscalculation caused them to run out of food, and to make matters worse, another Caribbean storm caught up with them. The tempest damaged their boat and injured Jose's pitching shoulder.

When a pleasure craft sailor picked them up, Jose arrived in America in near critical condition. After he recovered, Jose had lost weight and strength, and he also faced a steep medical bill he had no hope of paying off. So he fled to New York City and took upon a new identity.

Mephistopheles explained that while it made sense from a financial perspective, it was detrimental to Jose in so much as he was unknown as a baseball prospect. While his famed name might have enabled him to get his foot in the door with at least a few baseball scouts, he had to rebuild his baseball identity from scratch.

Jose joined a minor league team, but was a mere shadow of the pitcher he was in Cuba; he got cut from the team. He trained hard, but the damage done to his most valuable asset, his pitching shoulder, was too severe. Jose hadn't yet given up on his dream of making it as a pitcher. In the meantime, he snatched up odd jobs, which paid less than minimum wage under the table. He needed Mr. Condannato's help.

"I don't want to help him," protested Heinrich. "I want my revenge. I want him dead."

You know that, and I know that, said Mephistopheles, *but he doesn't know Mr. Condannato wants him dead. You will meet your adopted brother soon; be patient. We will have him brought here, and you will have your revenge. There couldn't be a more ideal arrangement for enabling this to happen, and you will make him suffer. Lucifer is confident about this.*

Heinrich observed two individuals in the lounge below him, and he noted how they didn't fully engage with each other. They both peered over each other's shoulder to watch if someone more important was near by. A beautiful woman sitting alone in the lounge distracted his attention.

"Who is she?" he asked Mephistopheles, pointing her out. She wore a red ombre knee-length dress. She looked exquisite to Heinrich, standing out as the most beautiful woman there with her reddish hair and pale angelic skin.

Does she please you? asked Mephistopheles. Heinrich nodded.

"Find out why she's here," he said. "I want to meet her."

"Excuse me, Mr. Condannato," said the voice of Heinrich's personal assistant. He shifted to Bianca. She held a dark, elaborate clipboard in her hands. "There are guests you must meet tonight."

Heinrich agreed to her request and followed her into the VIP area. She led him to a group of three people, who looked serious but hopeful as Mr. Condannato approached. A bartender brought over a glass of spiced rum over the rocks for Heinrich.

Bianca introduced Mr. Condannato to the three guests. The man on the right was Wallace Filburn, an ambitious entrepreneur trying to find a market for his internet software that would make investors millions. Seated at a high-top chair was a woman named Jayla Jordan, an African-American young woman who had started out as a fashion designer trying to find a buyer for her wares. Her potential was obvious, but her designs were too fringe for the mainstream.

On the left of her was a young man named Roy Berthus, struggling to get from underneath the shadow of his father's fame, Philip Berthus, a Senator from New Jersey. Roy served as the Chief of Staff for the Lieutenant Governor of the State of New York, but he was ineffective. Mephistopheles gave Heinrich all their back stories while he paid half-attention to each of them as they presented sugarcoated versions of each of their stories in their own words.

Heinrich's attention drifted from the conversation, as he had nothing in common with these souls. It perplexed him, though, as each was more successful than he could have dreamed to be in Cuba. Mephistopheles highlighted that each of them was depressed and unfulfilled with their success. They were all on the verge of quitting. They had all encountered one of the hardest decisions in life: to try harder or to walk away.

Heinrich scanned the room and watched others engaged in conversation while those in the VIP area still kept an eye on him as Mr. Condannato, though avoiding direct eye contact. He was uncomfortable with the attention and the expectation being placed upon him. He wondered if this fame and celebrity was what he truly desired. All these people just wanted his help. But is that not what all important people are known for? Their ability or potential to help others get what they want or need in life.

Heinrich excused himself from the group and went to his office with Bianca in tow. She closed the doors behind him as Heinrich reposed behind the desk.

"Your appointment for this evening is with Mr. Berthus," said Bianca, looking at her clipboard.

"Does he really need my help?" asked Heinrich in disbelief. "Can he not ask his father?"

Lucifer will have good use for him, said Mephistopheles. Bianca kept her opinion to herself.

"Bianca, would you take leave and fetch the man?" instructed Heinrich.

"Yes, sir. Right away."

After she left, Heinrich made his displeasure known to Mephistopheles. "How can these people be unhappy with their lives? Have they ever experienced hardship?"

Not as you had, but many a soul find their way here when they are unsure of where else to turn. One curse that the Almighty One placed upon mankind is giving him dreams of advancing himself, but in few places is this possible. The American Dream feeds these souls with the hope that anything is possible, but few can achieve this without the aid of another whether it be a guide or mentor. This is an innate human need. Alas, this is where you come in the service of Lucifer. Giving souls what they desire in exchange for their allegiance to the Master of Hell and making the will of Lucifer become a reality.

"But if they are here in my club, should that not be a testament to their arrival in higher society?"

One might assume, but you humans are very skillful at masquerading success, when in fact you might be on the edge of despair, nearing a fall into hopelessness, and crashing into the unmerciful ground of defeat.

"They live in New York City. How could they ever experience the paralysis of despair?" asked Heinrich with indignation.

Try not to judge the young man too harshly based on your experiences, said Mephistopheles, as the double doors opened with Bianca leading Mr. Berthus through. She instructed him to take a seat in front of the curtain while she took her place standing behind the desk and beside Mr. Condannato. *That would be the most rational thing one might do, but concern yourself not with trivialities.*

The young man cleared his throat. The curtain was set in such a way that Heinrich could see his guest, but his guest made out only the form of Mr. Condannato. Mr. Berthus straightened his tie and gave a pleasant, yet anxious smile in the direction he assumed Mr. Condannato to be. He waited to be spoken to, being mindful of the rules of respect for Mr. Condannato.

Worry not, I shall tell you exactly what to say, instructed Mephistopheles. *Say only what I tell you.*

Heinrich nodded in acknowledgement. "Mr. Roy Berthus, is it?"

"Yes, sir," said the young man. He leaned forward in his seat.

"My assistant tells me you have need of my aid."

"Yes, sir, I very much do."

"As I recall, you are the son of Senator Philip Berthus, is that correct?" asked Heinrich. His voice changed as he spoke. He retained full control of his speaking, but Mephistopheles's personality and intonation came through more within his vocal cords.

"Yes, sir."

"Tell me, why do you come for my help? Why not your dearest father?"

"Well, sir," said Mr. Berthus, "I am not a very good politician."

"Yes, that much is evident."

Mr. Berthus paused, absorbing the slight. "Yes, well, I hate my job. I cannot stand the blathering by the Lieutenant Governor. I want to do something that matters, be in a position that when I speak, people listen. The Lieutenant Governor is little more than a symbolic role, existing only for the outside chance that the Governor might die or be impeached."

"This much is true, I know," replied Heinrich. He grew impatient for the specific request.

"I've learned that you might have the connections necessary to make this happen for me."

"What else have you heard about me?" asked Heinrich.

"That you are a cruel man who knows no limits in having his justice. You take what isn't yours. You punish when slighted, and you have no tolerance for disloyal friends."

Heinrich wondered how such a man like Mr. Condannato had anyone seek out his service or company. But when he thought about it, few people care about who you truly are if you can help them achieve their success. This much he realized about people in the short time he had been Mr. Condannato. People sacrifice anything or anyone to make their dreams come true. Heinrich had a bitter taste in his mouth as he considered this reality. "And yet still, you seek my help?"

"I do, sir," said Mr. Berthus. "My father is a moral man. He lacks the courage to do what is necessary to change things in society. He is well respected, but accomplishes little save for maintaining a good reputation. He can be of no help."

"He got you your present job, did he not?" inquired Heinrich.

"That he did, but I tire of the mundane tasks with which I am charged."

"What is that you really want, young man?"

"Sir, what I truly desire is to become the Governor of New York."

"Is that all?" said Heinrich in mockery.

"I am aware it is strange, sir, if not ambitious, but it is what I desire the most."

"And what are you willing to do for this position?"

"*Anything.* Anything at all," said Mr. Berthus.

"You realize this would take considerable time?"

"I feared as much, but I will do whatever you tell me for as long as it takes."

Heinrich examined the young man's face. He looked eager. He might have the potential. He also observed a young man who hadn't received his father's approval, though Heinrich knew nothing of the man's father. He empathized with Mr. Berthus, having never experienced the love of his father himself.

"Mr. Berthus, if I am to help you," replied Heinrich, "you must know this: what you have learned about me is true. I do not tolerate disloyalty, but nor do I stand for disobedience."

"Yes, sir."

"This won't be something you can walk away from."

"Yes, sir."

"Should you try, I must assure you that you would never see the great State of New York ever again, should you see anything at all."

"Understood."

"And you must swear your allegiance not only to me and my name but the name of my master, Lucifer, ruler of Hades."

Mr. Berthus said nothing, as his mind caught up with the requirements that Mr. Condannato had just set out. But he was determined, he wasn't to be swayed. Plus, he learned what happened to those who walked out on agreeing to whatever Mr. Condannato offered during an audience. In Mr. Berthus's mind, when he received an invitation for an audience with Mr. Condannato, it only sealed it. He had already decided by responding to his invitation to the club.

"I will."

"Your words won't suffice, Mr. Berthus," said Heinrich. "Lucifer requires a blood oath. Bianca, would you fetch the sacramental knife?"

She reached into a desk drawer and produced an obscene, demonic knife. She also withdrew a thick piece of unbleached paper. It resembled that of the scrolls used in olden days. It had a contract written out and Heinrich's eyes skimmed over the agreement. When he was satisfied with what he read, Bianca produced a red-inked pen for Heinrich, with which he wrote Mr. Condannato's signature on the document.

Its ink is mixed with the blood of a goat, said Mephistopheles. Bianca came out from behind the curtain and produced the written contract. In her other hand, she held the sacramental knife. She gave Mr. Berthus the contract to examine and when he nodded, she handed over the knife to him. Yousef entered the room from the double doors and waited there until instructed.

"If this is what you will commit yourself to, take hold of the knife in your right hand. Place the blade in your left hand. Clasp your hand tightly around the blade and pull it slowly from your hand," Heinrich instructed Mr. Berthus.

The young man hesitated and braced for the pain. He took a deep breath and did as instructed. He extracted the knife, drawing blood and a painful grimace from Mr. Berthus.

"Now open your hand and place it palm-open on the space provided on the contract," instructed Heinrich.

Mr. Berthus did so, and as he withdrew his hand, Yousef attended to him. He provided First Aid to the young man's hand and produced a bandage for him.

"Now, Mr. Berthus, you are sworn to the service of Lucifer," said Heinrich. "In return for this, the Master of Hades shall ensure you have what you desire, providing you do as you are told, you say what you must, and you act when commanded. Failure to do so will not only stand as a revocation of this agreement but be a clear invitation to punishment how ever Lucifer may see it fit."

"Yes, sir," said Mr. Berthus, though the pain distracted him.

"Excuse me?" said Heinrich.

"I mean, yes, sir. It will be as you say, I swear," said the young man with conviction.

"Excellent. You may be excused, and with time, we shall watch you rise to your desired place in society."

"Thank you, Mr. Condannato," replied Mr. Berthus. "I won't let you down."

"Good," said Heinrich. "See that you do not."

Yousef invited the young man to take his leave and ushered him to the double doors while following him out. Heinrich exhaled. Seeing Mr. Berthus make his oath was difficult for Heinrich. The young man had a good life. Heinrich wondered if Mr. Berthus had any idea with what or whom he had involved himself.

Yousef returned to the office and cleaned the blood that had spilled on the floor. Bianca placed the written contract on the desk to allow the blood to dry. She left the room to head back out to the club.

"What will happen to the young man?" Heinrich whispered to Mephistopheles.

We spirits, nor the angels, can predict the future, but we see patterns in mankind; few of which are ever broken, but are bound to repeat, replied Mephistopheles.

"What pattern do you see with Mr. Berthus?"

He will fail. Were he a more selfish person, he might achieve his desired outcome, but he has his father's morality, despite what you might have just witnessed. He will not fulfill the contract, and he will meet his end.

A pang of sickness spread over Heinrich's stomach; a sense of responsibility for the man's downfall. When he reflected on Mr. Berthus's attitude of despair despite his good position in life, Heinrich had little grief for the young man. He had made his choice, and he lacked any gratitude for what he had received. Instead, he traded it all in for a dream.

The double doors opened yet again, Bianca passing through them this time. "Mr. Condannato, you requested an audience with your next guest?"

"Did I?" he said to Mephistopheles, though directed to Bianca as well.

The woman in red, said Mephistopheles.

"Oh, yes. Yes, I did," said Heinrich. "Yousef, would you draw the curtain back? Bianca, bring her in."

The young woman he had seen earlier entered the room. Bianca directed her to the chair in front of the desk. Bianca came around behind Heinrich's desk and returned to her station.

"Mr. Condannato, this is Felicia le Rêve," said Bianca. "She is from Canaan, New Hampshire and she is a ballet dancer. Is that all correct, Miss le Rêve?"

"Yes, ma'am," she said with a smile. "I've been dancing for—"

"Twelve years, if I'm not mistaken?" interrupted Heinrich, having been fed the information from Mephistopheles.

"Yes, that is true," she replied in surprise. "How did you know that?"

"No one receives an invitation to Babel without a reason."

She peered down to her folded-together hands.

"You are a dancer, and quite a good one I have heard," resumed Heinrich. "But you seem to be having trouble with getting your feet off the ground, is this true?"

"You could say that, sir," she replied.

"Something about a ballet director spreading negative rumors of some sort about you? Is that it?"

She nodded her head, but her expression grew with fear.

"And as I understand, you and this ballet director were at one time romantic."

She made no confirmation.

"But things went sour, which was made worse because others in your company already believed you were on your way to getting preferential favor or treatment. Your former lover, hearing this all from his colleagues sought to distance himself from you and protect his job security. He then treated you harshly and defeated your spirit?"

"How do you know all this, Mr. Condannato?" she asked. Her heart sank more with each word he spoke for it all was true.

"Little happens without my knowing in this city," he replied.

"You are well informed," she said. "I don't know what to do. I considered looking for a different company, but he is well known. His influence goes everywhere."

"You are in luck, Miss le Rêve," said Heinrich, sitting up in his chair, "for my influence also goes far beyond me."

"Can you speak to him for me?" she said, showing her first glimmer of hope in all this conversation.

"And more," replied Heinrich.

"But will he listen?" she asked.

"Miss le Rêve, what is it that you have apprehended

about me?" asked Heinrich, feigning indignation.

She withdrew to her seat. "That you are the most powerful man in New York City. You could have the police chief thrown into prison and no one would think anything of it. You are friends with the Mayor, all the judges, and anyone else that is important."

"Therefore, do you think it is reasonable to fear that this lover of yours will refuse me?"

"I suppose not, sir," she said.

"Tomorrow, you shall have your place in the company returned, Miss le Rêve, and your dance career resumed," encouraged Heinrich.

Her face lit up, "Mr. Condannato, you don't understand how much that would mean to me. If you could just say a few words to him. You know, help set him straight?"

"Certainly," he replied. "Bianca, will you ensure that this is taken care of tonight? And with urgency?"

"Of course," she said, taking her leave with the clipboard in hand.

"Mr. Condannato, what could I ever do to thank you for this?"

"Miss le Rêve, I hope it would not be too bold of me to make this request. Earlier this evening, I observed you in the lounge, and you were the most beautiful thing I have ever seen."

The young woman blushed, "You are kind, Mr. Condannato. As you know, I am just a girl from a small town in New Hampshire."

"Felicia, my darling, would you do me the honor of keeping me company this evening? I should like to get to know you better."

She smiled, "It seems you know everything about me already."

"Oh, I can assure you that there are few things I have yet to know about you," replied Heinrich. "Yousef, show Miss le Rêve to the VIP lounge, and Miss le Rêve, if you give me but a moment, I will be with you shortly."

She stood from her chair, her face still beaming with her beautiful smile. "Thank you again, Mr. Condannato!"

"Don't mention another word of it, I insist," said Heinrich. "Yousef, if you please?"

Yousef fetched the young woman's arm and led her out the chamber doors, as Heinrich nabbed his seat again. He spun it away from the desk and crossed his leg. As soon as the eye of his affections left the room, a weight came off his shoulders. His voice came back, and he was himself.

Well done, Heinrich, said Mephistopheles. *You are proving yourself adept to fulfilling the role of Mr. Condannato. Lucifer will be pleased.*

"What will happen to her lover?" asked Heinrich.

He will never dance again.

"Is that necessary?"

He won't do anything ever again, Heinrich.

"You will have him killed?" Heinrich asked in disbelief.

No, we will have someone else kill him, just as you have killed before as instructed.

"But she will never speak to me again!" suggested Heinrich. "I know I just met the girl, but I can tell that for certain."

Heinrich, you will forget about her before long. She shall be one of many women you meet in New York City. Worry not about her affections. You would grow bored of her in time.

Heinrich sensed discouragement taking him over, which Mephistopheles read in his body language. The young woman's willingness to spend time with him that evening pleased him, but he felt defeated knowing it wouldn't go anywhere.

Come now, your mistress of the evening awaits you. You mustn't keep her waiting long.

Heinrich climbed out of the chair and scurried over to the doors. He positioned his hand on the door handle, but stopped short of opening it. He released a heavy sigh and opened the door to walk through it.

Miss le Rêve sat in a reserved corner with a small table for the two of them. She held a martini in her hand, which she sipped. He made his approach toward her, and she lit up with a smile upon seeing him. She was the most beautiful woman, but something inside of him struggled to gather as much excitement as he had beforehand. He was pleased with the prospect of spending time with her, but something held him back. He cast a warm smile to her, as Yousef delivered another spiced rum for Mr. Condannato, who settled next to Miss le Rêve.

XVII

The next morning Heinrich awoke alone. The room was still dark from the previous night, the blackout blinds sealing out the light that might have risen him sooner. He still detected Miss le Rêve's scent, though she had left earlier in the morning. He remembered little of their encounter other that the red dress. The mental picture of her standing in that dress remained steadfast in his mind. Heinrich allowed himself to despair when Mephistopheles's dismissal of the woman returned to his mind.

He climbed out of bed and punched a switch to recede the blinds, bringing light into the room. He found his discarded clothes on the floor and intended to put them on again, but instead picked something comfortable and cleaner out of the walk-in closet. After he got dressed, he stepped into the living room and welcomed the even brighter light. It drew him to the window's edge to look upon Central Park. In the sky, partial clouds hung, providing a pleasant contrast to the blue skies above. He scanned below to the greenery and considered himself a lucky man for being alive again and for being far away from his previous life.

"Good morning, Mr. Condannato," said a voice, drawing Heinrich's attention away from the window.

"Good morning, Yousef," said Heinrich in recognition of his butler.

"I trust you slept well, my lord," Yousef said.

"Well enough."

"May I fetch you your breakfast this morning?" asked Yousef.

Heinrich agreed and strolled toward the kitchen. A dining table stood just beyond the kitchen, where Yousef invited him to take a seat. A place setting sat on the dining table anticipating his awakening.

Heinrich examined the genuine silverware. On the bottom of the handles, an inscription of Mr. Condannato's initials were etched. It drew a smile from Heinrich.

Yousef delivered a covered plate in front of Heinrich and withdrew the lid. Beneath it was a carved assortment of fresh fruit beside a plate of masterfully cooked sunny-side up eggs and bacon for protein. Heinrich consumed the meal while Yousef poured a glass of orange juice. Heinrich savored the meal, the most delicious breakfast he had ever experienced.

"Did you make this yourself?" Heinrich asked the butler.

Yousef nodded in acknowledgment, drawing a smile

from him.

"What did you do before working here? Were you a cook?"

"Oh, do not concern yourself with me, my lord," replied the butler. "I am but a common man with no good stories to tell."

"Nonsense," rebuffed Heinrich. "These are the best eggs I have ever eaten. There must be a story behind how you learned to cook."

"Nothing noteworthy, my lord, I assure you," said Yousef, as he stepped back to await Mr. Condannato and whatever else he might need.

"Yousef, a breakfast like this does not happen by chance," said Heinrich. "You must tell me where you learned your skill."

The butler looked uncomfortable in not wanting to refuse Mr. Condannato, but he hesitated. "All right, sir, but do not tell me I didn't warn you, my story is very dull," said Yousef. He almost sat at the table but thought better of it. "In Damascus, my hometown, back in Syria, I once operated my own café. It wasn't much, but I had a faithful clientele. We served such wonderful lunches, and the coffee was exceptional. I knew from a young age that food was my passion. Bringing people together around my food, it brought me such joy. The café, it wasn't famous, but the people came often, and they kept me in business. It wasn't until one afternoon that I had problems. Some of my guests, they complained about the government; as all Syrians do from time to time. Me, I didn't care about such matters, as long as I had my restaurant and my family close."

"Did you have children?" asked Heinrich.

"No, sir, just me and my parents. That was all," said the butler. "Anyway, it turns out that someone told the police that dissenters were at my restaurant, that it was a meeting place for revolutionaries of some sort. This was anything but the case, but there was no tolerance for any suspicion of it. The police, they arrived later that day, and they rebuked me for allowing such rebellion in my restaurant. They threatened to close my doors, but I promised them it wouldn't happen again. I pledged allegiance to our leader, and all that. It wasn't enough though. Several days later, they showed up again and flipped the tables upside down and threw them around. When I pleaded for them to stop, they gave me such a licking. I won't ever forget it. But then they left. I reasoned that the matter was over, that I had taken my punishment, but not so. I arrived the next morning to find my restaurant vandalized both inside and out. My family grew fearful, my mother especially. She told me it wasn't safe for me anymore, that I must leave, lest I bring judgment on my family. I refused. Instead, I grew indignant with my government. I had done nothing wrong. I wasn't a radical, nor was I a revolutionary. I was but a simple man who enjoyed food and sharing it with others. I promised to rebuild; not to be scared away."

"The next day, however, an arsonist razed my restaurant. I realized then I wasn't safe, nor would my family be if I stayed, so I fled. I determined to escape to Europe, whichever country would take me. It was terrible. My family got me in touch with friends who knew someone who knew someone who knew someone, if you catch what I mean, Mr. Condannato. By the end of the day, I went on my way, smuggled out of the country via Turkey in the back of a truck with only three days' wages. From there, I snuck into Europe by way of Greece and then ended up in Hungary, where I became stuck. It was difficult because the language was impossible for me to learn as much as I tried. But that is when I met a man who swore that he could get me safe passage to America. I was very interested, for I didn't have a future in Europe. I was stuck, but he said that there would be conditions once I arrived. I didn't have any choice as I was running out of money."

"The man got me onto a container ship by way of Greece. I was a stowaway for three months, stealing food as I could. How I was undetected, I am uncertain, but I am very thankful for that man's help. I completed the three-month journey to America unharmed and unnoticed. When the ship arrived in New York City, I evaded capture by the immigration authorities and was brought here to the club. They explained they would grant me my freedom here in America, if I pledged to serve Lucifer for ten years. And upon completion of my service, my family would be brought here to be with me in America, and that in the meantime, they would be protected. How such a thing was made sure, I wasn't certain. And here I am, in year three of my service, Mr. Condannato."

Heinrich stared at the butler and shook his head in disbelief. "Yousef, that is quite the tale. Tell me how much of that is true?"

"All of it, my lord," said Yousef with a confused smile on his face.

"It can't be," said Heinrich in denial.

"I assure you, Mr. Condannato, it is all true!"

"Does your family know where you are?"

"They know I am alive, and that is all that matters."

"Do you miss them?"

"Every day, my lord," said the butler, showing a strong face, though thinking about them made him emotional. "Without them, I have nothing in this life— I would have no reason to live. It is for that reason that I made my blood oath to Lucifer, who has assured me I will be reunited with them if I am faithful. If the only way we can be together again is by me swearing my soul to Lucifer for an eternity, it is the price to be paid. I accept it. I need to see them again, my lord. I will hold them again, I believe it. Whatever it takes."

"You care deeply about them; I can see that much is true," said Heinrich.

Yousef nodded. "Sir, may I clean your plate?"

"Allow me, I can take it to the kitchen—"

"No, sir, I insist. Permit me to serve you," he said, taking Heinrich's plate from in front of him. "It brings me happiness that my cooking satisfies you. It has been my pleasure."

"Thank you," said Heinrich, as he gave the butler a nod of thanks.

"You're welcome, my lord," said Yousef. "And if you should need anything else, do not hesitate to call for me."

When the butler left Heinrich alone in the dining room and headed for the kitchen, Heinrich turned inwards. "Mephistopheles?"

Yes, Heinrich.

"What will become of Yousef's family?"

I should expect that they will be reunited if he fulfills his duties.

"Good."

His story affects you.

"It does." Heinrich's mind pictured the life of Yousef's family back in Syria without their son, and how much they must long to hear from him. He wondered what efforts they must have made to contact him, or if they resolved to accept the news that he was safe for what it was.

"Tell me, Mephistopheles," said Heinrich, "might I ever meet my birth parents?"

It is not possible, replied Mephistopheles.

"Do they not wonder about their son?" asked Heinrich, as his heart sank to his stomach.

They do not.

Heinrich struggled with Mephistopheles's words. He had gone his life believing he was unwanted; this only confirmed it.

"How could they not?" whimpered Heinrich.

They are dead, Heinrich.

"Truly?"

Yes, it is true.

"But how?"

Your mother died by suicide. She hung herself. Your father, he lived out his final years in a depressive state before succumbing to Alzheimer's disease. They both died unhappy.

Heinrich failed to compose himself as his emotions got the best of him. He excused himself from the dining room table and took refuge in his bedroom. Alone.

XVIII

Heinrich entered his office and sat. Bianca called for him. Lucifer had requested the appointment, she said, and Mr. Condannato needed to facilitate the agenda. The purpose of that meeting involved a Mr. Ferdinand Brandenburg. The man, Mephistopheles informed Heinrich, was the CEO of the nation's largest print media corporation, and as it was, he had an arrangement with Lucifer. Mr. Brandenburg's company had damning photos that would ruin the reputation and electability of a man by the name of Terrance McMaster, a Republican from Rhode Island in the House of Representatives. Mr. McMaster also had a deal with Lucifer.

Heinrich's mind was belabored and heavy. He knew what he had to do, but he was distracted when Bianca entered the room with Mr. Brandenburg. She showed the man to his seat and took her usual place beside Mr.

Condannato. "Mr. Brandenburg," said Heinrich, as he again received instructions from Mephistopheles. "I appreciate you coming on such short notice."

"By all means," replied Mr. Brandenburg.

"You've been summoned here for a simple reason," said Heinrich. "It appears one of your papers has information that alarms us."

"Ah, yes," said the man. "The McMaster file."

"Good, then you understand why you must dispose of the photos," replied Heinrich.

Mr. Brandenburg chuckled and sat upright in his chair. He strained to look through the curtain. He wanted to make eye contact with Mr. Condannato but failed. "We won't be getting rid of anything," he asserted.

Heinrich paused, though he was aware what Mephistopheles wanted him to say already. He looked to Bianca, who avoided eye contact. "You do realize who Mr. McMaster is, do you not?" Heinrich asked the man.

"I do," replied Mr. Brandenburg with a condescending tone. "The man is a faggot, masquerading as a conservative Republican from Rhode Island. And I will crucify him."

"Mr. Brandenburg, I appreciate that you yourself are a homosexual," replied Heinrich, which drew an eye from Bianca. "But it matters not to us the sexual preferences of a certain Mr. McMaster, regardless of what he says and does to stay elected."

"Bullshit!" exclaimed the man. "We will out that coward. I am sick and tired of the anti-homosexual agenda rearing its ugly head and shaming people who have come out and have nothing to hide. The man is a coward! The world will learn it!"

"That is enough, Ferdinand!" shouted Heinrich as he stood from his chair. "I didn't summon you here to receive a lecture from the likes of you about honesty, integrity, and honor. In fact, I do not give a rat's ass about any of that. You had a deal with us, and you will obey. Period."

"You can't touch me, and you most certainly cannot scare me."

"What was it that ailed you when you called upon the heavens for help? Was it liver failure?" said Heinrich, changing his tone. "And who was it that ignored your pleas?"

"Damn you to Hell!" blasted Mr. Brandenburg. "How dare you!"

"You know we keep you alive, Ferdinand!" shouted Heinrich. "We kept you medicated when no one else could help you. You would be dead if it weren't for us."

"You wouldn't!" replied the man. "I have done everything you asked of me in return, but you won't take this from me!"

"Who was it that arranged for a suitable liver transplant, Mr. Brandenburg?"

He said nothing in reply. He squirmed in the chair not uttering another word.

"Who was it?" beckoned Heinrich. "Say it!"

The man slouched in his chair. He appeared on the verge of humiliation as Heinrich stared him down through the curtain.

"Lucifer," said the still voice of Mr. Brandenburg.

"And who is your master?"

A pause came before a reply. "Lucifer."

"Now then," said Heinrich before sighing, "you won't publish those photos. Better yet, you will destroy them and ensure that no copies ever exist, or you risk the fatal consequences. Is that understood?"

The man said nothing. His tail was between his legs. He sat upright and took a more respectful posture.

"Is that clear?" repeated Heinrich.

"Yes, Mr. Condannato."

"Good," said Heinrich. "That is all then."

Mr. Brandenburg rose from the chair and scrambled to leave, but paused before speaking. "Does Lucifer not care about the political fools who play into the evangelical vote and try to advance the cause of far-right religious values? Does Lucifer not care at all?"

Heinrich awaited Mephistopheles to speak, but nothing came for a moment. Heinrich spoke: "Mr. McMaster will come upon his downfall. His lusts will ensnare him, and he will be humiliated as you seek. He will be revealed as a coward. We are protecting him now, but there will be a day when we can no longer protect him, and he will have served his purposes to the Kingdom of Hell."

The man nodded and left the office.

XIX

Heinrich leaned on the railing overlooking the lounge below. He hadn't yet left the apartment since he arrived. Being Mr. Condannato fatigued him, and while he had the influence and fame he might have enjoyed, the role made him uncomfortable. The people didn't worship him because he was Heinrich Juarez, but because he stood in for the immortal Mr. Condannato.

He scanned the crowd. No woman in a red dress. He brooded over her and how he remembered little of their encounter after he had sat down with her. She had come to bed with him, but what happened when they got there was too fuzzy for him to recall, or even to enjoy again as a memory.

Below him, a group of women pleasing to his eye distracted him. He watched them. He discerned that before that night they were strangers to each other; that much was true. They connected on a level and banded together for the evening.

Heinrich's attention wandered to a sharply dressed young man who looked like everything Heinrich dreamed of being back in Cuba. The man had finely cared for hair, and dark stubble covered his face. He looked exotic and handsome, and as if he had little trouble being taken seriously or garnering a woman's attention. Heinrich wondered why they all were called to Babel that night. "Mephistopheles, do all these souls really hope for an audience with me this evening?" Heinrich asked.

Most are, but few will be so lucky.

"Why are some chosen, and others are not?" asked Heinrich.

It is simple, replied Mephistopheles. *Some are at their best service to Lucifer by continuing to live their lives the way they are—narcissistically and without meaning.*

XX

Heinrich slouched in his office chair. He listened to a young man speak about his band's ambitions to make it big. The fellow sat down as he spoke, while his bandmates stood behind him, full of optimism. They knew how rare it was to have an audience with Mr. Condannato. They didn't know how bored he was, nor that they weren't the first band that sought out Mr. Condannato's help.

Bianca looked to Mr. Condannato, which drew his attention. She nodded her head toward the band through the curtain. They had asked him a question which he hadn't noticed.

"Very interesting," replied Heinrich. He hoped Mephistopheles would fill in for him what he had missed.

"So yeah, totally, man!" said the lead singer of the band.

"Show Mr. Condannato respect," chided Bianca.

"Oh, so sorry, sir! I meant no offense," said the singer.

Heinrich asked Bianca for a piece of paper and a pen which she produced. He wrote a note and waited for Mephistopheles to see it. It read: "Do I really have to help these morons?"

Yes, replied Mephistopheles. *This is the will of Lucifer. The bass guitar player, if he does not remain in this band, Lucifer fears he will become a powerful man against the cause of Kingdom of Hell.*

Heinrich was puzzled. He studied the bass guitarist. He looked ordinary and unremarkable.

The Almighty One uses the strangest and sometimes simplest men of the world as his vessels for salvation, said Mephistopheles. *Do not be deceived by his appearance.*

Heinrich nodded. "All right, we can do something for you boys," he announced.

"Righteous!" exclaimed the bass guitarist, while nodding his head.

"But you must know that we will require a blood oath," said Heinrich. He motioned for Bianca to go around with the usual contract and the sacramental knife, after he had produced his signature on them with the blood ink. The other bandmates stepped forward in curiosity.

"Wicked!" said the lead singer, admiring the knife.

"Each of you will administer the blood oath," said Heinrich. "You must all know that such a blood oath cannot be broken and that you will pledge to serve the interests of Lucifer. And one day, the Master of Hell shall call upon you to return the favor."

"Whatever you say, man—"

"Respect!" beckoned Bianca again.

"Oh, sorry!" said the lead singer. He stepped up to take the knife. Bianca called Yousef into the office. Heinrich instructed the lead singer how to use the knife and blood flowed. The young man placed the palm of his hand on the contract. Yousef tended to the lead singer's hand.

Next was the drummer who followed the lead singer's example and made his blood oath with no apprehension or second thought. The bass player was next and after having seen his bandmates go through the ordeal, he was in a cold sweat.

"Yo' man, I'm not sure if I can do that hand cutting thing," he cautioned.

"Do it, man!" scolded the lead singer.

"But dude, we've got a show tonight. I can't play guitar with a fat bandage on my hand," he responded.

"Cancel the show then," Heinrich interrupted.

The lead singer turned to the bass guitarist. "Yeah, man," he said. "We'll postpone the gig. Don't even worry about it."

The bass guitarist shifted his eye away. He struggled with his apprehension. "All right, man. Let's do this."

He stepped forward and procured the knife and did as instructed. The bass guitarist grimaced in the process and panted. He placed his hand on the contract, and Yousef tended to his wound.

"Very well," said Heinrich as he rose from his chair. "Bianca will escort you, and my representatives will contact you by tomorrow evening."

"Thank you, sir!" said the lead singer, nodding his

head in approval.

"Man, we should write a song in honor of him?" suggested the band's drummer.

"No, you should not," said Heinrich. "You are never to make any mention of me or this place. Doing so would constitute a breach of contract."

"No way!" said the lead singer in surprise. "For sure, don't worry about it! We won't do anything like that!"

"Good," said Heinrich.

Bianca showed them out the door. Heinrich also went for the door once they left.

You have one more meeting tonight, said Mephistopheles.

"Another meeting?" said Heinrich. He exhaled in frustration. Bianca returned through the door. "I have another meeting, Bianca?"

"Yes, sir," she replied. "He is on his way now."

Heinrich returned to his seat in the office chair.

It is your adopted brother.

"What?" said Heinrich aloud in astonishment.

"Sir?" said a surprised Bianca.

"It's nothing," said Heinrich.

You will get your wish. He is headed here this moment.

"Bianca, would you fetch this man then?"

She looked confused, as Yousef was already bringing the man there.

"Meet him outside, will you?" Heinrich said. She conceded and exited the door to meet Yousef when he got there.

"Why didn't you warn me beforehand?" Heinrich chided the spirit.

You would've worried yourself sick, and you would've been useless with the earlier meeting you had.

The doors opened to Mr. Condannato's office. Bianca came through first. Another man walked in behind her. Yousef closed the door behind them and returned to Babel. Bianca led the man to a seat in front of the curtain.

Heinrich stared at the man, his adopted brother. It was him; that much was true. Anger welled up inside of Heinrich upon seeing Jose. He appeared frailer than when Heinrich had last seen him back in Cuba. He didn't possess his usual proud manner but appeared humble and nervous. Bianca took her place next to Heinrich.

Welcome your adopted brother, instructed Mephistopheles. Heinrich shook his head. He wouldn't welcome Jose. Silence carried the moment for at least three minutes. Heinrich sought to make Jose more uncomfortable and unsure of himself. Mephistopheles told Heinrich what to do, but he ignored all such instructions. He considered marching around the desk and bludgeoning Jose with his fists. He also considered taking the sacramental knife, which had yet to be cleaned. He would end his adopted brother's life that way. He brought to mind his bodyguards; they must be of use in killing him. Mephistopheles sought any sign of what Heinrich was thinking and how to gain influence over Heinrich's thoughts.

Heinrich, you must calm yourself! Mephistopheles rebuked him. *Now is not the moment. Your revenge will come later. This is all a part of the plan.*

Heinrich reigned in his anger but still struggled to calm down. Bianca produced a glass of water for him to sip.

"What do you call yourself, young man?" Heinrich asked to break the silence. He altered his voice to sound different from his own for fear of having it recognized. Mephistopheles told him that this was unnecessary, but he continued his attempts.

"My name is Jose Juarez," said Heinrich's adopted brother.

"What do you want? Why are you here?" asked Heinrich.

"Sir," he spoke, "I gathered that you, Mr. Condanna-to, could help me. Make my dreams come true, sir."

"Where did you learn this?"

"A man, or a lawyer-type, approached me while walking home from my job, sir," said Jose.

Heinrich had difficulty in paying attention to what Jose said. His thoughts swirled. Though Mephistopheles told him what to say, Heinrich wasn't sure what to do now that a moment had presented itself for revenge. Mephistopheles warned Heinrich against immediate revenge, but Heinrich's desire to avenge the humiliation and abandonment at Jose's hands was profound. This was the reason he had wanted to come back to Earth: to have his revenge.

"I don't know you from anyone else on the street," said Heinrich. "I don't understand why you need my help, nor do I see why I should help you. You come marching into my office and ask for my assistance, but I know nothing about you but your name alone."

"I am so sorry, sir," said Jose, sitting with a sense of earnestness. It was clear he doubted himself and whether he had already flubbed it.

Heinrich surveyed Jose and expected him to tell his

story and why he needed help, but his adopted brother still said nothing. He waited for a cue from Mr. Condannato. "Speak, damn it!" beckoned Heinrich.

What came next was a censored story about Jose's life growing up in Cuba, none of which made any mention of Heinrich or even that Jose's parents had died in a hurricane. Jose spoke volumes of the athletic promise he displayed in Cuba. He even suggested that it was his parents' idea for him to flee to America, hoping his baseball skill as a pitcher might lift his family out of poverty.

Still, he made no mention of Heinrich. He retold Mr. Condannato the story of his attempt to smuggle himself into the United States and achieve refugee status. It was everything that Mephistopheles had told Heinrich. The pitching arm was damaged by a dislocation that involved torn and pulled tendons and ligaments. Had he the money for physiotherapy and surgery by the most talented orthopedic specialist, his pitching arm might have survived. But as it was, Jose lived in the Bronx and worked three jobs, while also playing baseball in an unpaid adult league, hoping a baseball scout might see him. His arm wasn't healing, rendering him an unexceptional pitcher. The damage was done. The three jobs hurt his health. Even with those jobs, he struggled to keep a roof over his head and food on the table.

As Jose spoke, anger burned inside of Heinrich. His adopted brother didn't even mention Heinrich in any of his history. Jose had little regard for him his whole life, but listening to Jose's testimony made Heinrich hate him all the more. His desire for revenge was so much more real to him. His mind twisted to the prospect of murdering him in that office, and a rage revealed itself on Heinrich's face. The spirit regained Heinrich's attention and instructed him to send Jose away for a brief recess. Heinrich, thinking it was a good idea, complied and had Bianca escort Jose out.

You have got to hold yourself together, Mephistopheles chided Heinrich. *You will blow your chance at revenge if you don't focus.*

"When will I have my revenge?" insisted Heinrich.

The time is not now, replied Mephistopheles.

"I do not want to help that man," replied Heinrich. "I won't help him."

Heinrich, this much is true—Your adopted brother will never be a star in the big leagues. You will offer your help, but he need not know that you cannot even help him.

"So what is the plan?"

Call him back in. Heinrich did as instructed and rang for Bianca to return with Jose. The adopted brother took his seat again and awaited Heinrich to speak.

"I will help you, Mr. Juarez," Heinrich said. "But there will be a few conditions."

"Anything!" said Jose.

Heinrich paused. He relished the control he had over Jose. "Do you have any family?"

"No, sir," replied Jose.

"None whatsoever?" Heinrich pressed.

"No, I don't."

"Do you have a girlfriend?"

"Yes, sir."

"Good," said Heinrich. "Bring her here this very week."

"Sir?"

"You said you would do anything, did you not?"

"Yes, sir, I did, but—"

"Then you will bring her here as commanded, and she will sleep with me."

"Mr. Condannato, no! I can't do that."

Heinrich said nothing.

"Sir, why must it be so?" Jose asked.

"We must be certain you are committed to this arrangement; that there will be no other attachments more important than your service to the household of Lucifer. Is this clear?"

Jose's head sank in a depression.

"We will await your return," said Heinrich before handing a card to Bianca. She presented it to Jose, who lifted his head to see it. "Show this and you will be let in. Mr. Juarez, we will discover whether you want your dream to come true and how much you want it."

Jose nodded in acknowledgment, but it wasn't clear whether he intended to return. He looked defeated as if he considered resigning himself to the possibility that his baseball dream was finished. Bianca ushered him to the door, and he muttered a thank you to Mr. Condannato.

"Will he return?" Heinrich asked Mephistopheles.

We shall see. Lucifer waits in anticipation as do you, I am sure.

XXI

Heinrich left the office and entered the VIP area of Babel. Mephistopheles told him that a special treat waited for him there. At the far end of the room, three women lounged together at a high-top table while enjoying cocktails. The women appeared to be friends, or they at least put up with each other's company. They were lively and vivacious; the perfect distraction for Heinrich. As soon as they noticed Heinrich, their attention was his. They were youthful, exemplifying all the beauty of a woman that a man hoped to possess.

The most attractive one wore a shimmering gray dress that flattered her figure while the next wore a purple halter dress that gave Heinrich an alluring preview of her figure. The third woman wore a colorful midriff dress, revealing a toned frame.

They all saw his ring, and they knew who he was. Heinrich drank up the attention, but he still felt his

mind consumed with seeing Jose and seeking his revenge. Mephistopheles witnessed that such matters
weighed on Heinrich, so Mephistopheles gave Heinrich
instructions to lead the women to his office. From
there, he directed them through the passageway to his
private residence.

He entertained them in the living room and shared
drinks. The liquid anti-depressant helped clear his mind
from his other desires. The three women became the
primary object of his desire. When he had made them
comfortable, he led the three women to follow him to
his master bedroom. He shut the door behind him.

XXII

When Heinrich awoke the next morning, his head pounded. It was hard to open his eyes. Through his squinted eyes, he determined it was well into the morning. His whole body ached, but again, he remembered almost nothing of the night previous. He was pleased that something must have happened last night, but his spirit grew sad when he accepted that it was a memory he couldn't retain or recall. His eyes opened more. His bed was a tattered mess while he was naked. Waking up alone wasn't what he wanted. Heinrich had that his whole life, and even as Mr. Dante Condannato, it was still his reality.

He gazed around the room. It bore little resemblance to who he was as a person. He lived in someone else's house. Heinrich threw on pajamas from his closet. The realization occurred to him again: he still hadn't left the penthouse since he arrived. Heinrich hit the switch to open the curtains and scurried over to the window to take in the view over Central Park. He needed to get out of the house and explore, not as who he was when he arrived, but with the advantages that came with being Mr. Condannato. Once he envisioned this, though, his heart changed. He wanted to explore, but he didn't want to bring along the baggage and expectation of being Mr. Condannato.

Heinrich called Yousef, who presented himself. Heinrich requested that he be taken somewhere for relaxation. Yousef asked if he would like to go to a museum, but Heinrich declined. Mephistopheles suggested a spa, saying that Heinrich might get lucky, but he dismissed this as well.

"I haven't left this stuffy house in a few days," declared Heinrich. "I want to enjoy New York for a day. Get away from all this business for a little while."

"A baseball game then, sir?" asked Yousef.

"No. Too many people," Heinrich declined again. "How do most New Yorkers relax?"

Yousef looked at Mr. Condannato with a desire to please, but he was also at a loss in finding something to please his master. "Sir, how about a visit to a coffee shop?" asked Yousef. "Maybe to read or just to take in some people watching?"

"Is that what New Yorkers do?" asked Heinrich.

"Some, yes."

"Great. Send for a car and take me to a coffee shop," requested Heinrich.

A coffee shop? There are other things you could do. Heinrich shook his head.

"Right away, sir," said Yousef.

"And Yousef, no bodyguards, okay?"

"Sir?"

"I don't want a bunch of oafs following me around and making me look like somebody."

Heinrich, it's best to bring protection! Heinrich again shook his head to decline.

So be it.

XXIII

As Heinrich trekked from the parked car to the coffee shop that Yousef had picked out, it felt good to breathe in fresh air for once; even though to many others, the New York air was hardly fresh. For Heinrich though, it was a breath of fresh air. He slipped off the ring of Mr. Condannato, as he didn't want to be approached or recognized for the role he played.

He opened the coffee shop's front door and took a step in. He overlooked the room. Tables sat empty or occupied. Pleasant conversation filled the atmosphere. It seemed unremarkable, but it brought a pure comfort to Heinrich. He could be himself, whatever that meant. The café had a clear line toward the cash register from the door. On the left, booth seating was open for groups and on the right two rows of free-standing tables sat with chairs. Farther to the right, high-top chairs against the wall were available for those seeking study or solitude. At the far end of the café were the cash register and bar area. A small lineup waited to place their orders, so Heinrich took his place at the back of the line.

As he waited, he overheard the conversations going on. A few engaged in a business discussion, while at another table, a book club deliberated over the latest literary trend. Though coffee shops existed in Cuba, he had never gone to one. He never had money for it, let alone the desire. Here in New York City, he was keen to experience a small slice of Americana.

Heinrich's attention slid to the line in front of him. A businessman stood in front of him with a briefcase, checking his watch on repeated occasions. Ahead of him, a woman was in conversation with the young woman behind the cash register. They knew each other, or the barista was at least friendly and cheerful. The barista talked to the woman about her daily plans, and brought an empty cup over to the bar area to be made by another barista. The young lady walked with either a limp or a physical disability. Her movements were sudden and jerky, and it necessitated a good deal of effort for her to move around, but the young woman seemed pleasant and happy.

The man in front of Heinrich came next to the register and barked his cappuccino order, specifying it had to be a certain way. None of it made any sense to Heinrich. He assumed this was New Yorker behavior. The girl was pleasant to the businessman, but he made no response in kind. The young lady's patience and kindness to the businessman impressed Heinrich, even though the man failed to be gracious to her.

When Heinrich's turn came, he noticed that the girl wore a name tag with Greta on it. She greeted him with a smile. "How are you doing today?" asked the young woman.

Heinrich smiled at her kindness. "I'm okay. Have a hangover," he replied.

She laughed, "You came to the right place. What can I get to cure your headache?"

Heinrich requested a latte; it sounded familiar to him. A medium size. She placed the cup in the production queue and asked him if he needed anything else like food or a newspaper. Heinrich never read the newspaper, but he said he would take one. After he paid, he stood near the bar as an emotionless barista produced drinks. He made no eye contact with Heinrich or the businessman in front of him, nor the other woman waiting for a drink.

The difference between the two baristas surprised Heinrich. The first barista was so friendly, cheerful, and engaging; the other uninteresting, muted, and dull.

Heinrich gave his attention back to the girl who served the other customers behind Heinrich in the lineup. He wondered what her disability or ailment was. She was prone to laughter, and she asked every customer how they were doing. She recognized a fair number of the customers. They were regulars, or she made people feel at home. She loved her job, even if customers like the businessman in front of Heinrich were condescending and pretentious.

But still, Heinrich struggled to understand how she was so joyful when her physical disability made her job more difficult than the able-bodied robot working at the bar making drinks.

"How can someone like her have such joy?" he whispered to Mephistopheles.

It is hard to understand, knowing the life she has lived.

"She's had a difficult life?" Heinrich whispered.

Yes, you could say as such—

"Excuse me, sir," said a stranger, jarring Heinrich from his thoughts, "but are you Mr. Condannato?"

Heinrich's guard went up, and Mephistopheles told him what to say. "I am not. Now leave me alone."

"You really aren't Mr. Condannato?"

"No, my name is Henry. Leave me in peace."

The stranger apologized and excused himself, which was a relief for Heinrich. The stranger meandered back to their high-top table along the wall. He had seen Heinrich from a distance and concluded it worth his while to come all the way over to introduce himself to Mr. Condannato. Nearby that fellow, though, a beautiful young woman studied. She had long blonde hair and focused on whatever textbook she was reading. The woman's features appealed to Heinrich, but his hangover rendered him hesitant to approach her.

The dull barista behind the bar called out Heinrich's latte. He grabbed it and searched for a seat. The lineup was extinguished, so the young barista girl excused herself from the cash register and went to tidy tables. Heinrich decided where to sit. Mephistopheles encouraged him to sit nearby the attractive woman, but Heinrich was hesitant since the stranger was so close to her. He gave his attention to admire the young woman's beauty.

As he glided among the tables, Heinrich tripped over

something hard. He couldn't recover his step as the latte went flying and Heinrich fell. The hot latte splashed on him and upon a man who Heinrich identified as the impatient businessman in the earlier lineup. Heinrich had tripped on the man's briefcase on the ground beside him. The businessman stood and screamed at Heinrich, "You clumsy idiot! Look what you've done! Can you not watch where you're going?"

Heinrich froze in fear but remembered that he was Mr. Condannato. He was about to ask the man if he had any idea who he was, but Mephistopheles told him not to reveal himself. The man screamed at Heinrich as he brushed the hot latte off his pant legs. "You will pay for my dry cleaning, you fool! Do you have any idea how much this suit cost me?"

"All right, quiet down!" said the voice of the young disabled girl. She arrived on the scene with the cloth in hand she had used to clean the tables. "It was a simple mistake—"

"He will pay for—" the man shouted at the barista.

"Enough!" she said, raising her voice. "You need to calm yourself down, sir!"

"Don't tell me to calm down!"

"That's enough!" said Greta, as she offered him the cloth to clean himself. "It was an accident, and we'll get you cleaned up."

Heinrich still reclined on the floor. The hot drink had soaked through his clothes.

"You stupid imbecile!" bellowed the businessman, as he made a move toward Heinrich with a newspaper rolled up in his fist. Heinrich tried to rise from the floor, but the young woman stepped in.

"That's enough, sir!" she shouted at the businessman. "If you can't calm yourself down, I will ask you to leave and I *will* call the police!"

The man grunted at her and stared her down, but she had none of it as the entire café stared at her. He threw the newspaper to the ground as a statement and stormed out with his briefcase. "This is the last time you'll see me here!" said the businessman as he exited. He slammed the door.

Greta turned to Heinrich and though she was physically disabled, she helped Heinrich up. "Are you okay?" she asked him.

"I am," he said, as he stood, brushing the latte from his pant legs.

"Don't mind him," she encouraged him. "He was never the most pleasant customer. Accidents happen."

Heinrich nodded but said nothing. He was surprised that it had been her to help him. The other able-bodied customers of the café sat and watched as that interaction had went on. A part of him felt weak for having been helped by a woman who had physical challenges of her own.

She told him to take a seat and that they would get him another latte. He did as instructed and pulled out his damp newspaper. He pretended as though nothing had happened. Others' attention returned to whatever they were doing before he had taken his tumble. His eyes caught sight of the civil war in Syria in the newspaper, which made him think of Yousef, but he couldn't keep his eyes on the paper with any focus. He still reeled from what had happened. He was disappointed for not making a stand against the businessman. But even his own disappointment was short as he recollected how the young woman helped him. "That was the most kindness anyone has ever shown me," Heinrich muttered to Mephistopheles, "albeit by a disabled girl."

Don't think too much of it. Besides, remember the beautiful woman. You must approach her!

"I can't. My clothes are stained, and I am covered in coffee," he said.

That would appear to be a valid point.

Greta returned with a latte, though this time in a paper cup with a lid. "I figured this might help keep it in the cup for you this time," she said with a laugh. "Plus, I spill things if I try to carry liquids."

"Thank you," Heinrich said, as he plucked the cup. Even with the lid, the latte had spilled through the lid's spout during its journey to the table.

"Oh, I'm sorry," she said, realizing what Heinrich stared at. "Looks like even that didn't work. Sometimes that happens with my muscles."

"It's okay," he said, smiling for the first time since the spill. "I made more of a mess."

"Anything else I can get for you?" she asked. She studied his face which made Heinrich worry she knew he was Mr. Condannato.

"No, no, I think I'm all right. Thank you for your help," he replied. "It was very kind."

"Don't mention it," she said. "I like to help."

She had spun to leave when Heinrich blurted out a question. "Tell me, how do you like your job when you have to deal with men like that?"

She shrugged, but her face lit up. "I enjoy it well

enough," she said. "It can be a little harsh sometimes with some people, but my customers make me happy. I get to make a lot of friends and help people start their day."

Heinrich nodded. He had never seen someone so full of joy.

"It can be a little tough to make rent though; it is New York City," she said. "But it is a good job for me right now."

"What do you want to do with your life?" he asked her. Mephistopheles was quite impressed with Heinrich for the possibility of recruiting a soul for Lucifer.

She paused, as she studied Heinrich's eyes before answering. "I want to help people," she said. Her voice grew serious. She had an evident passion for helping others. Customers passed through the door as she spoke. "I would love to open a home and training center for disadvantaged people."

"Why?" Heinrich asked.

She was about to answer when customers arrived in the queue.

"Greta! I need your help!" barked the previously emotionless barista behind the espresso machine; it was the first emotion he had managed to show during Heinrich's visit.

"He's a charming fellow…" muttered Heinrich to the girl.

"It's okay," she said. "He's my manager."

Heinrich raised his eyebrows in surprise.

"As I said, charming," said Heinrich.

Greta excused herself and said she would return. She marched to the cash register. She had to work hard just to move and take control of her muscles to get her to where she wanted. This was a job that required her to stand on her feet all day and provided little relief in that area.

Heinrich watched her as she served the customers in line who talked to her about their plans. She knew everyone in the café that day. Heinrich waited for the line to diminish so he could finish his conversation with her, but the line never let up. After waiting for a while longer, Heinrich rose and went back in the lineup. He had barely consumed his latte. He watched the girl named Greta the whole time.

The young lady was so consistent, even if a customer didn't want to talk much. When Heinrich got to the front of the lineup, she greeted him with another smile and apologized that she hadn't been able to return. A lineup stood behind Heinrich, so he withdrew a card from his pocket. "Take this," he said, as he handed it to her. "I would love to talk to you more about your dreams and maybe I can be of some help."

She smiled and inspected the card which read the name of Mr. Dante Condannato and had the address of Babel. She had never heard of it, which surprised Heinrich.

"Certainly!" she said with excitement. "Thank you so much."

Heinrich said his goodbye and left the lineup.

Impressive, Heinrich. You did all that on your own. You truly are becoming Mr. Condannato.

XXIV

A hideous cat screech came from outside the room. Light filled the poorly lit bedroom apartment. Every electronic device was on, including the alarm clock radio. The young woman jolted up in her bed in fear. She felt a heavy presence, and terror came over her. She wanted to crawl back into her bed, but took courage and willed herself out of it.

Light came from underneath her bedroom door. She opened it to discover every single light illuminated throughout her small apartment. She called out to ask if someone was there, but no response came back. The young woman extinguished the lights to her bedroom. As she passed through the hallway, she turned off the lights there as well. She hopped forward to the open kitchen and living room across the hall from the bedroom. She entered the kitchen and spotted the microwave's clock, which read 666. It startled her, which almost made her stumble and fall.

The young woman backed away from the kitchen and into her small living room. An inverted cross was painted on the walls in crude red paint; it looked like blood. She froze in fear and rotated her head to the perpendicular wall. She discovered a painted inverted pentagram with a foul demonic goat face in the center, exuding evil, murderous intent. The detail paralyzed her eyes from moving away from it, and it ushered her to scream in utter terror. Other symbols she didn't recognize or identify were etched on her walls, and they were not a part of her decor.

She went to flee to her bedroom, but when she gazed down the stairway to the front door of her apartment, she found that the entrance was wide open. She wondered in fear if she had forgotten to lock the door and was the victim of vandals. The young woman struggled her way down the stairs, using every ounce of courage in her spasming muscles to shut the door. She slammed it and hobbled up the stairs. She jetted down the hallway and shrieked in terror when she found that her bedroom lights were on again. She swore that she had switched them off. She entered the room and looked around, but found no one. She climbed back into bed and grabbed her cellphone and dialed a number in panic.

"Please pick up, please pick up…" she whimpered in fear. It rang and rang. Her eyes cast a glance toward her alarm clock, which also read 666. It was dark outside, and she had no idea what time it was, but the clock wasn't correct. Finally, an answer.

"Father Cavanagh! I am so sorry to wake you…" she

shrieked into the cellphone.

"What is it, my child?" said a tired voice on the other end.

"There's something very scary going on in my apartment," she cried. "I'm so scared."

"What is happening?" asked the man, still attempting to wake from his interrupted slumber.

"My lights keep turning on," she murmured. "My clocks say 666 and awful symbols are painted on my walls. The front door was knocked open. I am so scared, Father. I am so scared…"

The man startled at her revelation but tried to ground the situation. "Are you sure you have not been dreaming, Greta?"

"No, Father," she replied. "A noise awoke me and I discovered it. I'm so scared, Father… what should I do?"

"We must pray," he commanded her. "In the name of the Lord Jesus Christ of Nazareth, I stand with the power of the Lord God Almighty to bind Satan and all its evil spirits, demonic forces, satanic forces, principalities, along with all kings and princes of terrors, from the air, water, fire, ground, netherworld, and the evil forces of nature… I take authority over all demonic assignments and functions of destruction sent against your daughter, and I expose all demonic forces as weakened, defeated enemies of Jesus Christ. I stand with the power of the Lord God Almighty to bind all enemies of Christ present together, all demonic entities under their one and highest authority, and I command these spirits into the abyss to never again return. Their assignments and influences are over… I arise today with the power of the Lord God Almighty to call forth the heavenly host, the holy angels of God, to surround and protect, and cleanse with God's holy light all areas vacated by the forces of evil. I ask the Holy Spirit to permeate your servant's mind, heart, body, soul and spirit, creating a hunger and thirst for God's Holy Word, and to fill your servant with the life and love of my Lord, Jesus Christ."

XXV

In his bed, Heinrich lay still and asleep. The curtains were closed, and it was dark. Heinrich rested in a deep slumber, not about to wake. As he lay motionless, a reddish glow formed in the master bedroom's far corner. An apparition appeared, and it approached the bed. With its hands, it motioned over Heinrich's body as if to draw something from it. Another glow flowed from Heinrich's body, which, like the reddish glow, resulted in an apparition appearing. The two figures floated toward the window away from Heinrich.

"Mephistopheles," said the apparition coming from the red glow.

"Lucifer," replied Mephistopheles.

"I've come to alert you of your grave mistake," replied Lucifer. "You've risked the entire operation."

"My lord?"

"You should not have allowed Heinrich to go that

café yesterday," imparted Lucifer.

"My lord, you know as well as I do that I cannot make that soul do anything—"

"Do not get smart with me, Mephistopheles," chided Lucifer. "You know exactly what I mean."

"As that may be, Heinrich wanted to do so—"

"Enough!" Lucifer scolded Mephistopheles. "I warned you what the consequences of failure would be this time around, should you fail as you did with the last mission you were given."

"Do *not* threaten me, my lord," replied Mephistopheles. "I am no fool. Though you are the Master of Hell and I am but your servant, do not think I do not remember who it was that led us to our condemnation. Do not speak contritely to me, or you will regret it. I understood my mission, and I have accepted it. You have my word."

"Do we?"

Mephistopheles stared at Lucifer's apparition without yielding. "Yes, my lord."

"Good," said Lucifer. "Now wake Heinrich."

"My lord?"

"Do it now," said Lucifer without patience.

Mephistopheles's apparition flowed back into the glow from which it came out of Heinrich's body.

Lucifer watched as Heinrich's body stirred. From Heinrich's eyes, he wondered if he was dreaming, but he detected the voice of the devil calling him forward. "Heinrich Juarez, awake!"

Heinrich rose out of bed and rubbed his eyes. He realized it was Lucifer who appeared the same as in the bowels of Hell. "Lucifer," he said in acknowledgment.

"You needed to see me at this hour?"

"Yes," replied the devil. The apparition approached Heinrich, throwing a cold breeze against Heinrich's shirtless body. It gave him a brief chill which drew Heinrich to rub his arms. "We have your master plan for revenge against your adopted brother. All is coming together."

Heinrich nodded. "We asked him to bring his girl-friend sometime this week, and we're waiting to see if he will," said Heinrich. "I don't understand why I couldn't have just killed him when he was here earlier."

"Is that what you really want?"

"Yeah."

"I don't think so," replied Lucifer.

"What do you mean? How would you know?" asked Heinrich. "You can't read my mind. I've been able to tell that much is true."

"As that may be," replied Lucifer, "but we can tell you do not simply want your adopted brother dead. You want to make him suffer. When he beat you and left you behind in Cuba, he might as well have been dead to you. You knew not where he was, nor did you make any attempt to follow after him to find him. He was dead to you, can't you see?"

"I guess that makes sense," conceded Heinrich.

"So then, this is part of the plan to make him suffer," Lucifer said.

"Am I to make love to his girlfriend in front of him and make him watch?" asked Heinrich, thinking it would be twisted.

"Tempting as that might be for you, no," asserted Lucifer.

"Then what?"

"All you need to know is you won't be sleeping with his girlfriend," replied Lucifer. "But you will make him lose her trust, and he will be alone like he made you feel. Then you will have your revenge."

"So I'll be destroying his relationship with her?" asked Heinrich.

"Yes, you could put it that way," affirmed Lucifer.

Heinrich nodded his approval of the plan.

"And you will witness the agreement drawn up this very evening," confirmed Lucifer.

"But I don't want to help Jose—"

"I know that, but he does not know that," replied Lucifer.

Heinrich's face gave way to a mischievous smile. "Okay."

"There is one other matter I came here to tell you about," volunteered Lucifer.

"Oh?"

"There is a woman you will meet this evening—"

"I meant to talk to you about that," interrupted Heinrich.

"Yes?"

"I'm not really enjoying these drunken rendezvous. It's not quite what I hoped for."

"As I recall, you told me you wanted multiple girl-friends, and multiple women," Lucifer reminded him.

"Yes, I said that," said Heinrich. "But I don't believe that's what I want. It's hard these people leaving and me waking up alone. It's not what I was hoping for."

"You are in luck then," replied Lucifer. "Because the woman coming to see you tonight will satisfy you, I am confident."

"Really?"

"And she will be eager to fulfill all your fantasies, I assure you," said Lucifer. "And you will help her get what she wants."

"But…" said Heinrich. "I don't think that's what I want either. I want to experience someone who wants me, not Mr. Condannato."

Lucifer looked at Heinrich with bemusement. Heinrich gazed at Lucifer's apparition and waited for a reply, but nothing came.

"Lucifer?"

"Heinrich, you humans are so strange," said the devil. "First, you know well that we cannot make someone love you, nor do I estimate that's what you want."

Heinrich looked unimpressed. "Why don't I spare you the question and you tell me what I really want?" he stated.

"That is unnecessary," said Lucifer. "But trust me. This woman will please you, and you won't ever express these feelings to Mephistopheles or me again."

"Truly?"

"Truly."

Heinrich didn't feel comfortable trusting Lucifer that his wishes were understood, but he didn't have much of a choice to believe otherwise. As he relented his suspicion, he became more excited about meeting this new woman, whoever she was.

"I will let you sleep, Heinrich," said Lucifer, turning from Heinrich before remembering something. "Wait, there was one more thing I needed to tell you."

Heinrich showed he listened.

"Stay away from the cripple," commanded Lucifer.

"I'm sorry?"

"You know exactly who I am talking about," said Lucifer in a sterner tone.

"Suppose I do?"

"She is trouble," replied Lucifer. "And she cannot be helped. She is a redeemed individual."

"What does that mean?"

"That there is nothing that can be done for her. She has made her choice."

"But I told her to come visit me—"

"She is off limits," said Lucifer. "And should she show up to Babel, you are to reject her. There is nothing to negotiate. Do not entertain her. Send her away."

Heinrich cast Lucifer a puzzled look. He wanted more information. "But Lucifer!—"

"Goodbye, Heinrich," said Lucifer before the apparition shrank to a reddish glow and disappeared.

XXVI

"Greta Falk?" said the voice of an older woman behind a reception desk.

"Yes," replied Greta, as she stood from her chair. In her hands was a manilla envelope. She brushed her combed hair away from her face. She approached the reception desk.

"He will see you now," said the secretary, motioning her hand to the closed door that led to an office.

Greta thanked the secretary and opened the door. Within the office and behind a solid oak desk, a balding man sat looking at a computer screen. "Come in," he said without casting a glance at her. As Greta approached the desk, the man offered her to take a seat. It wasn't until she neared the desk that he saw her. When he did, it was apparent that her physical condition surprised him. He recoiled but tried his best to mask it. It didn't work.

"I've brought my resumé, sir," said the young lady. She opened the manilla envelope and approached the desk to hand it over.

"Thank you," said the man, though it was clear to Greta that he was distracted.

The man scrutinized the resumé and cover letter. Greta sat waiting, though her mind replayed the planned answers she conceived to any question he might have. She was prepared. The man glanced at her a few times. She smiled each time, waiting for him to comment. The man made no comment.

"So you're applying for the office mailroom clerk posting," said the man with little to no interest.

"Yes, that's correct," she said. She reminded herself to speak with as much enthusiasm as possible, even if for others such a job was a poorly paying entry-level position.

"You have a lot of volunteer experience at your parish," he said. He raised an eyebrow which she read as him being impressed, if only mildly. "And you've been active in your community."

"Yes, I am. I enjoy helping others, and interacting with a variety of people," she said with a broad smile, "some needier than others."

"I see," he said. "I'm not sure if there is much relevant experience for the position you're applying for, though."

"I can do the job," she boasted, "and I'll be good at it."

"What experience have you neglected to list that would show this?" he asked.

"I work at a coffee shop right now; I'm a bar—"

"Young lady, everyone is a barista these days," he replied with condescension. "It doesn't mean you'll be any good in the office workplace."

She paused. She didn't expect such apathy about her application. "Well…" she said, pausing again to think through her response. "My whole life, I've had to fight; to earn people's respect. So in my mind, this challenge won't be anything more difficult than what I've already dealt with before. I will find a way to not only make it work but to exceed your expectations."

"How can I be certain your obvious physical limitations won't impede upon your ability to perform the job to the basic expectations we have?" he asked with a smirk.

"My ability or disability won't get in the way—"

"Yes, but how can I be certain?"

She exhaled. "Again, I've had to deal with far more challenging circumstances, which were way more demanding," she stressed. "I can do this."

The interviewer became frustrated. "I have my doubts," he said.

Greta's brain considered another angle with which to persuade him.

"What exactly is your condition?" asked the man.

A perturbed look fell over Greta's face. "I didn't think I would be required to share such information, so long as I can do the job," she replied.

"That's just it, Miss Falk," he said, tiring of the interview and growing more so with each minute that passed. "I am trying to determine if you *can* do the job and whether your disability will interfere with executing the tasks and role."

"Listen, I know I can do this. Just trust me!" she pleaded as she leaned forward to speak. "Just give me a chance to prove myself. In fact, if it makes you feel more at ease, you can hire me on probation. And if, before three months pass, you find I can't do the job: fire me!"

"That's not how we do things here—"

"I need someone to give me a chance, please!" she begged. "Just give me an opportunity to gain experience. I need this!"

"I am sorry," he said, "but I won't be able to recommend you for hiring, or for bringing you onto our team."

She looked away. Rejection settled in yet again. "Tell me," she said. "Is it because of my disability?"

"Listen, I've already made my decision, and I need not explain it to you. You must accept my decision."

"But it's against the law to discriminate against someone because of a disability if they can do the job —"

The interviewer lost it with her response. He stood to speak. "Yes, damn it! It is because you are disabled, and you probably can't do the damn job! I said it, fine. And I don't regret saying it at all. You listen, young lady! I am sick and tired of taking the heat for hiring staff who just aren't physically or mentally cut out for the work and end up costing the company in the form of medical benefits. I am done with my boss coming down on my ass for hiring a bunch of cripples, who drain more money as liabilities than they do in wages. So yes, I am discriminating against you. Sue me, I don't care. But chances are if you are applying for this entry-level job, you can't afford a lawyer. So good luck on that front!"

Greta slumped in shock over the man's outburst. She had miscalculated. She didn't expect to receive an answer so candid or honest. Greta sat and avoided eye contact. She couldn't think of an adequate response. Inside, her anger burned. This was a wasted fight that got her nowhere. She stood from her chair and collected her resumé, which the man had dropped on his desk.

"Good day then, sir," she said, opening the door to leave. She passed through it but couldn't control her anger. Greta slammed the door shut. She overheard something fall from the office wall of the hiring manager. It ended with a smash. Anger filled her eyes as she stormed out of the reception area. She couldn't hide it.

XXVII

The face of the Christ looked cast down to its right side as it hung on the cross. Greta gazed upon the Christ. She reclined on a pew in silence at her parish. The quiet murmur of someone in the confessional was evident, but it was undecipherable. It wasn't any of her concern though. She had come for another reason.

She searched the defeated eyes of that body on the Crucifix. She wondered, did He know that He would die as a common criminal on a cross? Somehow in the past, she looked upon the crucifix as a symbol of strength. In her present condition, she struggled to view it as anything other than a figure of weaknesses. Did He know that He must die such a torturous death?

Her thoughts turned to her present condition. She viewed her legs. When she didn't move, they looked as ordinary as any other person's legs. Whenever she wanted to move them though, she struggled to control them. She reconsidered what she had already accepted about herself many times: what benefit could be had in God giving her such a disability?

"Greta, my child?" said a comforting voice. A middle-aged man of the cloth called her forth. He waved his hand to invite her toward the confessional. She crept over, entered the booth, and closed the door behind her.

She kneeled down and signed the cross over her chest. "Bless me, Father Cavanagh, for I have sinned," she said. "It has been one day since my last confession."

The priest nodded. His shadow came through the separation.

"Father, I have sinned," she said. "Forgive me for my sin of unbelief. Today, I was rejected for another job. I feel doubt rising in my soul. I don't understand the Lord's purposes in all of this; for what reason has He made me continue to struggle through life, after everything I've already been through? Is this all a part of God's plan for my life? Father, you know I try to do good and serve others. But it seems sometimes that God has rejected me like the hiring manager did today. Has He cast me aside? Is this why He gave me this broken body?"

"My child," said the priest in response. "The Lord knows all things, even the things we cannot yet comprehend. He operates in ways that are confusing to our minds, and in His ways, we have often yet to understand them until all has come to pass."

"I know, Father," she said in reply. "It's just very hard. And I am struggling."

"Take courage, Greta," said Father Cavanagh. "You know the Lord is trustworthy and ever compassionate."

"Yes, Father," she said. "I am sorry for these sins and all of my sins."

"One Hail Mary will suffice, my child," said the priest. "But if you would like to discuss this matter more, I am available."

"Thank you, Father," said Greta. "My God, I am sorry for my sins with all my heart. In choosing to do wrong and failing to do good, I have sinned against you whom I should love above all things. I firmly intend, with your help, to do penance, to sin no more, and to avoid whatever leads me to sin. Our Savior, Jesus Christ, suffered and died for us. In his name, my God, have mercy."

"God, the Father of mercies," said the priest, "through the death and resurrection of your Son, you have reconciled the world to yourself and sent the Holy Spirit among us for the forgiveness of sins. Through the ministry of the Church, may God grant you pardon and peace. And I absolve you of your sins, in the name of the Father, and of the Son, and of the Holy Spirit. Amen."

"Thank you, Father Cavanagh," said Greta as she rose from her knees.

"Thank you for coming, Greta," he said, as she opened the door to the confessional. He too exited.

"Father, I wanted to ask you about something."

"Yes, Greta?"

"The other day, a man offered to help me," she volunteered. "He asked me about my dreams and said he would help, but I don't understand why."

"Did he ask for something in return?"

"No, Father," she said. "I mean, I helped him after he fell with his coffee. It was at work."

"Perhaps it isn't so strange," replied Father Cavanagh. "You showed him kindness. He wants to repay you. You responded as our Lord did to those who suffered."

"I suppose," said Greta.

"It may be of God," said the priest. "He could be going before you and leading you to the path He has set out for you."

She smiled at such a thought. "I hope so, Father," she said. "I think I will go visit him tonight."

Father Cavanagh patted her arm with care and nodded his head with encouragement.

"Father, can I ask a favor?" she asked.

"Certainly, my child."

"Could you pray for me?"

XXVIII

Heinrich sat in the chair in his office with the curtain drawn in front of the desk. He slouched while holding a highball in his hand. He received word that Jose was headed there that evening as Lucifer had suggested he would.

Outside the office, it was a busy night at Babel as many hoped for an audience with Mr. Condannato. Heinrich though grew tired of the meetings. On his mind alone was the opportunity for revenge, and he wondered how it might present itself that night.

Bianca stood off in the corner of the office. She looked through papers, which drew Heinrich's attention. Bianca was an attractive woman. She made no notice of his passing glance but instead focused on the evening's schedule.

"Bianca?" Heinrich called out to her.

"Yes, sir?"

"For how long have you been serving Lucifer?" asked Heinrich.

"Some time, I suppose," she replied.

"What arrangement did you make with the devil?" he asked her.

"Nothing particularly noteworthy."

"Really?"

She shrugged her shoulders and returned her attention to the papers in front of her.

"Come now," Heinrich pushed further. "With what deal did Lucifer approach you?"

"Mr. Condannato, it was of little significance," she replied. She looked more uncomfortable as he probed her with questions.

"Humor me," he asked her out of boredom.

She turned away before responding. "He helped me escape."

"Escape what?"

"My father," she said.

"Some people would do anything to be with their father."

"Not me," she said. "He was an abusive, controlling man."

"And Lucifer is not?" asked Heinrich with a smirk.

She didn't respond with any humor. "My father beat me," she said in a plain manner.

Heinrich regretted making the jest.

"Lucifer helped me gain my freedom and lead an independent life of my own away from my father," she said.

"Are you free though if you are serving Lucifer and me?" asked Heinrich. He gave her his full attention.

"It is more independence than I have ever known," she replied. "I sometimes wonder what my life would be like without Lucifer's help, and I know it wouldn't be like my life now."

"How do you know?" he asked.

"I would be in prison," she said with no remorse.

"Why do you think that?"

"Because Lucifer helped me kill my father and get revenge," she said. Her matter-of-fact approach made Heinrich uncomfortable, even if he was seeking his own revenge against Jose.

"I wouldn't peg you as the type."

"Killers don't have a type, Mr. Condannato," she stated. "If I have learned one thing in your household and in meeting all the people we do, there is no type to a killer. There are simply those who have had enough and can no longer go on with things as they are: either they kill, or they kill themselves."

Heinrich's mind drifted back to Cuba and his Cuban mindset. "Why do you stay in Lucifer's service?" he asked. There had to be a deal.

"If I don't, Lucifer will release the police on me for the murder of my father. It is a cold case. Lucifer is the only reason I haven't been charged. I did not try to hide the murder, or my father's body. Lucifer has the prosecutors on the payroll."

"And it was worth it?"

She nodded her head as she worked on her papers as if allowing herself the distraction. "I couldn't live that life anymore. It was him or me."

"How long does Lucifer possess you?"

"For life," she said. She didn't seem bothered. "And

for the rest of eternity."

Heinrich considered his deal with Lucifer, and while in a different circumstance, he saw himself in Bianca's situation. She received what she had wanted, and she seemed content with life. Jose deserved the justice that Heinrich sought. He was a selfish person and caused so much of Heinrich's grief in life. Had Jose been more welcoming and kind to him, Heinrich's life might not have been so miserable.

"How do you envision an eternity in Hell?" Heinrich asked.

"I choose not to dwell on it," she replied with a strong face, though Heinrich read that she didn't like the question. It made her uncomfortable. "If Satan is my master though, I trust it won't be torment. I serve Lucifer faithfully, and I expect to be treated as such."

Heinrich nodded.

"Okay, yes, I do sometimes wonder about it and whether it was worth it all," she conceded. "But I am glad I am free. Once and for all."

A knock came at the door. Bianca went to answer it, and there was Yousef. He whispered to Bianca, who strode over to Mr. Condannato and closed the curtain in the front of the desk. She took her place behind the desk and beside him.

"Mr. Jose Juarez is here," she whispered into Heinrich's ear. "And he has brought a guest."

Heinrich motioned to Yousef to bring in his adopted brother. In came Jose as Yousef held the door open, and behind him sauntered a woman. She had a warm smile on her face; she was excited. What Jose had told her about the reason for the visit mystified Heinrich.

They took seats in front of the desk and sat until spoken to.

"Mr. Juarez," said Heinrich. "You have returned."

"Yes, sir."

"And who is this?" he asked, playing up his ignorance of her identity.

"This is Dominica," Jose said, clearing his throat. "She is my girlfriend."

"Welcome, Miss Dominica," said Heinrich.

"Thank you, sir," she replied with excitement. "We are so happy to be here."

"Mr. Juarez tells me he dreams of being a baseball player?" Heinrich asked.

"Yes, sir," she said as she sat upright in her chair, but stopping herself from speaking more. She disciplined herself from getting carried away or speaking out of line.

"And he tells me he was injured in an accident at sea and that times are very challenging for you both."

"Yes, it has been," she said.

"You are both working?"

"Yes, we are," she said. The reminder of work tired her. "I work at a daycare during the day and serve at a restaurant at night."

"Mr. Juarez is working three jobs, is this true?"

"Yes, sir," she said. "He works very hard. I am very proud of him."

"Very good," said Heinrich. "Well, Dominica, I suppose he has told you why you are here tonight."

"Yes. He told me you wanted to meet me and get to know us better," she volunteered.

Heinrich beheld his brother. It wasn't unlike him to

lie. He had fooled this poor woman and convinced her he was a good person. Not a good bone resided in Jose's body. Heinrich's blood boiled in considering how Jose's devious nature knew no end. Heinrich would enjoy taking him down a level and humiliating him.

"Good, then we may begin," he spoke to the woman. "Please stand up for me."

She took a look at Jose, but stood and smiled in Mr. Condannato's direction.

"Good, now take off your clothes," said Heinrich without emotion.

She glanced again to her boyfriend and back to Mr. Condannato. "I'm sorry?" she said.

"Undress."

"But why?"

"It is necessary," said Mr. Condannato with no further explanation.

She shifted to Jose again, searching for support or a response.

"Do you want to help your boyfriend's dream come true?" asked Heinrich.

"But why is this necessary?" she asked. "What's all this about?"

Jose sank farther into his chair. He became flustered. He made little effort to defend his girlfriend's honor.

"Mr. Juarez, you know why you brought your girlfriend here," Heinrich chided Jose. "Do something about it!"

"Listen to Mr. Condannato," said Jose at Heinrich's urging. Dominica sneered at him with incredulity. She struggled to speak, but twisted back toward Mr. Condannato and shook her head.

"Miss Dominica," said Heinrich. "You were brought here under the explicit pretense that you sleep with me, and I would have my way with you. This is the condition of your boyfriend receiving my help."

She slapped Jose across the face, "*Cabrón!*" she shouted at Jose. "*Me cago en tu puta madre!*"

Jose slumped in his chair and avoided eye contact with his girlfriend. He was a coward in Heinrich's eyes. No one defended him; no schoolyard bullies protecting him from his raging girlfriend.

"After everything we have been through together," she scolded him. "After the lives we've made together, how could you ask me to do this?"

Jose gazed away without a care in his eyes, but mere frustration.

"I already sacrifice so much for you and your dreams," she said. "How could you bring me here for this?"

"Listen," Jose replied, "we have a chance here. Do as Mr. Condannato says!"

"No!" she shouted back. Heinrich witnessed her passion. He admired her. "I can't do this. If you believe this is reasonable to expect of me, I can't be with you anymore, Jose. I can't!"

Jose again shifted away from her. Anger resonated on Jose's face for her refusal to comply. She darted closer to Jose and glared down on him. She grabbed her coat that was on the chair and went to walk away from him, but stopped and slapped his face once more.

"After everything I've done for you, how could you?" she said before storming out. She fumbled with the door, but Yousef waited on the other side and opened it for her. She shoved her way past, which surprised Yousef. He closed the door behind her, leaving Heinrich, Jose and Bianca in the room alone. Heinrich examined Jose as his adopted brother looked agitated. He had slouched even farther into his chair and exhaled.

"She was a part of our agreement," said Mr. Condannato. Jose peered toward Heinrich, but before he spoke any words from his open mouth, Heinrich spoke again: "But since you showed good faith, I will honor our arrangement."

Jose's jaw dropped farther. He tried to speak, but few words came. "I don't understand," said Jose when he could finally put a sentence together. "She walked out on us, though?"

"Don't worry about the details, Mr. Juarez," said Heinrich. Inside him, he didn't like that Mephistopheles told him that revenge wouldn't be had this night either. After what he witnessed from Jose, Heinrich would feel no remorse in handing out justice upon him.

"Leave your address with Bianca and you should expect a visit from me."

"Thank you so much, sir!" said Jose with a look of relief.

"Go on," said Heinrich to dismiss him. Bianca passed around the desk and collected his information and showed him to the door. As the door shut behind them, Heinrich let out a heavy sigh. "When do I kill him?"

Patience, Heinrich, said Mephistopheles. *Patience.*

XXIX

Heinrich's mind replayed what he had witnessed between Jose and his girlfriend. He felt bad for the woman who loved his adopted brother, yet Jose gave that all up for his selfish dream. What Heinrich would have given for a sacrificial love like Dominica's. He wondered what the woman would do next. As for Jose though, Heinrich grew frustrated in waiting for his revenge.

Bianca returned to the office. She came around to Heinrich and interrupted his pondering. "Your next visitor is here," she said. "She is in the VIP area waiting for you."

Heinrich rose from his chair and straightened out his suit. He followed Bianca out of the office. He passed through the doors. Bianca led him to a hightop table where a tall, thin woman stood with a drink in her hand and her back turned to Heinrich's direction. She waited and wasn't in any rush. As Heinrich came around to view her, she was the most beautiful vision. She had long, straight blonde hair, and on her face was a warm, genuine smile. She wore a knee-length silver dress, which paired with her pale skin. She was as much of an angelic sight as Heinrich had imagined.

Unlike any woman before, Heinrich trembled as a weakness came over him. Her eyes were blue as a clear sea while her shoulders were soft and gentle. Her figure was exquisite. It was clear to Heinrich that she took great lengths in maintaining her body and her beauty. Her innocence made an impression upon Heinrich; such a woman didn't belong in his company, let alone in Babel. It only made him love her all the more. If such a thing as love at first sight existed, Heinrich concluded he was experiencing it.

"I don't believe we've had the pleasure of meeting yet," said Heinrich. Mephistopheles was to be his guide again.

"No, we haven't, Mr. Condannato," said the woman. She extended her hand, which Heinrich scooped and kissed. "I'm Jezebel Saval."

"Pleased to meet you," replied Heinrich as he let go of her hand. Despite the confidence of having Mephistopheles to guide him, Heinrich was the most uncomfortable he had ever been with a woman on Earth.

"You look nice tonight."

"Thank you," replied Heinrich, "and if I may say myself, you are ravishing in that dress."

The woman blushed, "You are sweet."

Heinrich smiled and invited her to follow him to his

office. He took hold of her hand and led her to the doors, drawing the surprised glances of others in the VIP area. Mr. Condannato wasn't known to be seen in public with women in such an obvious manner. Heinrich didn't hide anything. The two entered the office, and he led her to take a seat. Rather than sitting behind the desk, he sat beside her. He rotated his chair toward her, so they were face to face.

"Now, tell me," said Heinrich with a still grand smile on his face, which she witnessed. "Why are you here?"

She let out a nervous sigh. She looked away with a smile and then shifted back to him, "I heard that you could help me."

Heinrich nodded.

"And I'm willing to do whatever you need me to do to make that happen."

Heinrich blushed as a smirk came across his face. He considered a few things he would like her to do. "What do you want me to do for you?"

"Gosh, this will sound so stupid now that I say it out loud," she said.

"No, nonsense. Tell me; I want to know."

"My dream is to become a fitness instructor on television," she confessed.

"Why is that?"

"I'm a fitness model," she said, "and the money is decent, but I want to do so much more. I want to help people feel better and get into shape. Most people just view me as something they can never attain, but I want to show them it is possible."

"What's stopping you?" asked Heinrich.

The woman paused. Something under the surface

was difficult to say. He told her she didn't need to hesitate to share it with him.

"I used to be married, but my husband is dead now," she stated. She took her time in speaking. Heinrich perceived pain was there, so he grasped her hand to console her. "I could never do what I wanted to do while we were married. Now is my chance to do what is best for me: what I want to do with my life."

"What help do you think I can provide with this goal?" asked Heinrich. He was more than content for her to keep talking.

"Well," she said, again pausing due to her nervousness, "you're Dante Condannato. The most helpful, yet elusive man in New York City."

Heinrich laughed, as he reclined back in his chair and took another moment to enjoy her delicate, angelic features.

"I will do *anything* you need me to do," she pleaded, though it was unnecessary. Even if Mephistopheles told Heinrich not to help her, he wouldn't have been able to comply.

"Anything?" replied Heinrich. "Do you mean that?"

"Yes."

Mephistopheles told him what to say, but Heinrich froze. It seemed bold to him, though it was what he wanted. After all, this woman, Jezebel, had come to satisfy him. He went with it. "I do have a request in mind," he said, as he leaned forward and gazed into her eye. "It involves you being my lover."

"Done," she replied without blinking, though she smiled after saying so.

Heinrich was surprised, though he knew he shouldn't

be. This was the realm of Lucifer. "Why do you not even hesitate when I ask you that?"

"After losing my first husband," she said, "I realized that while I loved him, it didn't get me what I wanted in life. This time though, if it will get me what I want, I would be happy to try again."

Heinrich turned away from her. He was disappointed to hear her speak what she had said. "It would be difficult for me not to feel used and untrusting in such an arrangement."

"I will learn to love you, Mr. Condannato," she replied to assuage his fears. "It won't be very hard. I can tell you are a good man. I want to fulfill your every desire, whether it be companionship, romance, or something more risqué."

"I do find you the most beautiful, desirable woman I have ever seen with my eyes," he confessed.

"Likewise, I admire you, and I would be honored to be your lover," she said.

"If such an arrangement is to be made, there would need to be something signed by you."

"Will I need to marry you?"

"No, that isn't necessary," Heinrich replied. "Rather, you will need to sign a blood oath to Lucifer, and promise your soul for eternity. Lucifer in exchange will grant you your dream come true through my maneuvering and influence."

"I will do it," she said. "How soon can I sign it?"

Heinrich called out to Bianca, who entered the office. He passed along the instructions, and Jezebel produced a contract and the sacramental knife. Heinrich considered it a shame she might scar her delicate hand, but Mephistopheles assured him it was necessary if Lucifer was going to make it happen.

Heinrich watched Jezebel with pleasure as she signed the contract and performed the ritual under Bianca's supervision. Jezebel winced as she removed the knife from her grip and placed her hand upon the contract. Heinrich helped to mend her hand. Once she was bandaged, Heinrich kissed her hand with grace. It drew a smile from her face, which produced such a pleasing warmth within Heinrich's heart.

"What would you like me to do for you?" she asked with a mischievous smile.

Bianca interrupted, "Mr. Condannato, you have one more visitor tonight that requires your attention."

Heinrich exhaled in disappointment. "Who is it?"

Bianca informed him it was a girl named Greta who had a business card from him, and while the girl was plainly dressed, she had arrived to meet him. Heinrich turned to Jezebel and apologized for the intrusion, "Would you wait for me in my private residence?"

She complied. Bianca escorted her to the bedroom. Bianca had Yousef send Greta into the office. Mr. Condannato took his usual place behind the desk and waited for Bianca to return.

XXX

As Heinrich sat waiting for Greta, the woman in his bedroom consumed his mind. He readied himself for Greta as Mephistopheles gave Heinrich instructions for turning her away. He asked Mephistopheles why it wasn't possible for the guards to just deal with her that night and prevent her from coming. Mephistopheles told him that a Dante Condannato business card carries great power and respect. In Lucifer's eyes, Heinrich had given it too easily.

Bianca came into the office from the bedroom and took her usual place beside Heinrich with the curtain pulled closed.

"Have you met this young woman?" Heinrich asked.

"I met her outside in Babel," she replied. "I had to verify the invitation, or your business card I should say."

"What do you think of her?"

"I know her eyes."

"Do you?" Heinrich asked in surprise.

"I have seen myself in those eyes," she said.

"Whatever do you mean?" Heinrich asked, but the office door opened. Yousef produced Greta and showed her to the seat in front of the desk.

As she approached the desk, it became apparent that she was uncomfortable in the office. The darkness of the room imposed a constricting presence. On the walls, satanic symbols and other grotesque pieces of art unsettled Greta. She sat and placed her hands under her legs. She was nervous and reconsidered her decision to come to see Mr. Condannato. Heinrich watched her as her eyes recalled the same imagery that had haunted her in her house.

Do not entertain her requests, or humor her, Mephistopheles reminded Heinrich. *Show no weakness. Send her away.*

"Did you design the office yourself?" she asked to break the silence.

"Do not speak unless you are spoken to!" Bianca chided the young woman. Heinrich waved her off.

"It's all right," said Heinrich. "It is nothing more than art. Don't mind it. I have unusual tastes."

"So it seems," replied Greta. She waited for Heinrich to speak as she feared another scolding. She wondered if that was a sign she shouldn't have come. The place was creepy and unnerving.

"Nice of you to come so soon," said Heinrich with an air of politeness. Mephistopheles pushed him still to send her away.

"Yeah," she said. She couldn't decide where to look as glaring into the curtain was uncomfortable. She had never been to such a place. "My priest told me I should come today; that you might be my lifeline."

"Your priest?" replied Heinrich with bemusement. "The Lord certainly works in mysterious ways."

"That's what he said," she said after receiving a moment of comfort in Heinrich's words, but that dissipated. "Do you believe in God?"

"I do in a roundabout way," he replied, "but let us leave our religious convictions for another time."

Send this cripple away. You have no use for her! Mephistopheles scolded Heinrich.

Heinrich refused. Greta looked no more comfortable than the moment she first arrived. "Tell me about your dream."

Greta considered excusing herself, but not wanting to be rude or unkind, she decided that telling him couldn't hurt. "I guess you could say I want to help people."

"Don't we all," said Heinrich in a mocking manner.

"I suppose," she said. She wanted to back out, but her conscience prevented her, even if it also told her to flee. "I guess I want to serve people and help them, you know, get better, or improve."

"You want to be a doctor?" asked Heinrich.

"No, not that. I want people to talk to me if they need to."

"You want to talk to strangers on the street?"

"No, oh my goodness, I'm terrible at this," she said in frustration at herself.

"No, no, go on," said Heinrich, drawing another sharp rebuke from Mephistopheles.

"I want to be a counselor," she blurted out. "That's

what I want to be. I want to open a home for others with disabilities or victims of abuse. I want them to come and stay and work through their issues."

"Why are you so passionate about that?"

"I'm sure you and everyone else can tell that I have a disability—"

"Yes, what is it exactly?" he asked.

"Cerebral palsy."

"Which is?"

"It's hard to explain. Let's just say I know first-hand how challenging it can be for those of us who are disabled. It can be isolating and lonely."

"How does your condition isolate you, Greta?"

She gazed down to the ground and sighed. Her heart reasoned it right to be open, but her mind told her it was time to go. She gave way to her heart. "My mom killed herself when I was a little girl. She thought it was her fault I was disabled. She killed herself over her grief in giving birth to me. And ever since my dad passed away, it has been just me. There's no one else in my life but my church."

Her story moved Heinrich, having known such a reality. Mephistopheles didn't let up on the commands to send her away, regardless of her sob story. Heinrich was playing too much of a risk, but he saw himself in her and wanted to help her.

"I'm grateful for my parish," she said. "They've been so kind, but I want to do more with my life. It has been so hard to get an opportunity. So many people see me as just a disabled girl. I could do so much more for my community; if I could just get a decent job to pay for school and get money to open a home, or a resource center, or safe house, whatever you want to call it. For once, I'd be able to contribute to society rather than people looking at me like I can't do anything. I can do so many things! As it is now, I'm relegated to working at a coffee shop, making minimum wage and counting my tips to get me through each month's rent and bills —"

"It is done," said Heinrich.

"I'm sorry?" she asked. Greta realized she had rambled. She was so caught up in the emotion of telling her story that she had almost forgotten Mr. Condannato was listening, or that someone else was a part of the conversation.

"It's done. I will take care of it all for you," said Heinrich.

Mephistopheles couldn't be contained. *What the devil are you doing?*

"I will take care of all the details," said Heinrich, "but there will be conditions."

"I'm willing to listen," she said. "I've never been so shocked before. No one has ever believed in me like this. Not even Father Cavanagh!"

"I will make it happen," Heinrich assured her. "You can take a job in my service. If not, you can go straight to school and get the education you need. I'll pull the strings and arrange enrollment. Hell, I'll even put the financing in a trust for when you finish school."

"I don't know what to say!" she exclaimed. "What are the conditions though?"

"They are simple," said Mr. Condannato. "You will sign a blood contract and swear your service for a time at my discretion."

"A what?" said a disturbed Greta.

"A blood contract," he said. "You must make an oath to the devil and swear your soul to Lucifer."

Greta stood. "I can't do that!" she said, almost shouting it.

"Why not? You'd rather live your boring, lonely life?"

Greta scowled at Heinrich with disgust. "I'm Catholic. You know this. My soul is God's and I can't turn my back on Him."

"Why?" he asked. "It appears He has done so to you."

"How dare you!" she shouted.

"Lucifer has open arms to you to make your dreams come true," replied Heinrich. He tired of her self-righteousness, even if but a moment ago he was empathetic toward her. She deserved her life if that was how she would respond.

"No! That's not true!" she insisted. "I have not been abandoned. He has a plan! He does!"

"Does he?" said Heinrich.

"If I knew what you meant when you told me to come, I never would have!" she said. She found the courage to leave and looked away from Heinrich.

"So be it," he replied. "If you aren't interested, you are more than welcome to leave. I have business to attend to."

Bianca came around the curtain and motioned the direction to the door. Greta stared at her with contempt, but Bianca made no emotional response visible to Greta. She was a true professional.

Greta turned back toward the curtain. "I can't believe you would ask me such a thing," she chided Heinrich.

"If you change your mind, you know where to find me," he said with an air of condescension.

Greta shook her head in disbelief and trotted out the door that Yousef opened as she approached.

Bianca returned to Heinrich's side with the contract, which she had torn up. She tossed it into a rubbish bin. "She is weak," she said. "I can see it in her eyes. She is at her wit's end."

Heinrich nodded.

"I know those eyes. I told you earlier," she said.

"So it may be," he replied. "But for now, I have someone to attend to."

"Have a good night, Mr. Condannato."

"Good night, Bianca."

Heinrich strolled to the entrance of his bedroom. He unbuttoned his tie in the process and opened the door to find Jezebel lying on his bed with a smile on her face. The blanket covered her body, but her shoulders were bare. Heinrich smiled. He would have a good night.

XXXI

A sprinkling rain drizzled upon Greta as she exited the tower. Tears streamed down her face. A sense of utter defeat numbed her from caring about anyone seeing her tears. She held her coat close to keep warm amidst the weather. She questioned herself. How was she so foolish to have bothered seeing Mr. Condannato, let alone not leaving earlier?

She couldn't decide what bothered her more: that her hopes were dashed, or that Mr. Condannato had asked her to sell her soul to the devil. But when her tears subsided, she determined not to think about the earlier events anymore. She pushed it as far from her mind as she could. As she felt a semblance of normalcy again, an uneasy sense came over her. While she passed by alleyways, she witnessed a bizarre masquerade of shadows. They didn't come from anything moving, but they moved as they desired. They made no figure recognizable, but it was enough to alarm her. She veered as close as possible to the side of the road whenever she passed an alleyway. She grew frustrated with her muscle spasms as she powered through her fear on her journey home.

As she passed another alleyway, a man stood with a trench coat. He wore dark sunglasses. It made no sense to her as it was evening. He looked at her and didn't try to hide his staring. She looked away but stole another glance at him to realize his gaze hadn't left her.

Greta jaywalked across the street away from the man. She peered over her shoulder to discern that he still gazed at her. She said a quiet prayer asking for protection and that the man would leave her alone. The man's gaze still never left her the farther she drifted from him, but he didn't try to follow her. Greta experienced relief when she passed around a street corner and out of the man's sight. She exhaled and thanked God for keeping her safe.

Greta cleared two more city blocks on her walk home when she found another man in a trench coat, the same color and style as before, wearing dark sunglasses. She froze when he stared at her like the previous man. She went another way. The man in the trench coat never let his gaze stray from her. Greta went down another street but stopped when the same man manifested there staring at her. She didn't know what to do.

To her left was an alleyway which exposed a clear path to another street. She studied it longer, resisting the urge to go down the darkened escape route. She never walked down such an alleyway at night in New York City, but she was scared. She wasn't thinking, but she had to get away.

Her leg muscles grew more tired with all the walking, and she couldn't keep this up all night. She went against her better judgment and proceeded down the alleyway. It seemed like it was a safe decision, but after several paces, three people stood in the distance. Where they were when she had looked before, she didn't know, but they made notice of her. She prayed again, though questioned if she should just turn around.

They were three teenage boys, each under the influence of some substance. She prayed that they leave her alone as she moved forward through the alleyway.

"*Hola malparido!*" shouted one younger man at her. She didn't understand. The other young men made comments in Spanish. Her breathing increased as she grew fearful. She wasn't about to fight them, but she focused on fleeing.

"*Niña! Espera!*" said one of the bolder young men, as he grabbed her arm.

Greta surveyed him with fear in her eyes, "Please don't touch me," she said as she lumbered forward. Another young man stepped in front to block her.

"What's a matter? You don't speak Spanish?" mocked one boy.

"No!" she barked at them. "Now let me past!"

"Hold on, we won't hurt you," said another of the boys with a mischievous smile. "We just want to get to know you."

"I'm late," Greta replied. "I don't have time."

"Now, now, no need to be rude, girl," said the third boy blocking her. He gripped both of her arms and held her.

"Leave me alone!" she shouted. The other boys jeered and asked in Spanish if the third boy would take that from her. "I have to go home!"

"We will take you home, won't we, Armando?" said one boy, as he grazed her cheek with the back of his hand. "You look like you could use the help."

"No, I'm all right on my own," she said, almost whimpering as she spoke.

"Have you ever made love to a man?" asked another of the boys, laughing. The others joined him in laughter.

"Leave me alone! Stop touching me!" she said again, this time trying to break free from them. The boys began pushing her around and fondled her inappropriately. She struggled to keep her balance, let alone stay up. "Stop it!"

The boys shoved her more, and Greta screamed for help. A man at the alleyway's end shouted at the boys to stop, but they made no recognition of him. The man sprinted down the alleyway and hollered at the boys again. He had an athletic build and was taller than the young men. He commanded them to stop harassing the girl. One boy stepped away from Greta to approach the man as the other two boys fought to keep hold of Greta's arms. She still struggled to escape, but they were too strong for her. The Alpha Male of the group darted closer to the man and clenched a fist to take a swing at him. The man was too quick as he grabbed the young man's fist in the air, and twisted the boy's arm into a lock. It drew a painful cry from the young man who begged to be released. The rescuer threw the teenager to the ground, and the boy whimpered.

"Any of you other boys care for a turn?" shouted the man at the two remaining hoodlums. They let go of Greta and ran opposite from the man and down the alleyway. The fallen boy ran the other direction to flee. Greta collapsed to the ground in tears. The good Samaritan helped her up. "Are you okay?" he asked her.

She threw her arms around him and sobbed. "Thank God for you," she said amid tears. "Thank God!"

He held her for minutes as she had a good cry. She gathered herself and decided that she was okay.

"Can I call you a cab?" the man asked Greta.

"No, I can't afford one," she confessed as she wiped the last of the tears from her face.

"Don't worry about it," said the man as he reached into his pockets. "I'll cover it."

He hailed a cab with a whistle, which resulted in the cab pulling into the alley. Greta gaped with amazement: how does one get a cab to pick you up from an alleyway?

He helped her into the cab, and the driver asked where she wanted to go. She provided the address, and the man handed the driver a $20 bill and asked if it should cover it. The driver nodded in affirmation.

Greta stared at the man. She couldn't believe the help of a stranger. "Thank you so much," she said again. "You saved my life."

"Don't mention it," he said, as he shut the door to the cab. She rolled down the window.

"But what is your name?"

"I must be off!" he said as he waved at her.

"But at least tell me your name!" she begged.

"It's Mike," he said. "I'm glad you're okay, and I was happy to help."

The man tapped the top of the cab. The driver exited the alleyway. "You have yourself a good night!"

The cab drove onto the street and made its way to Greta's home. She didn't understand what just happened. She wanted to ask the driver to turn around and take her back to the man so she could understand, but she stopped short. Greta sighed and thanked God for His protection of her. That was what she assumed it was.

XXXII

As Heinrich lay peacefully in his bed, Jezebel wrapped her arms around him, and her head rested on his chest. It was early in the morning, and not a soul in the house stirred. A familiar red glow appeared, and from it sprang Lucifer's apparition. Lucifer performed the same ritual as before to draw Mephistopheles from Heinrich's body. Mephistopheles's apparition stood at attention. Something was amiss.

"Mephistopheles, I don't intend to spend much time in telling you this, but you have been an utter failure," said Lucifer to the other spirit with indignation.

"My lord?"

"You knew perfectly well that Heinrich was not to make any offers to that pathetic girl!"

"But my lord—"

"You were well aware of what was at stake for you with this assignment, Mephistopheles," said Lucifer.

"My patience with you is finished!"

"I could not stop him!" Mephistopheles defended. "He would not be dissuaded."

"Heinrich is hardly the most complicated soul you've ever been assigned to," said Lucifer. "You were overcome by someone who has been an abject failure his entire life. A loner. A worthless soul. A human who couldn't stand up for himself, but he resisted you—"

"But my lord, there is goodness in him—"

"Don't start! Not even the Almighty One concerned Himself with Heinrich!" Lucifer bellowed. "Not *even* the Almighty One!"

Mephistopheles said nothing. Any further rebuttal would only heightened Lucifer's anger and fury.

"You have *one* last chance, Mephistopheles!" declared Lucifer. "*One* last chance! You deliver this cripple's soul to me or you are finished. Not even I, the Master of Hell, will have any use for you. You will be little more than one of the other condemned souls."

"Yes, my lord," said Mephistopheles.

"Do I make myself clear?" demanded Lucifer.

"Yes."

XXXIII

"Mr. Condannato?" said the calm voice of a woman. She nudged Heinrich as he lay asleep in his master bedroom. "Mr. Condannato?"

Heinrich stirred from his slumber and opened his eyes. He couldn't make out who it was. When he focused his eyes, he realized it was Bianca and not Jezebel. He turned to where Jezebel had slept the previous night. She was gone.

"Mr. Condannato, you have your meeting with Rufus Harper in thirty minutes," said Bianca.

Heinrich sat up in the bed. "Where did she go?"

"She left early this morning, sir."

A cringe of disappointment arrived in Heinrich's heart.

"She left you this, though," said Bianca, as she handed over a small handwritten note. It reassured him that Jezebel wouldn't be like the other women who came through his bed.

"What's this meeting about?" asked Heinrich with a smile once he finished reading the message.

Bianca explained that she arranged for Mr. Harper to come over that morning to discuss the arrangements for Jezebel's fitness instruction program. She excused herself once Heinrich got ready for the day.

Lucifer seeks an audience with you, mentioned Mephistopheles as Heinrich dressed.

"What for?" asked Heinrich in the midst tying his tie.

Lucifer would like to tell you personally.

Heinrich finished dressing and entered into his office chamber. He passed through the door and found Lucifer's apparition standing there. Heinrich went to take his seat at the table, but Mephistopheles cautioned him otherwise. *Never take the seat behind the desk in Lucifer's presence.*

Heinrich thought better than to go against the advice he received, so he approached Lucifer. "I apologize for keeping you waiting," he said to Lucifer.

The apparition faced Heinrich.

"To what do I owe the pleasure?" Heinrich asked.

"I am well aware of the meeting you had last night," said Lucifer.

"Which one?"

"I think you know which one I am referring to."

Heinrich said nothing.

"The girl I warned you about—"

"There is nothing to worry about with her—"

"Excuse me, but I will not be interrupted!" declared Lucifer.

Heinrich raised his hands to concede to the devil.

"I am not worried about her any longer," said Lucifer. "Quite the opposite. There might be potential with this woman."

"You didn't see how things went down last night," said Heinrich.

"Oh, I did. I know well how things played out last night," retorted Lucifer. "Despite Mephistopheles's failure to arrest you from making an offer to that crippled god-forsaken woman, you have discovered potential use for her in my kingdom."

"She said she wasn't interested—"

"You must pursue her and the deal you offered her," Lucifer interrupted Heinrich.

"I don't understand."

"She is weak. I can sense her frailty," said Lucifer with an intent stare toward Heinrich. "We might yet draw her away from the hands of the Almighty One, by her own volition no less. I am commanding you to seek her out."

"I don't think she has any interest in ever speaking to me again, nor I her," said Heinrich.

"You must trust me," replied Lucifer. "There is an opening to her soul. You are bound by our agreement to obey me, or suffer the consequences like Mr. Condannato did before you."

Heinrich exhaled in frustration. The last thing he wanted to do was waste time on Greta when he had the embrace of another woman. "Do you have a plan?" asked Heinrich in a patronizing fashion.

"You know where she works," said Lucifer.

"I do."

"I want you to go see her at work and visit her during her break," ordered Lucifer. "We will send you there when it is her break time. We will watch the café."

"But what do I say?"

"You went alone in your conversation with her last night," said Lucifer. "Mephistopheles is not any help to you. I trust you will know what to say."

Heinrich sensed something inside of him burning with a rage, but it wasn't him.

"I must be off now," said Lucifer.

"But wait!" said Heinrich before Lucifer's apparition disappeared into a fading red glow. Heinrich sat behind his desk and slouched in the chair. He waited for Mephistopheles to say something, but nothing came. Heinrich considered in his head what Lucifer wanted him to say to Greta, but nothing intelligent came.

A knock arrived at the door. Bianca came through and alerted Heinrich that Mr. Harper had arrived. Heinrich asked her to send him in. A man of medium stature entered. He looked like an executive; he was well-dressed in a pinstripe suit tailored to his body. He strode into the room with a confident smile and sat as directed by Bianca. She came around with a manilla envelope.

"Mr. Harper," Heinrich greeted the man. "Thank you for coming on such short notice."

"Don't mention it," said Mr. Harper. "Happy to be of service to you after all you've done for me."

"Excellent," replied Heinrich. Mephistopheles fed Heinrich instructions again, but clear agitation came through in the instructions. "You were summoned today because Lucifer would like to call in the previously agreed upon favor."

"Certainly," said the man as he sat forward. He was comfortable in the chamber of Mr. Condannato, which Heinrich presumed to mean he was a frequent guest. "I would be pleased to be of service. Lucifer has been splendid to me. I've gotten my ratings and kept my job. I owe everything to Lucifer. I have Lucifer to thank for it all."

"I am pleased happiness finds you," replied Heinrich. "There is a woman to whom we would like you to give a televised fitness program."

"A fitness program?" said the man, almost laughing, but he held it back. "There hasn't been a market for fitness programs on television for some time, except infomercials."

"Lucifer has a plan, and this girl will be a big star. I guarantee you," replied Heinrich. "Are you able to do it or not?"

"I will make it happen," said Mr. Harper, "so long as Lucifer knows that I will still get my ratings."

"It won't be a problem," said Heinrich. "She will be a phenomenon. She is beautiful."

Heinrich told the man more about her charming, charismatic personality and how she was a fitness model. He directed Bianca to hand over the contents of the manila envelope to Mr. Harper. Attractive head shots and body shots of Jezebel filled the envelope.

Mr. Harper nodded. "I will send over the paperwork and contracts later this afternoon then. We'll make it happen," he affirmed.

"Excellent," said Heinrich. "Thank you for your cooperation. You have always been a faithful servant. With this act, you may consider your earthly service to

Lucifer rendered complete."

"Is it true?" said the man. "Mr. Condannato, I will serve Lucifer until the day I die. I hope I may continue to turn to you for counsel if need be?"

"Certainly," said Heinrich. He admired the man's loyalty. "The eternal obligations, though, will still be outstanding."

Mr. Harper nodded. "Is there anything else I can do for you, Mr. Condannato?"

"That is all, Mr. Harper," said Heinrich.

Bianca escorted the man out of the office and returned to Mr. Condannato's side. "He was most cooperative, as always," she said to Heinrich.

"Bianca, I want to take Jezebel out to one of the finest restaurants in New York City," said Heinrich. "We have something to celebrate."

Bianca agreed to put the plans together and make it a memorable night.

"And Bianca, please send protection along with us," said Heinrich.

"Of course."

"I don't need another experience like the coffee shop," he said. "I'm not accustomed to being shouted at, and not in front of the object of my affections."

XXXIV

Later that afternoon, Heinrich's heart warmed with a call from Jezebel. She asked if he was free for a brief coffee break visit as she was between photo shoots. Heinrich got himself together and had a car fetched to get him to the coffee shop of Jezebel's choosing. His heart filled with excitement at the prospect of seeing her. Heinrich pressured the driver to hurry through traffic as fast as possible.

When the car arrived, Heinrich's heart sank. The address that Jezebel provided to him was the same coffee shop where he had first met Greta. Heinrich sat in the car. He tried to decide if it was a good idea. When he recalled Lucifer's demand of him, he wondered if this was something Lucifer had arranged. The puppet strings were in full motion.

He summoned the courage to take the chance. For all he knew, Greta had the day off, and all this awkwardness was for nothing. He told the driver he would be less than thirty minutes and requested that the driver wait right there for him. Heinrich entered the familiar café but didn't see Greta. He joined the line and kept an eye out for Jezebel. Still no sign of Greta. He calmed himself more. He wouldn't need to execute Lucifer's requested interaction in front of Jezebel.

Heinrich neared the front of the line. Jezebel was at the bar waiting for her drink. She was talking to the barista making her drink, so Heinrich ordered a latte. After paying, Heinrich went over to the bar where Jezebel was, and she noticed him. She smiled as he approached. She still listened to what the barista was saying to her. Once Heinrich stood beside her, he discovered that the barista who made his drink was none other than Greta!

Greta hadn't yet seen Heinrich. "So yeah, we will see if I can get another interview somewhere else," said Greta, looking up and recognizing Mr. Condannato. She froze.

"I'm so sorry, Greta," said Jezebel. "I know how much you wanted that job. I'll keep my eyes open if I hear of anything that might be good for you."

Greta gave her attention back to Jezebel. She did her best to mask her recognition of Mr. Condannato. "That would mean a lot," she said. "You know how hard I've been trying."

Jezebel nodded her head. It was much worse than Heinrich had imagined. They knew each other! "But what would I do without my favorite barista here?" asked Jezebel in a playful manner.

Greta laughed. Her awkwardness upon seeing Mr.

Condannato became more evident to him.

"Babe, can you guard my drink?" Jezebel asked Heinrich. "I will freshen up a little."

Heinrich agreed as his lover parted for the washroom.

"Babe?" Greta questioned out loud to Heinrich.

Heinrich ignored the comment, "How long have you known her?"

"At least seven months," she replied as she crafted the other lattes. It was difficult for her to focus; she was frazzled. Mephistopheles strangely did not push Heinrich to act on Lucifer's request regarding Greta. The spirit remained silent. Heinrich was certain this wasn't the time to discuss Lucifer's business; not when Jezebel might return at any moment.

"Are you friends?" asked Heinrich.

"We've talked almost every morning for the last seven months, at least whenever I'm working," stated Greta.

Heinrich was surprised.

"How do you know her?" she asked.

"None of your business," said Heinrich.

"All right, fine," said Greta as she dropped the question. "You had better be careful with her!"

"She's a great girl," replied Heinrich.

"No, that's not what I mean," replied Greta. "She's been through a lot."

"I love her and would never hurt her," said Heinrich. "So if you don't mind, refrain from giving me advice."

"If you knew what was best for her, you'd know that the last thing she needs right now is a relationship."

Heinrich scoffed at Greta. "I care deeply about her,

as she does about me as well."

"She's never mentioned you before," contended Greta.

"Ours is a new love."

"Love?" said Greta as she furled her eyebrows at Heinrich. Jezebel was returning from the washroom. "You don't know who you are dealing with."

Heinrich shook his head in disbelief.

"I worry about her," said Greta as Jezebel approached Heinrich.

Jezebel gave him a peck on the cheek. Heinrich turned to Greta with a boasting, if not mocking, smile. Heinrich snatched his lover's hand, and they grabbed their drinks. Jezebel waved goodbye to Greta and promised to stop in the next morning. Heinrich and Jezebel found a table together while Greta excused herself from the bar. She took a moment in the café's back room.

XXXV

Heinrich reposed alone at an intimate table at the Rue de l'essence. Bianca had selected the restaurant for him and his lover that night. It was one of the most exclusive venues in New York City.

He held a half-consumed glass of Shiraz. His joy at being able to see Jezebel yet again made it difficult to wait for her. He surveyed the other tables and studied the guests that evening. A strict dress code was in place, and everyone dressed well. Bianca told Mr. Condannato that it often took months to get a table at Rue de l'essence, but for Mr. Condannato, all things were possible.

"Mephistopheles, who are these people?" asked Heinrich. "Are these not the elites of New York City?"

Several could be classified as such, replied Mephistopheles. *Some have made deals with the devil. Some did so more easily than others.*

"Have any of them made an arrangement with Mr. Condannato?" asked Heinrich.

Yes, but long ago. Worry not, you won't be disturbed this evening.

Bodyguards stood still in the shadows by the walls in order to not disrupt the atmosphere or ambiance for him and his lover, or for any of the other guests that evening. Heinrich's eyes affirmed the bodyguards' presence.

Jezebel arrived accompanied by another bodyguard, who had been sent to collect her for the date that night. Heinrich didn't know it was possible for her to be any more stunning than when he first saw her. She wore a gorgeous red dress both flattering and revealing of her figure. Her smooth pale skin captured his eyes. He admired her accentuated curves. With each step closer she took toward him, his heart melted all the more. It was difficult for him to speak, but when he did, it was simple. "You look so beautiful," he said, standing upon her arrival.

She looked happy to see him, her face filled with joy. She knew how rare it was to come to such a place. Plus, Mr. Condannato had a surprise for her. She didn't know what the occasion was, other than that the driver and bodyguard arrived to pick her up from her photo shoot and to bring her home. There, a dress of Heinrich's choosing waited for her, while the driver remained in the car to deliver her to a celebration.

"This is so beautiful," she stated as Heinrich helped seat her. "Now tell me, what is the big surprise?"

"I will get to that," he replied. "But first tell me, how was your day?"

"It was okay," she said. "It got a lot better once the car picked me up. The photographer was controlling and demeaning today. Just get sick of it sometimes."

"I'm sorry, my dear," Heinrich comforted her.

"I get a little tired of dealing with dramatic, prima donna photographers sometimes—"

"All right, I can't wait any longer," he interrupted her, "but let me first tell you that you won't have to worry about any of those photographers ever again."

"What do you mean?" she asked with a hopeful smile.

Heinrich produced a small stack of stapled together papers. On the top was a header that read: "Service Contract." Heinrich flipped to the last page which had her name printed along the bottom with space for her signature.

"Is this what I think it is?" she asked.

Heinrich gave her the cover letter to the contract which she read out loud. "Dear Miss Savel, we are so excited to work with you here at WNYC network and to shared your passion for fitness with the greater New York area, and beyond. This is the beginning of a beautiful partnership, and I look forward to producing your own televised fitness program for the duration of this three-year contract." She paused. "A three-year contract?" she said, turning to Mr. Condannato. He nodded.

"You must be kidding!"

Heinrich shook his head. "I took care of it this morning," he confirmed. "As I said I would. You had my word."

"Why didn't you tell me earlier?" she said. Jezebel

beamed with excitement, which gave way to a joyful shout. She quieted herself down, remembering where she was when others stared at her outburst. "I can't believe it!"

"It is our night to celebrate," he replied. "In fact, it is your night!"

She leaned over from her chair, kissed Heinrich, and thanked him. For the first time in Heinrich's life, he felt appreciated.

"I was happy to do it," he said. "I love you."

Jezebel paused at those last three words. Hesitation came over her. "I care about you too," she said.

The joy from Heinrich's smile faded.

"I'm sorry," she said, realizing that it was her words that had precipitated his reaction.

"No, it's okay," he said, dismissing her need to apologize. "It was a little quick for me to say it."

The two were relieved when the waiter came and asked them if they were ready to order. Heinrich's demeanor changed. "Yes, we are here to celebrate!" he told the server. "Bring the most expensive champagne you serve. We will drink to this beautiful woman's success!"

Jezebel blushed, as the server obliged and went to collect the champagne. "You don't have to do that," she said.

"I insist," said Heinrich. "I will have it no other way."

She leaned over and kissed him again.

Heinrich enjoyed the kiss, but a man calling out stole his attention, "Dante!"

Heinrich searched for his security detail, who slipped out of the shadows. Upon seeing them, Heinrich motioned for them to hold up. A poorly dressed man approached the table and threw himself at it. He begged Mr. Condannato for mercy. Jezebel startled and pushed her chair away to keep a safe distance. Her attention bounced back and forth from Mr. Condannato and the man.

"What the devil is this about?" barked Heinrich both to the man and to Mephistopheles.

"Do you not remember me?" asked the man.

"I've never seen your face before in my entire life," said Heinrich. The man grazed the leg of Heinrich's pants, resulting in Mr. Condannato motioning for the bodyguards to come and assist.

"Dante, I want to be free!" the man pleaded. "Free from my contract with Lucifer! I must be ridden of it! Lucifer has deceived me, and now, my family wants nothing to do with me and my gambling addiction."

Heinrich looked away from the man as the bodyguards approached. *His name is Archibald Argent. He made a deal for money with Lucifer to enter a worldwide poker tournament as a last-ditch effort to keep his family's home. Lucifer promised the money for his soul and service. While the man won a fair amount of money, he had to keep gambling to save the home. Eventually, he could afford the house, but he couldn't quit gambling. He has no career, and his family is leaving him.*

Heinrich shifted to pretending to recognize the man. "I remember you," he said. "And I will have none of this!"

"Please, Mr. Condannato, please!" he pleaded. "Please release me, I beg your pardon from the deal! Release me from my addiction!"

The bodyguards gathered the man's arms and yanked him from the ground. The restaurant's security detail also approached.

You must deal with this man now, Mephistopheles instructed Heinrich.

"Must I deal with this now in the midst of our celebration?" Heinrich asked out loud in frustration to his audience, and to Mephistopheles.

It is so. Lucifer commands it.

Heinrich showed his disgust. "Jezebel, you will forgive me," he said to her, giving instructions to one bodyguard to take his lover back to his house.

"But what about you?" asked Jezebel.

"I will find you at my residence," he replied. He gave his attention back to the bodyguard, "And send the bottle of champagne home."

The bodyguard understood his instructions and did as told, taking Jezebel from the scene. The other guard still held onto the begging man, who didn't try to escape his clutches.

"Come, follow me," said Heinrich to the bodyguard. They passed through the restaurant. Other guests were curious about what was going on. Heinrich assured the restaurant's security detail that they were leaving.

As they made their way to exit the dining area, Heinrich directed them instead into the kitchen and out of the sight of the restaurant's security detail. He knew where he was headed, for Mephistopheles led him. They passed through a surprised kitchen and rounded a corner to find a large walk-in refrigerator. The bodyguard went in first with the whimpering man, and Heinrich followed them.

"Please, Mr. Condannato! Give me my life back! Have mercy on me!" cried the man as the refrigerator door closed.

The man sensed the cold chill from the fridge and shivered.

"You shouldn't shudder at the cold," Heinrich rebuked him. "Embrace it. It will be the last time you ever experience such a sensation."

The man's face went pale, which led to him pleading again for his life to be spared. "Please, Mr. Condannato, forgive me! I shouldn't have bothered you this evening," he said. "I apologize for ruining your dinner! This much I regret. If you release me, I won't ever bother you again. I will accept my fate."

"That isn't possible any longer," said Heinrich without a hint of sympathy in his voice. "Lucifer is calling in the deal."

"Please! Don't do this! Forgive me!" he begged. He was on his knees with his hands held in front of him.

"Tape his mouth shut," Heinrich instructed the bodyguard. His whimpering became more pathetic and forced as tears formed in the man's eyes. Heinrich motioned to the bodyguard who produced a silenced pistol and handed it over to Mr. Condannato.

Heinrich accepted the gun and pointed it at the man's head. The man closed his eyes as he cried.

"Mr. Argent, your luck has run out," said Heinrich without mercy before firing the gun twice into the man's skull. The man dropped to the ground in a mess. Heinrich handed the gun back to the bodyguard who extracted a cloth and wiped the gun down.

"I will see you back at the residence," said Heinrich

before exiting the walk-in cooler, as the dead man lay
still on the cold floor.

XXXVI

Heinrich took heed of a muted cry as he lay in his bed the next morning. He glanced over to check on Jezebel, but she wasn't there. He listened closer and discovered the sound of the shower running in his washroom.

Heinrich climbed out of bed and approached the washroom. He discerned more crying. It wasn't a heavy cry, but something more gentle. He opened the door to see his lover sitting on the shower floor with her knees curled up to her breasts as the water flowed over her naked body.

"Are you okay?" he called out.

She hadn't witnessed him opening the door. She twisted her head to him and looked embarrassed. "I'm sorry," she said. "You weren't supposed to see me this way."

Heinrich opened the shower door and turned off the stream of water and squatted down to her level.

Even in her tears and wet hair, she was a beautiful sight to Heinrich.

"I didn't mean to wake you," she said.

"Not to worry about it," he dismissed her. "What were you crying about? Was it last night? Did the news not bring you joy?"

"Oh no, that made me so happy," she said, as she held her knees closer to her chest. "I have you to thank for it."

"Then whatever is the matter?" Heinrich asked. He needed Mephistopheles's help with this conversation, and it was forthcoming.

"I don't know," she said. "I don't know how to explain it."

"I've got time," encouraged Heinrich.

"I don't get it," she said. "You've been amazing. You're making my dreams come true. It is wonderful, but there is a deadness I feel inside of me."

Heinrich shot her a look, hoping to understand better.

"You've been so kind. You've made me feel like a queen," she said. "But something inside of me I can't feel anymore."

"Can you help me understand?"

"Well…" she said before considering her words. "Last night, you told me you loved me. And while I ought to love you for how you've taken care of me, I realized last night when I came back here and waited for you; a part of me wasn't allowing me to love you or anyone else."

"Is it because of your deceased husband?" asked Heinrich. It was difficult for him not to experience a wave of rejection coming over him again, but he fought it.

"I don't know, I'm scared it might be," she replied, "but I really don't know."

Heinrich placed a consoling hand on her bare shoulder. He needed her to know he cared about her.

"Ever since losing him, a certain listlessness to life has carried on, the routine, and the mundaneness," she said. "And while I don't think I've ever been happier than these past couple of days with you, because you have been amazing and you've already given me so many opportunities, I can't shake this feeling."

Heinrich wrapped his arm around her shoulder to comfort her. "I wouldn't worry about it too much," he told her. "It will take time transitioning. And with today being your first day of work, you might find yourself feeling differently by the evening's end, when we are back together again."

"I hope so," she conceded. "You probably are right."

"Can you give it a shot for me?" he asked.

She nodded her head in agreement. "You are sweet. I don't know what I did to deserve your love."

Heinrich smiled at her acknowledgment of his clear feelings for her.

"I hope I will love you as fully as you deserve," she said.

"That would please my soul ever so much if you could find it in yourself," said Heinrich.

She smiled at him. "I will finish up in the shower, okay?" she said. "Thanks for listening."

Heinrich left her and went back to his bedroom. He lounged on the side of his bed. He pondered his lover's words and hesitations about loving him back. Heinrich realized it was too soon, but he struggled to shake his nervousness regarding her apprehensions about loving him. "Mephistopheles?"

Yes, Heinrich?

"Is something about me unlovable?" he asked. "One of the primary conditions of the deal I made with Lucifer was that I would find love. I've been here how long already and I'm still searching for it."

You know it is impossible for Lucifer to force someone to love you, cautioned Mephistopheles. *It is contrary to the nature of love and free will. Rest assured though, the conditions will be met, and I will make sure you experience real, honest love soon. I promise you.*

"I hope so," said Heinrich in a defeated tone.

XXXVII

Heinrich spent much of the day in a quiet, reflective space. He canceled all appointments in his chamber and gave strict instructions to both Bianca and Yousef that Babel not be open that night. He had tired of the continual stream of souls walking into his office and asking for something. Jezebel was at her first day of the production shoot for her televised fitness program, which left him to consider her difficulty in loving him. He still possessed strong feelings for her. He didn't deny his own feelings, but his heart struggled with opening itself up to be spurned yet again.

A call from Jezebel interrupted his solitude. She had a mid-day production schedule break. She asked him if he could come over to her house that night. She wanted to properly thank him for the blessing he had been in her life. Such a statement revived his listless heart's desire for her. It drew him out of his funk and gave him reason to get dressed and out of his bed attire.

Bianca summoned a lift to transport Heinrich to Jezebel's home. The drive was uneventful other than Heinrich thinking fondly of Jezebel. What were despairing thoughts gave way to hope. His love for her was stronger than anything he had ever experienced, and he wouldn't allow this love to get away from him. He would fight for this love, no matter the obstacles. She wouldn't be able to take herself away from him. He would prove his love to her as long as was necessary for her to be able to love him.

The car dropped Heinrich off outside a tall apartment building in Manhattan. A doorman welcomed him in and directed him to an elevator operator, who brought him to Jezebel's floor. He knocked on the door to her apartment, which drew an invitation to enter.

He opened the unlocked door and within her apartment, Jezebel stood in an elegant robe. The apartment was dark, but candles provided a romantic ambiance. Rose pedals led to her from the door and into the bedroom. She held two champagne flutes in her hand while on a table beside her was a bottle.

Heinrich's heart warmed at the sight of her efforts to please him. And while he felt joy in his heart, she recognized that something depressed him. Heinrich dismissed it as nothing more than a hard day. She poured him a glass and one for herself. She handed him one, and they clinked glasses and consumed a sip.

"I wanted to find a way to thank you for everything," she said, as she undid the knot on the front of her robe. There in the dining room, she let her robe drop to reveal her gorgeous figure in a stunning piece of lace lingerie, all for Heinrich's pleasure. He smiled and enjoyed what he saw, which made her feel confident. He reached to grab her hips and caress her. Heinrich brought their faces together and kissed her. She gripped his hand and led him into the bedroom. She entered first and climbed on top of the bed and lay waiting for him.

Heinrich undressed, undoing his tie first. He looked upon her as he removed his shirt and joined her on the bed. She leaned forward and kissed Heinrich with passion, pulling him down closer to the bed. Heinrich's heart raced, which helped to make his earlier concerns far away and irrelevant.

The two made out and rolled around the bed. They took their time kissing each other all over their bodies. She removed the lingerie's straps from her shoulders, dropping it on the bed as she stood on her knees. She gave him a moment to enjoy the view of her body. Jezebel undid his belt buckle to remove his pants, which he did his best to help with. He was naked with her, and the two made out. How she massaged him drove him crazy and made him only want more of her.

As they were about to make love, a banging came from the front door. Heinrich ignored it, but screaming rushed from the entryway. Jezebel froze on top of Heinrich when it sounded as if a blunt objected smashed the door open. Rapid footsteps thumped the floor, causing Jezebel to drop beside Heinrich on the bed. Heinrich withdrew to a defensive posture near her when a scream beckoned Jezebel's name.

A man entered the bedroom and was hysterical upon

seeing Jezebel naked with Heinrich. Jezebel recognized who it was. "Get out!" she screamed. "Get out of here and never come back!"

"I can't!" he shouted back. Heinrich gazed back and forth between Jezebel and the man. He wanted Mephistopheles's help, but there even was a sense of shock on Mephistopheles's end.

"I need to see you!" the man shouted.

"Who the hell are you?" Heinrich yelled.

"You can't see me!" Jezebel shouted.

The man pulled out a handgun and pointed it at Heinrich to suggest he stand down. Heinrich startled and backed farther against the wall and headboard.

"There is a court-order! You aren't allowed to see me!" she shouted back at the man.

"Please, Jezebel!" the man pleaded. "I only need to see you!"

"No!"

"I need you to forgive me!" the man pleaded in a calmer, more emotional tone.

"I can't!" she shouted back. "And you know I said I never could."

Heinrich fixed his gaze upon Jezebel. He was so confused and scared. "Who are you?" asked Heinrich.

"Shut up!" the man barked at Heinrich. "Keep your mouth shut and get the hell away from Jezebel."

Jezebel turned to look at Heinrich. "He's my ex-husband," she said in tears.

Heinrich backed away from her toward the other side of the bed. His mind raced. "I thought you said he was dead?" Heinrich said.

The man shifted his gaze to Heinrich and back to

Jezebel. "You told him I was dead?" he shouted in disgust. "Jezzy, you know I love you! You need to forgive me, please! I beg you!"

"I can never forgive you!" she shouted back in anger. "How many times do I have to tell you?"

"Please!" he pleaded again.

"No!" she shouted back. "Not after you let our little girl die."

"Jezzy, no!" he pleaded further. "You know I didn't!"

"You killed our baby girl!" she shouted in raw emotion. "Why couldn't it have been you who died in her place?"

"Baby, no! Stop it!" He was crying.

"You were her protector!" Jezebel shouted. "You failed to protect our little girl."

"Baby, please!"

"I loved you," she said, as her shouts quietened down to a crying whisper, "but you took away my little girl. Our little girl."

Heinrich struggled to watch Jezebel in such a state, so broken and defeated. Why had she never told him anything about this? Why had she lied?

"There will be no forgiveness to be had in this life," she affirmed to her ex-husband.

"Please, Jezzy," the man asked again. "Please forgive me! It was an accident! I shouldn't have been driving that night!"

Jezebel shook her head. "I can't. I just can't."

Heinrich tried to think how to escape, but the man turned the gun on himself.

"If no forgiveness can be had in this life, then maybe in the next," the man said, placing the gun's barrel in his mouth. He pulled the trigger, sending fragments of his skull and brain onto the wall and ceiling behind him. Jezebel screamed in horror while Heinrich was so shaken he fell onto the floor. He struggled to breathe. Jezebel howled louder and louder in sheer terror at what they witnessed.

While a part of Heinrich compelled him to comfort Jezebel, he was terrified and struggled to move. He wanted to be anywhere but there. He collapsed and breathed his way through what he had witnessed. Jezebel climbed off the bed and approached the corpse of her ex-husband. She drew his lifeless chest to her naked chest, covering herself in blood.

She turned to Heinrich in hysteria, "I'm sorry for not telling the truth," she said. "I'm sorry for not telling you about my husband, but now I know I will never love again. I know that now."

Heinrich said nothing. He couldn't speak, but he wanted to dissuade her from that truth. Jezebel seized the handgun from her dead husband's hand and stuck it against her head and merely said, "I'm sorry!"

"No! No! No! No!" shouted Heinrich just before Jezebel pulled the trigger and killed herself. Heinrich screamed in horror, but couldn't put together a single syllable. He crawled on the floor toward the dead woman and pulled her dead body close to him. He screamed in agony and held her corpse against his. He tried to console himself and make sense of what he had witnessed. Nothing processed in his head. His crying stopped about the same time he detected the soft wail of sirens. He needed to leave, so Heinrich searched for any of his clothing he could find. His shirt was nowhere to be seen. He left with only his boxers and a pair of pants and exited her apartment in bare feet.

XXXVIII

Heinrich sat on the side of his bed as he had earlier that morning. It seemed so long ago, but in reality, it was less than twenty-four hours since he had comforted his lover in the shower. Blood was spattered on his bare chest from the two victims of suicide earlier that night. He wept over where he found himself. His eyes skimmed over his bed. It was where he shared himself with Jezebel, and while he tried to comfort himself with those memories, they hardened his heart.

Heinrich, I am so sorry, said Mephistopheles, seeking to comfort him. *Not even I had seen that coming this evening.*

"Did you know her husband was still alive?"

I did not know, no.

"Did Lucifer?"

I do not know.

Anger burned in Heinrich's heart. Someone must have known.

"Mephistopheles?"

Yes?

"I want revenge tonight," he told Mephistopheles. "I want to kill my adopted brother."

No, this is not the time, Mephistopheles cautioned.

"No, damn it! I want my revenge tonight!" Heinrich shouted. "Make it happen!"

I cannot!

"Are you unable?" Heinrich mocked.

I will not go through with it, Mephistopheles said. *I have led many a soul to the path of destruction. With many, I was happy to do so, but I cannot do the same for you.*

"I can't believe this!" said Heinrich in disgust. "You are refusing to help me! What about my deal with Lucifer?"

I know the arrangement you made with Lucifer, but I cannot aid you in this endeavor. There is something yet redeemable in you; a soul that doesn't have to follow this path. Lucifer wants only to use you for Hell's advancement. You will not find what you desire in killing your adopted brother. You must not follow the path of the fallen ones, like Lucifer and I. You possess a soul that is yet capable of love—

"Damn you, Mephistopheles!" Heinrich shouted. "Don't you understand? I'm unloveable!"

No, Heinrich! It is not so! replied Mephistopheles. *You've just had everything taken away from you.*

"No!" said Heinrich. "I won't listen to this bullshit. Will you or won't you help me get my revenge?"

I will not.

"Lucifer!" Heinrich screamed in his bedroom. "Show yourself!"

A red glow manifested, giving way to the dramatic

appearance of Lucifer's apparition.

"Hello, Heinrich," said the voice of Lucifer.

"I will have my revenge tonight," said Heinrich. "I don't care about any of this love bullshit. I don't care about women. I don't care about anything. Give me my revenge tonight!"

"We can make that happen," said Lucifer.

"Mephistopheles refuses to aid me!"

"Mephistopheles! You deceiver! How dare you stand in the way of this soul's desire for revenge!" Lucifer rebuked the spirit. "You who were unfaithful back when we first went to war against the Almighty One."

Anger flowed from the devil's apparition. Lucifer instructed Heinrich to lie on the bed and close his eyes. Lucifer began an incantation, using its hands to guide Mephistopheles out of Heinrich's body. Mephistopheles fought back though, struggling to maintain its residence within Heinrich. "Come out, you unfaithful viper!"

Heinrich screamed out in pain. "Get out of me!" Lucifer waved its hands again and what followed was such an intense pain in Heinrich's chest. A glow struggled against being sucked out of his chest. Lucifer cast it out of the bedroom, and Heinrich sensed a heavy tiredness come over him.

"Worry not, Heinrich," Lucifer said. "We will indwell you with a spirit much greater than Mephistopheles."

Heinrich tried not to fall into unconsciousness.

"Legion, we call upon your faithful service," said Lucifer. "Enter this servant of the Master of Hell. Bring him his desired revenge, and your service will be rendered complete."

A rushing wind blew into the room. A glow larger than Lucifer's entered the room. It was bright enough that Heinrich knew it was there even though he found it difficult to keep his eyes open. Lucifer gestured with its hands, and the glow threw itself against Heinrich's chest. It drew a painful scream from him. In only three seconds though, Heinrich was alert and had his energy returned to him. He sat upright in his bed and his body moved robotically. It was hard to control his movements as another power guided them.

"Legion, do you swear allegiance to the Master of Hell?" asked Lucifer.

Heinrich's voice spoke through him, though not from his own doing. It sounded like the growl of a wolf. "*We do, our Lord!*" said the voice. Heinrich rose from the bed and exited the bedroom with only the clothes he wore before.

XXXIX

In an alleyway stood a tall man with an imposing figure. His shoulders were strong, his stance intimidating, and his gaze terrifying. Beside him were two companions, who served as bodyguards. A glowing apparition came down the alleyway toward the group of three. The two guards took a defensive stance against the apparition. The tallest of the three waved for them to stand down.

The apparition made a humble, respectful prostration before the tallest figure.

"Identify yourself, malignant spirit!" said the most towering figure.

"Michael, it is I, Mephistopheles," said the apparition. "Do you not remember me?"

"I do recall you, you traitor against the Almighty One," said imposing figure. "What is the deception behind your appearance this day?"

"Michael, I swear that I have nothing to keep hidden

—"

"You are the servant of the father of lies. How could I trust you?"

"Yes, I have been servant to Lucifer," replied Mephistopheles, "but I can do so no longer."

"I am listening," said Michael in a suspicious reply.

"I was commanded to assist a soul in achieving revenge against its sibling, but—"

"We are aware of whom you speak," interrupted Michael. "We are familiar with the arrangement that Lucifer made with him."

"Yes, I know," replied Mephistopheles. "I have seen you watching us."

"You are observant."

"Heinrich is a redeemable soul who has suffered greatly. For what reasons the Almighty One has behind allowing him to suffer so, I do not understand, nor do I believe Lucifer knows. But I can see within Heinrich a heart capable of change. I cannot bring myself to help this soul to have his revenge. I cannot lead him down the path of destruction. I seek your help in sparing him."

"To spare a soul from Lucifer's grip?" said Michael, almost laughing at Mephistopheles's request.

"I renounce all allegiance to Lucifer," Mephistopheles interjected. "I repent for my wickedness against the Almighty One."

"Repent?" said Michael. "You know that there is nothing for you to gain in renouncing Lucifer, or even in repenting. Your judgment was eternal and final. You were there when the Almighty One handed down your punishment."

"So it may be," replied Mephistopheles. "But I must help spare Heinrich from heading down the path to the same end as which I am headed for my service to the father of lies, even if I myself cannot be spared."

"You realize that in doing so, you accomplish nothing more for yourself than to be cast into the abyss; subject to torture and annihilation in the final days as any other human soul?"

"So shall it be," said Mephistopheles without hesitation.

Michael inspected Mephistopheles to discern the spirit's real purpose behind its renunciation of Lucifer. Nothing was ascertained from the demon. Michael spoke. "The Almighty One has heard your plea, and the Kingdom of Heaven shall intervene."

"Thank you, Michael."

XL

The legion of demons within Heinrich wasted no time at all in driving him toward his revenge. Legion possessed the driver of Heinrich's car, as the vehicle blew through red lights with no caution or hesitation. Heinrich's mind was overwhelmed and perplexed the entire ride over. Unlike with Mephistopheles, it was difficult to perceive what were his own thoughts and what were those planted by the demons within him.

The car pulled up to a closed sporting goods store. The demons ushered him forward to the entrance. A steel garbage can sat beside the door. With a strength superior to anything he had known before, Heinrich took hold of the can. He threw the trash can through the glass windows, setting off a security alarm. Without hesitation, Heinrich entered the store. The spirits directed Heinrich to the baseball gear section. There, Legion instructed Heinrich to take the strongest wooden baseball bat. He collected it and marched out of the store with little haste. Heinrich had no fear of getting caught for breaking and entering. He jumped back into the car, which sped off toward their next location: the home of Heinrich's adopted brother.

The car stopped down the street from the address that Jose had supplied him. The demons within told Heinrich to not yet act. It was an hour before the demon gave Heinrich the go-ahead. Jose had been working, but after the long wait, Heinrich saw him finally arrive home in the middle of the early morning.

The driver of the car asked Heinrich where he would like him to wait, but Heinrich told him to go home. Heinrich had nothing to go back for. The drive of revenge coursed through Heinrich's veins. He knew what he would do to Jose with the baseball bat. He galloped up the front steps and banged on the front door with the bat.

No answer. Heinrich beat on the door again. "Open the door!" he shouted. A man answered the door, but it wasn't Jose. It was a roommate. Upon seeing Heinrich, the man cowered in fear.

Heinrich forged his way through the door, despite the door chain locking the door. The door crashed, knocking the roommate to the ground. Heinrich's physical strength grew more potent the angrier he became. The roommate crawled and ran down the hallway away from Heinrich.

"Juarez! Where are you?" Heinrich called out with a vocal force of all the demons within him speaking. It was a terrifying sound.

A door opened at the hallway's end. Jose took a step

outside, but cowered back and slammed the door shut. Heinrich rushed toward the door and stood before it. He smashed it open with the baseball bat. The door didn't stand a chance against his ever-increasing rage.

Jose stood in front of his bed, wearing only his boxer shorts. Heinrich never saw such fear in Jose's eyes. Such a realization did little to give way to any mercy. Heinrich landed a violent kick to Jose's chest, knocking him onto the floor.

It elicited a pained scream from Jose, who cursed Heinrich in Spanish. Jose didn't know who the stranger was. Heinrich kicked him once more before taking a firm grip of the baseball bat. He readied to swing without mercy. He produced a heavy strike at Jose's rib cage and another to his left leg. All the while, Heinrich screamed a torrent of curses in Spanish for everything that Jose had done to him.

"Do you have any idea who I am?" Heinrich screamed with a demonic fury in his voice.

"No!" Jose screamed in pain.

"We are Heinrich," he replied. "For we are many, and we will have our necessary revenge for all the agony and suffering you have caused us!"

Heinrich swung the baseball bat again at Jose, this time to the face. He expected it to render his brother unconscious, but it didn't. The hideous screams from his adopted brother's body made that obvious. Without hesitation, Heinrich swung the bat. With each blow, bones broke. He hacked at Jose's rib cage again.

"*Por favor! Para!*" screamed Jose in Spanish. "Have mercy on me! Please, oh God, stop!"

"No mercy shall be shown," Heinrich said in Spanish

with each swing he took. "For no mercy was given while you tormented us at home and at school. This is the just payment for all the misery you wrought upon us."

"Forgive me," Jose pleaded with a slur as it was evident his jaw was broken. "Forgive me, please!"

Heinrich didn't experience the slightest bit of sympathy toward Jose. "How convenient that you now ask for forgiveness when finally we are able to overcome you!"

"Forgive me, my brother!" screamed Jose. "I have wronged you, please, brother, forgive me!"

Heinrich's grip on the bat weaken as it was the first time that Jose had ever called him his brother. But his adrenaline fueled his rage to the point that he could push through such interfering thoughts. He repeated his swings at Jose's body. Each swing brought another scream of agony and pain. "Have mercy on me! Please forgive me!"

Heinrich might have wailed more on Jose, but he found his next swing interrupted by a high-pitched shriek. He expected it to be that of a woman, perhaps Jose's girlfriend, Dominica, but instead he rotated to see a little boy. The boy watched in terror as blood covered Jose's mangled and torn body.

"Please," pleaded Jose, struggling to breathe. "Spare my son."

Heinrich looked at Jose and back to the boy in tears. The little boy had wet himself in fear. Heinrich became paralyzed, though the demons within told him to finish the job. The little boy ran to his bloodied father, showing no fear of Heinrich. The boy clutched the thrashed body of his father. Heinrich stumbled backward away from Jose. He examined the blood-drenched baseball bat. The adrenaline had worn off. He dropped the bat in shock of what he had just done and of what was in front of him. Jose had said earlier that he had no family.

He watched the little boy crying over his father. The boy spoke in Spanish, "Papa, don't cry. I'm here. I'll take care of you."

The child brought blankets from his father's bed to keep him warm. Heinrich struggled to contain himself as he sobbed in realizing what he had done. Heinrich could endure the sight no longer and fled the room. His pants were soaked in blood as tears streamed down his face. As he stepped out onto the street, he flagged down a cab. Once he got in the car, the taxi driver shrieked in terror upon seeing the blood all over Heinrich. The driver refused to take Heinrich. He told him to take another cab. Sirens wailed in the distance. Heinrich assumed they were for him.

"Drive the cab, damn it!" Heinrich threatened the man amidst his tears. "Or I will drive for you!"

The cab driver jolted out of the car and fled the scene. He wanted nothing to do with Heinrich's threats.

Heinrich jumped into the front seat and sped off. When he was far enough away from the scene of his attempted murder, he ditched the cab on the sidewalk. He felt no peace or satisfaction over what he had just done, despite having wielded the revenge he so desperately craved.

XLI

Heinrich hoofed it in the chilly New York night with no shirt. He sobbed with each city block he passed. His soul was in turmoil, yet he felt as though he had nowhere to go. He couldn't return to the residence. It was the last place he wanted to be. He didn't want to be reminded of Jezebel and her passing.

As Heinrich was lost in his thoughts, Legion inserted the consideration in his mind to seek Greta. The idea was met with revulsion for how she frowned upon Heinrich's relationship with his lover. Jezebel was dead because of Heinrich being a part of her life. Greta also didn't want to have anything to do with Mr. Condannato or Lucifer's deal. Might she reject Heinrich as all others had beforehand?

The demons within Heinrich provided him with an address, and he soon discovered that he wasn't that far from Greta's home. He decided he would find Greta.

Soon, he found a building with an address that matched what the demons had given him. In tears, he banged on her door and called out her name. Anyone in the street overheard his sobbing. Lights came on as neighbors sought to see what was going on. A light went on in Greta's apartment.

"I have to see you, Greta!" Heinrich shouted. "Have mercy on me, please! Forgive me!"

He rang the doorbell more than a few times. He begged for a response. Tears poured down his chest. The faceless man's blood was still on him, as was Jezebel, and he imagined Jose's blood too. His spirit agonized at the memory of both events.

Greta came down the stairs and cracked the door open, but a chain locked it to prevent Heinrich from entering. This time, Heinrich didn't force his way in.

"What are you doing here?" she asked. In her voice, he picked up fear, annoyance, and concern. Her eyes went to the satanic scar on his chest, which she hadn't seen before. It alarmed her. It looked similar to a symbol painted on her living room wall. "What has happened to you?"

Heinrich's body convulsed as a satanic scream exited his throat. Heinrich fought for control of his body. "Please," he pleaded. "I have done something terrible. I need your help."

She was too scared to let him in. She had never seen someone so distraught in her life, and something tormented him.

"Please, let me in!" screamed Heinrich, though his voice sounded deeper and twisted. "I won't do anything to you. I won't let them!"

Greta recoiled. She feared whoever they were. She almost shut the door.

"I need to talk to you," he said. His voice changed mid-speech between his own and the voices of the legion of demons. A visible battle went on within him as his bare torso contorted with different muscles moving while he stood there bent over at her door.

"I'm sorry," she said, "but I can't let you in. You're scaring me."

"Please! Have compassion on me," he begged. "Don't let them take me."

Greta's terror grew further, but she felt compassion stirring within her, even if she feared for her life. Heinrich wailed in tears and begged to be let in. In a split-second decision, she decided against her better judgment again. She unlocked the chain and ushered Heinrich in. As soon as he crossed over the threshold to her apartment, the physical torment subsided. He threw himself to the floor at the base of the stairs to her apartment.

"Come on, Mr. Condannato," she said. "Let's get you inside. You must be freezing."

Heinrich glanced up the stairs, and there stood a black cat. It meowed.

"Don't worry," she said. "That's my kitty. Her name is Delilah. She's harmless. Friendly in fact."

Her spirit was more at ease with each step she helped him take up the stairs. Once they got to the top of the stairs, Heinrich whispered, "Lucifer is tormenting me."

Greta didn't know whether to believe Heinrich, but she was certain that something haunted him. It wasn't out of character from everything else that she experienced that week.

"I need to tell you what happened," he whispered as she helped him to her bedroom. She wanted to get him warmed up with her blankets. Heinrich coughed as he spoke, but his voice sounded warped the more he talked. It startled Greta even more so. "I'm not who I appear to be, nor who I want to be. I've become something vile and disgusting—"

"What is going on with you?" she said, helping him onto the bed. She grabbed a blanket and flung it over his shoulders.

"*I am Satan!*" Heinrich screamed out. He tried to regain control of himself, which caused her to jump in fear. "I'm sorry, they are trying to control me—"

"Who are they?" she demanded to know. Any relaxation of the battle within Heinrich had ceased.

Without so much as even answering her question, he spoke, "I believed the key to happiness was getting what I wanted. But all it has accomplished is that it has destroyed me and all those around me. It has all been a path of destruction."

"What have you done?" she insisted he tell her.

Heinrich told his story of hopelessness, even starting with the story of his life back in Cuba. As he spoke though, he had to fight for control as the demons within turned on Heinrich. They didn't want him to seek Greta's help; they wanted to follow Lucifer's orders to steal Greta away from the Almighty One's grip. They fought to stop him. He took control as he confessed his whole life story, sharing that he had killed himself, ended up in Hell, made a deal with the devil, and concluded with how he wasn't Dante Condannato, but his name was Heinrich Juarez. His stated mission was revenge upon his adopted brother, but he had come from failing to do so. He tried to talk about what happened to Jezebel, but he was incapable of speaking whenever he tried. Instead, he talked about how he feared he had made his adopted nephew an orphan like he had become himself when his parents left him in Cuba.

Greta couldn't believe it because she didn't want it to be true. She stood by the door away from Heinrich. She was terrified to be next to him, but neither could she allow herself to abandon him. He needed help, but she felt powerless. Something seemed so familiar about him as if he was a friend she needed to help.

"Greta," he said, "could God forgive someone like me after all this?"

She couldn't imagine herself saying yes, because even in her soul, she didn't know if someone could be forgiven for such demonic chaos. Still, she said yes. "I believe God will forgive any soul that is penitent."

"But what if I don't have a soul anymore?" he asked. He explained more about the deal he made with Lucifer, and how he was damned to return to Hell, and that it was sealed with an eternal oath. He referenced the satanic scar on his chest. It was meant to be a sign to the Almighty One that he was the property of the devil now and forever more. He told her what he had said before the Almighty One at Judgment Day and how he had rejected any attempts by whom he only imagined was Jesus to stand up for him. "I sound delusional. Perhaps I am delusional. Maybe I'm hysterical, and I've lost it, but it's the truth. I hope you believe me. I don't know what to do. Am I finished?"

The demons hurled condemning thoughts and judgment; that he was too far gone; that he couldn't be forgiven; that no one had ever caused as much destruction, heartache, and chaos as him; that he was beyond saving; and that he was the property of the dark lord, and his soul would be returned to Hell no matter what he tried. He had made an oath that not even the Almighty One was capable of breaking. His destiny was sealed with that of Lucifer and the legion of demons. The demons screamed at him to stop this train wreck and that he needed to leave.

"Yes. I believe you can be spared," she said. She mustered the most confidence she could in saying that. She stepped forward to approach Heinrich, but the demons fought for control of Heinrich's body and caused it to convulse.

"*Away from us, whore of Babylon. This is the son of the fallen Lord. You have no right to this soul. We will curse you, and you shall be tormented should you seek to save this soul. His soul is damned to an eternity in the Lake of Fire.*"

Greta shrieked in fear. She couldn't pray for him; she was too terrified. Greta left the bedroom to get the phone, but Heinrich howled in agony. "Pray for me, Greta! They are tearing me to pieces!"

She turned around to face Heinrich. She dropped to her knees and prayed for him, petitioning against the powers and forces of Hell, commanding them to begone. She asked the Almighty One to send His guardian angels to protect Heinrich. All the while, Heinrich contorted yet again, screaming in the pitches of a wild beast. Greta screamed her prayer that God send His guardian angels to provide shelter for Heinrich's soul from the attacks of the soldiers of Satan.

At once, Heinrich's body collapsed into complete stillness on her bed. Heinrich's body slipped off of the bed as an immense load lifted off of his chest. His body flopped to the floor as he shed weak tears from his eyes. He couldn't speak a word any time he tried as his vocal cords had been damaged. He shivered, so Greta got him back on her bed. She wrapped her arms around him and sought to warm him. He looked so weak. She tucked him in so he retained what little body heat he had. He almost passed out but still breathed. She kneeled beside the bed and recited the Lord's Prayer out of fear for what was going.

"Our Father, who art in Heaven, hallowed be thy name; thy kingdom come; thy will be done on Earth as it is in Heaven. Give us this day our daily bread; and forgive us our trespasses as we forgive those who trespass against us; and lead us not into temptation, but deliver us from evil."

XLII

The next morning, Greta stirred from her sleep. She lay on her bedroom floor. She had passed out while praying and spent the whole night there. Greta rose to find Heinrich still lying on her bed. He looked in much better shape than the previous evening. Her cat sprawled at Heinrich's feet and meowed at Greta. Heinrich stirred from his slumber and saw Greta overlooking him.

"Why have you been so kind?" Heinrich asked.

She opened her mouth to speak but hesitated before she spoke. "At first, I guess I did what I reasoned God wanted me to do, even though you scared me."

"I'm sorry," he whispered.

"But I realize now that's not all of it."

"What do you mean?" he asked.

"Don't you understand?"

He shook his head.

"I know who you are."

Heinrich looked more confused.

"As soon as you told me your name was Heinrich, and that you were abandoned in Cuba, I knew something was familiar about you."

Heinrich stared at her to suggest she explain further.

"You're my long-lost brother, Heinrich."

Heinrich said nothing but blinked. "How could you say that?"

"It all fell into place," she said. "It probably makes no sense to you."

"It doesn't."

"Do you remember how I told you that my mom killed herself after I was born?" she asked him. "I told you it was because she was beside herself with grief for having given birth to a disabled girl like me. She thought it was her fault I was born this way. Well, that wasn't all of it."

"Get to the point!"

"My mom never admitted it, but I remember as a little girl hearing my dad talk in his sleep," she said, growing more excited. "He said your name. I would ask him about it. It was almost impossible to get him to speak about it."

"None of this can be," Heinrich rebuked her. "My parents lived in Sweden!"

"They did!" she said, "but after Mom died, Dad moved us to New York City for a teaching position when I was a little girl."

"I can't believe this—"

"You must!"

Heinrich's mind raced. It was hard to think when he

had just woken up. "You said that it was impossible to get him to talk about it."

"Almost. He admitted on his deathbed that I had a brother taken from them. He said it was his biggest regret that he hadn't been able to go back to Cuba and rescue his son," she told Heinrich. "He was barred entry every time he tried. I used to think he was going to academic conferences whenever he went away, but he was trying to rescue you, his son."

Heinrich's eyes filled with tears. "It can't be," he cried. "It can't be."

"You're my brother, Heinrich," she said with a smile. "I had to help you."

Heinrich reached out his arms to hug her and sobbed in her arms; the most powerful cry he had ever experienced. All the grief he experienced couldn't overcome the emotion he felt. Greta comforted Heinrich and held him close. While it was an emotional meeting for Heinrich, it was a joyous one for her.

After some time, Heinrich's sobs subsided, and he let go of his sister. "Thank you," he said. "Thank you for everything. I've treated you so poorly."

"Nonsense," she said. "I should get you something to eat. You must be starving. Then we'll take you to my priest, and he will pray for you."

"I would appreciate that."

"I'll be right back," she said. She went to the kitchen. She first fed her kitten, who made it known she was hungry. She threw a breakfast burrito from the freezer into the microwave for both her and Heinrich.

While it cooked, she went to freshen up in the washroom. She switched the light on and turned on the tap.

She bent her face forward to the sink and splashed water on her face. When she finished, she turned off the tap. She looked at herself in the mirror, but instead of her own reflection, she observed the face of a demonic figure. It startled her, knocking her to the floor with its eyes looking like they were filled with blood. On its head were sharp horns, but not like that of any animal. It had no lips, but instead its face looked like it consisted of bare muscle tissue. It had no nose, but it looked murderous and threatening. It spoke in a warped high-pitched voice that didn't match the fierce anger that burned within its eyes. "*Under no circumstances are you to help the fallen soul. He is the property of Lucifer, and should you attempt to interfere with the devil's possession, rest assured, your soul shall be damned for eternity. If you refuse to be warned, you will face the consequences not only in this life, but the next life.*"

Greta prayed: "Saint Michael the Archangel, defend us in battle; be our protection against the wickedness and snares of the devil. May God rebuke him, we humbly pray: and do thou, O Prince of the Heavenly host, by the power of God, thrust into hell Satan and all the evil spirits who prowl about the world seeking the ruin of souls. Amen."

Greta looked up from the floor. The demon had disappeared. She pulled herself up. She saw no reflection but her own. She left the bathroom and returned to her bedroom. "Heinrich, we have to leave now," she said as she shook him. He had dozed off again. "We have to go."

Heinrich stirred. "Where am I?" he asked Greta.

"You're in my bedroom," she said as she pushed

273

him. She was confused how he could have forgotten already. "You're safe. For now. But we need to get you to the parish." She scrambled to her closet to find something to fit him and his bare chest. Heinrich rose from the bed and sat on its ledge. She found sweatpants of hers for him, even if it was tight.

"You mustn't interfere with the plans of the Master of Hell," said the demons cryptically through Heinrich. She shifted to see Heinrich sitting motionless, but his eyes looked bloodshot. It sent a chill up her spine. She backed into her closet out of fear when Heinrich's eyes changed again. "Please! It's not me. It's them. They are overtaking me—"

"I will get you help!" she said. She threw the sweatpants and a hoodie she found next to him. "Put these on. I will be right back."

She exited the bedroom and went straight to her telephone near the top of the stairway.

"You will not stand in the way of Lucifer!" shouted the demons from Heinrich's mouth.

She dialed her priest's phone number as quickly as possible, but her fear caused her to misdial the first time. She tried again, and it rang. A church secretary answered it, and Greta demanded to speak to Father Cavanagh. She was connected with haste. "Father Cavanagh, please! Can you come to my house?" she begged.

"What is it, my child?" the priest replied.

"There's something terrible going on again," she pleaded. Her cat screeched. Greta twirled from the phone for fear that the demons were doing something to her cat. Instead, the cat ran out of her room and showed its teeth to Greta while coming at her. It lunged at her, clawing at her face, which caused Greta to lose her balance and scream.

As she fought with her cat, she slipped off the top step of the stairway, sending her down the stairs. She felt a painful crack in her back as she tumbled down the stairs. Her neck made a snapping sound. One of her legs impacted every step on the way down. She screamed in pain until she landed with a hard thud at the base of her stairs. As she lay there, she made no sound but stared at the ceiling with wide, pain-filled eyes.

Heinrich rose and left the bedroom to see what havoc was caused. The kitten stood at the top of the stairs, licking its paws like nothing had happened.

You have caused this, screamed Legion. *It is you, who have wrought this carnage upon this woman.*

Greta lay on the floor in a crumpled mess. Her right leg was behind her head. She was contorted, but in far too much pain to even cry. How she was even conscious was impossible to understand. Heinrich descended the stairs to attend to her. "I'm so sorry, Greta," he whimpered. He wasn't sure if he should touch her. He feared himself more than ever and what other harm he might cause her.

"Heinrich…" she said, gasping in pain. "Talk to Father Cavanagh. He can help you. It's your only hope. He's coming; I know he is."

Father Cavanagh shouted Greta's name through the phone's speaker as its cord hung swinging back and forth. Heinrich climbed back up the stairs to grab hold of the phone. He drew it to his mouth, "Father, please help me!" he pleaded into the phone.

"Who is this? Who is speaking?" demanded the priest through the phone.

"*We are Legion, for we are many, and as many, we have come to destroy,*" the demons said as they overpowered Heinrich's voice. "*Fuck yourself with the cross, adulterating slave of that whore Mary. Stay away from this place.*"

Father Cavanagh hung up the phone. Heinrich was in anguish with what was happening inside of him and his inability to control himself any longer. He had to leave. He descended the stairs and stepped over Greta.

"Don't leave," she said in mustering all her little strength as she spoke. "He's coming—"

"I'm sorry, Greta," he said. "I will only harm you. *Silence you faithless woman!*"

"Heinrich!" she whimpered with a weak cry.

XLIII

Heinrich fled Greta's apartment in her sweatpants and hoodie. He bawled. He felt like a condemned man on the run with no place to go. He avoided eye contact with any who passed him as his eyes were bloodshot. Heinrich was so distraught that those who passed by him made a point of walking as far away as possible from him on the sidewalk. Heinrich gazed before him, and a subway station escalator withdrew to the underground.

Heinrich descended and shoved his way through the crowd with force. A subway train came into the station as masses of people exited and entered the train. Heinrich stood at the edge of the station ledge and watched trains come and go. He didn't get on a single one of them. The rushing wind flowed around him as he stood there. It provided momentary relief from the agony upon his soul.

This is the only fitting end for the beast you have become, said Legion.

"I'm not the animal you think I am!" Heinrich said out loud, which drew strange glares from passersby. "I am not an animal!"

You are nothing more than an animal with a corrupted soul. No better than the dogs that roam the streets looking for whatever scraps or filth with which they might satisfy themselves.

"I am a human being!" he shouted. He alarmed others in the station with his behavior, drawing someone to call for security.

There is no redemption for you; not even the Almighty One could forgive a soul that has done what you have done, let alone a soul sworn to Hell with all the other demons and sinners who reside there.

Heinrich teared up as he collapsed under the persistent attacks. He was too weak to protest further.

You are the worst of all sinners; you've destroyed the lives of countless others at your own gain. You remember that whore to whom you gave your virginity. She is dead. We dumped her body in the Hudson after you had your way with her. And those three women that you ravaged in a drunk rage? All dead. Their families will never hear from them again. And what of Jezebel? Her spouse killed himself and then she turned the gun on herself. And your brother and his son, what have you wrought upon them? And now, you've caused the destruction of one of the Almighty One's servants! You are destined to Hell for eternity. The Almighty One will take pleasure in damning you a second time. You are filth.

Heinrich was filled with such despair that he sought an end to his suffering. He couldn't bear it anymore. A train was coming. He panted and prepared for what he was about to do.

"Hey man! Are you all right?" asked a male by-stander approaching Heinrich. He peered into Hein-rich's eyes and recognized reckless intent. "What's going on? You need to talk?"

The train came closer, and Heinrich ignored the man, readying to jump.

"Don't do this, buddy!" said the bystander. "I don't know what you're going through, but it ain't worth it!"

The train was almost in the station, and Heinrich went to jump, causing the bystander to leap and grab hold of Heinrich's hoodie. He yanked him out of the way of the train with which Heinrich seemed destined to come to his end. The bystander caused Heinrich to fall backward onto the station platform. Heinrich was in shock as the bystander fell on top of him. "Are you okay?" the man asked.

Heinrich looked into the man's compassionate eyes.

"Everything will be okay," the man said. "You're safe now."

"Who are you?" asked Heinrich.

"Mike," the man said. Heinrich lifted himself up. "Hey, hold up! Help is coming!"

"I can't stay here!" shouted Heinrich. He clawed at his ears as the demons screamed at him for his failure to end his life. He fled from the bystander who gave chase, but Heinrich sprinted away.

"I can help you!" the bystander shouted in futility.

XLIV

Heinrich kept running in no particular direction. Something in his legs just made him run hoping to flee the demons tormenting him. He terrified people everywhere he went until he retreated to shelter in an alleyway out of the sight of passersby.

As he leaned against a building wall, he gazed down the alley opposite from where he entered it. A hospital entrance identified itself as a Catholic hospital. His thoughts went to Greta. He feared that he had killed her, his only living blood relation. He needed help, and she was the only one who understood what he was going through.

The demons raged inside of him to tell him to stay out of the hospital; it only confirmed that she must be there and that she must be alive. He stumbled his way over. She had to be be there. He passed through the automatic doors and presented himself to the front desk. He asked if a person named Greta stayed at the hospital.

"We have a Greta here," said the nurse in a bureaucratic manner. "What is your relation?"

"We are family," said Heinrich, which warmed his battered heart by speaking it out loud.

"Can you specify?"

He panicked. He had nothing to prove that they were family. He didn't even know his family name. "I'm her brother," he said. He wondered if the nurse believed him, but in case she didn't, he spoke further and lied. "I've looked all over for her. I've been calling her cellphone, and she wasn't at home. I've been so worried."

The nurse paused, but relented. "She is in the Intensive Care Unit; room number 777."

"Thank you so much," he said to the nurse who smiled at him after being all business beforehand. He scampered over to the elevator to go to the seventh floor. Once there, he marched his way down the corridor in search of room 777.

It is much too late. She is already dead. You've killed her.

"Shut up!" Heinrich shouted, but quietened himself down. He wanted no one to think him a crazy person. "They don't put dead people in the ICU."

He found room 777, but the door was locked. He looked through the window to see Greta lying there on a hospital bed with too many tubes to count hooked up to her. Her neck was in a brace. Bruises were all over her face and arms while her right leg hung in traction. Heinrich grimaced. He knew the role he had played in her present suffering. He searched for a doctor to let him in. When he found one, the doctor told him it wasn't the time for visiting hours and that Greta was resting.

"If you want to come back in two hours, you will be welcome to return," the doctor told Heinrich.

Heinrich waited. The demons tried to persuade him to leave. He was a murderer and a damned one at that. The two hours seemed like an eternity because of the verbal jarring from the demons. This time, they seemed restrained from their previous capabilities. Heinrich didn't understand why.

You have two options: one, finish the job, or two, leave now.

Heinrich again refused. The demons tormented him, but he fought against succumbing to their nagging condemnation. When the two hours had passed, the doctor told him he could enter. Heinrich stepped through the door. She didn't stir as he entered. She looked asleep. He sat next to her hospital bed and tugged the chair closer. She wasn't much different from him, in that, neither of them had anyone there for them at their lowest but each other. Tears filled his eyes as he mulled over all the pain she must be in. She had done nothing wrong, except for crossing paths with him.

"I'm sorry," he said, wiping a tear from his eyes. "I'm so sorry."

He grasped her hand. He was careful not to disturb the IV tube connected to her. "I'm sorry for everything I've brought upon you," Heinrich whispered. "I'm sorry for ever tripping on that damned briefcase and having you reach out to help me. I wish you ignored me like everyone else has. Perhaps you'd be okay if I never came to New York City. All I've ever accomplished is bringing pain and suffering into others' lives, and for that, I'm sorry. Especially since all you ever did was the opposite for me."

You're wasting your time, Legion shouted. *She will never forgive you. What you have done is unforgivable.*

Heinrich ignored the voices, not even acknowledging them, but continued speaking. "I'm sorry for how I have harmed you, Greta. But I also wanted to say thank you for caring about me and reaching out. You're the only one who has ever cared about me in ways beyond mere words. You risked your own well-being for me, and now I can't help feeling like all I've done is repay you with misery and agony. I'm so sorry."

Heinrich studied her battered face and wished he could make her better. "You know, when I made the deal with the devil, meeting someone like you is what I wanted deep down, Greta," he confessed. "Not the sex, lust, and pleasure I asked Lucifer for, but I said I wanted those too, so I guess I have to take responsibility for that. All I ever wanted though was the friendship and kindness of a stranger. I never experienced that until I met you. But I guess you aren't a stranger."

Heinrich listened to the heart monitor beep. She still had a strong pulse it seemed. "Maybe if things were different, in perhaps a different life, a different place, or a different time, we could've been the brother and sister we were meant to be," said Heinrich with a hopeful smile. A self-loathing thought came after it. "Even though I don't know what I could offer you as a brother…"

Greta stirred from her slumber. She opened her eyes.

Heinrich leaned in closer but backed away for fear of scaring her. She didn't look startled at all. "Heinrich," she murmured in pain.

"Should I leave you?" he asked, worrying that the sight of his face might terrify her.

"Don't go," she whispered.

Heinrich teared up again. He didn't understand her. "How is it even now, you can be so caring after all I've done to you?"

She grimaced, as she shifted her eyes toward him. She struggled to move with her neck brace and her leg restrained in traction. "Because. You're my brother," she whispered.

Heinrich smiled.

"You have our father's eyes, Heinrich," she said. "You were the one that my mom suffered in agony for having lost. It was too much for her; she felt like she failed by losing you and then giving birth to me, I suppose."

"Don't be ridiculous," said Heinrich. "She had to have loved you."

"I've always struggled to forgive my mom for abandoning me, but when I met you, and it hit me that you're my brother, it all made sense."

"What do you mean?"

"She couldn't forgive herself for losing you and leaving you behind. When you came to my door yesterday, you terrified me. But I couldn't abandon you in the same way. I had to help you."

Heinrich grasped her hand. He hoped she would recover. It wasn't fair to see her suffer so.

"Daddy never forgave himself for leaving you. He

never did," she confided.

Heinrich's emotions overcame him. For the first time in his life, he experienced love. The love of his blood, the love of his own flesh. He sobbed and leaned his head onto her bed. She stroked his head and ran her fingers through his hair. He cried for what was several minutes until his tears let up.

"I love you," she whispered.

Heinrich tried to say it back to her but struggled with his words. He had never found someone else to say it to who had already said it to him. Twice he tried to repeat it back to her before he could. "I love you too, Greta."

She grimaced and closed her eyes.

"Are you in much pain?" he asked.

"It's difficult to think of anything but the discomfort," she confessed. She winced again.

The heart monitor changed its beat, causing an alarm to go off. "Greta? Are you all right?" Heinrich asked, as his own heart rate increased.

"Heinrich!" she said in a barely audible voice.

He stood and stuck his head out of the door, "Can we get a doctor here?" he pleaded with a shout. He turned back to his sister, "Stay awake, Greta!"

Her breathing became labored as Heinrich embraced her hand. She struggled to maintain consciousness. "Greta, stay awake!"

A team of nurses and a doctor rushed through the doors to attend to her. They told him to back away. Greta held his hand. He didn't want to let go of her.

"Back away!" said a large male nurse, who restrained Heinrich. Greta and Heinrich's hands separated.

"Greta!" he screamed. "Don't fall asleep!"

"Sir, you will have to leave," said the male nurse.

"Don't leave me!" he shouted over the nurse to Greta. The heart rate went flat and gave a constant off tone. The doctor administered CPR to resuscitate her heart with the help of the nurses. Heinrich howled in agony. He knew what it meant. After several more tries, the doctor called off the attempt. They declared Greta as having passed with a time of death at 759PM. Heinrich collapsed into the chair just outside ICU room 777.

Heinrich sobbed and sobbed. His sorrow knew no end. He blamed himself for her death. There again, he was alone.

A man in black approached the door but stopped before entering. He placed his hand on Heinrich's shoulder. "Are you all right, son?" asked the man.

Heinrich looked up to see a priest. Heinrich wiped tears from his face. "Are you Father Cavanagh?"

"Yes, I am," said the priest.

"You're too late," said Heinrich between sobs. "She has passed."

The priest looked shocked, but entered the room to speak to the doctor. The doctor nodded that Greta had passed. The priest hustled over to Greta's bed. Heinrich watched from outside the room. The priest administered the Last Rites upon Greta. Tears still poured from Heinrich's eyes for having lost his last blood relative.

Once the priest finished with the Last Rites, he sat down next to Greta and prayed. He held the dead girl's hand. After spending ten minutes with the girl, he rose from his chair. The priest's eyes were wet. As he was about to pass, Heinrich tugged the sleeve of the priest's jacket.

"Father, can you help me?" Heinrich asked. "Please help me!"

The Father settled next to Heinrich and gave him his attention.

"Greta was attempting to help me when she fell down the stairs," he confessed. "She was my sister."

"Greta had no family, my child," said the priest.

"As I thought, but Greta told me otherwise," he said. "How can this be?"

"Father, I don't understand myself," replied Heinrich, "but she wanted you to help me. She said you could help me."

"Why don't we go somewhere we can talk?" the priest invited Heinrich.

Heinrich agreed. The priest led them to the hospital cafeteria; not quite where Heinrich imagined they would go. The priest gave him his full attention and asked him to tell him his story.

While Heinrich shared, as he had with Greta, he found no judgment from the priest, even if it was a high-tale for any mortal soul to believe. He also shared how Greta convinced him they were related. Heinrich confessed everything he had done, even all the murders, the fornication, and his attempt at suicide a second time. He pleaded for the Father's help, as he was too weak to resist the devil alone.

"Father, would God be able to forgive a sinner like me?"

"The Lord is compassionate and gracious, slow to

anger, and abounding in love," the priest replied.

"But can even He save me?" Heinrich asked. "I am so scared. I don't want to be away from Greta. I don't want to spend an eternity in Hell away from her while she lives in peace for an eternity with the Almighty One in Heaven."

"Listen, son," the priest said as he fixed on Heinrich's bloodshot eyes. "The Lord is exceedingly powerful. I have learned over the years to never pretend to decide what is and isn't possible with the Lord. I cannot deliver you alone, but with the Lord, there might be salvation had through prayer. I will help you. We will come to your home tonight. I need help; I cannot do this alone. The Lord will be with us."

XLV

This will not end well for you, for have you not forgotten that it is we who keep your heart going? Legion told Heinrich as he hunkered down in silence in the office chamber of Babel. He had barricaded himself in the room to ensure that Yousef and Bianca didn't disturb him.

"You cannot kill me!" Heinrich shouted. "You do not have power over the mortality of humans. Mephistopheles told me!"

The demons were drawn to silence before taunting Heinrich again. *Did not Greta die? Agony is before you should you continue down this path.*

"Do your worst!" Heinrich taunted Legion. "There is nothing you can take away from me, or do that has not already been done."

At once, Legion caused such a foul noise in Heinrich's mind that he clutched at his ears as if to silence the painful sound. Screams unheard of before in the earthly realm tormented his mind. It was near impossible for Heinrich to concentrate on anything but the noise. The sounds made it feel like knives stabbed his ears. Heinrich fell and writhed. His mental anguish was far worse than anything he had ever experienced at their hands. He crawled on his hands and knees within the chamber as he screamed in pain.

Heinrich fought for control of his mind. Amidst the agonizing screams of Legion, Heinrich clung to the image of his sister. The demon let up for only a moment as Legion taunted Heinrich. The spirit attacked him with an even greater vengeance. From Heinrich's vocal cords came the howl of a bear. Heinrich struggled to crawl as Legion made Heinrich's body twitch and contort against his will. He battled for control of his entire body, almost giving in against his will. Legion threw him to his stomach, but Heinrich resisted. The demon waged war for Heinrich's soul.

The agony lasted for the entire afternoon and early evening as Heinrich stood firm against the assaults of Lucifer's minions. Heinrich's whole body ached, and bruises and cuts marked his flesh. Around his ears, scratches from his fingernails drew blood as he had clawed at the sound. His chest cavity burned as Legion made Heinrich's heart beat faster.

Father Cavanagh arrived with two other priests. The entrance to the residence was barren. No security guard stood there, but the barricade beyond the doorway impeded their entrance into the office. Once they forced their way into the chamber, the priests found a complete mess of the furniture. Documents and papers were strewn throughout the space. Heinrich was curled into the fetal position in a far corner away from the desk. The satanic symbols and demonic imagery adorning the walls startled the priests. Father Cavanagh sensed the demon within Heinrich, as he writhed in pain with blood all over his body.

Father Cavanagh set the other priests, Father Flanagan and Father McNally, to work. Father Cavanagh instructed them to take hold of Heinrich. They grabbed him, but Legion made Heinrich resist their grip. Yet, they didn't let him go. They dragged Heinrich's body to the chair behind the desk but brought it around in front of the closed curtains. Father Cavanagh handed them ropes. "Heinrich Juarez, this is for your own safety," said the Father.

Father Cavanagh prepared them for the Rite of Exorcism. He told the others they were battling against time in a war for Heinrich's soul. He gave them instructions to dispose of the satanic symbols present in the chamber.

"*Leave them alone!*" howled Legion from within Heinrich. "*Or we shall kill whoever touches them. This is the domain of Lucifer!*"

"Ignore him, brethren!" shouted Father Cavanagh. "They have no power over you! This place must be rid of debauchery."

Nothing happened, save for Heinrich wrestling around in his chair as the priests disposed of the symbols. Heinrich bellowed animalistic screams and roars as if trying to distract them from the task at hand.

Once the priests were ready, they prepared each other with Father Cavanagh taking the purple stole and surplice. He traced the sign of the cross over Heinrich, which drew a demonic roar from him like that of an angry lion. Father Cavanagh made the sign of the cross over the other priests and himself. He sprinkled the holy water over Heinrich, which drew an even more foul scream from him. The water burned on his skin, causing sores to rise. Father Cavanagh sprinkled it on the other priests and himself.

After that, Father Cavanagh began with the Litany of the Saints with the other priests speaking in response. Little retaliation came from Heinrich's body as the priest began, but when they spoke of the Almighty One, Heinrich's body writhed. When it came to calling upon the saints, starting with the Saints Michael, Gabriel, and Raphael, the demon spewed verbal filth about each saint and cursed their names. Upon Saint John the Baptist, the spirit called him worm food. For Saint Joseph, Legion denounced him as a eunuch, of Saint Peter, a denier, of Saint Paul, an apostle killer. Of each saint, the demon showed disrespect to worsening degrees as the priests continued the Litany.

"From all evil, deliver us, O Lord," said Father Cavanagh as he gazed upon Heinrich with compassion. He carried on by asking the Almighty One for deliverance from sins through the resurrection of His Son before continuing with the Lord's Prayer. "Our Father, who art in Heaven—"

"*Nema. Live morf su reviled tub, noitatpmet otni ton su dael dna,*" bellowed the demon from within Heinrich in unison.

"Hallowed be thy name; thy kingdom come—" Father Cavanagh responded before being interrupted again by the spirit.

"*Su tsniaga ssapsert ohw esoht evigrof ew sa sessaapsert ruo su evigrof.*"

"Thy will be done on Earth as it is in Heaven—"

"*Daerb yliad ruo yad siht su evig.*"

"Give us this day our daily bread;—"

"*Nevaeh ni si ti sa htrae no enod eb lliw yht.*"

"Forgive us our trespasses as we forgive those who trespass against us—"

"*Emoc modgnik yht. Eman yht eb dewollah.*"

"And lead us not into temptation, but deliver us from evil—"

"*Nevaeh ni tra ohw,*" bellowed the demons in a thunderous voice, "*Rehtaf ruo.*"

"Amen."

The other priests peered upon Father Cavanagh in fear over what they overheard. They took a moment to realize what the demon had spoken. Weariness overcame Father Cavanagh. The demon mocked the Almighty One without fear of retribution. Father Cavanagh led them into a prayerful reading of Psalm 53 as Legion writhed and cursed the names of the priests.

"God, whose nature is ever merciful and forgiving, accept our prayer that this servant of yours, bound by the fetters of sin, may be pardoned by your loving kindness," said Father Cavanagh. He braced himself for the full display of the demon's power. "Holy Lord, Almighty Father, everlasting God and Father of our Lord Jesus Christ, who once and for all consigned that fallen and apostate tyrant to the flames of hell, who sent your only begotten Son into the world to crush that roaring lion; hasten to our call for help and snatch from ruination and from the clutches of the noonday

devil this human being made in your image and likeness. Strike terror, Lord, into the beast now laying
waste your vineyard. Fill your servants with courage to
fight manfully against that reprobate dragon, lest he
despise those who put their trust in you, and say with
Pharaoh of old: 'I know not God, nor will I set Israel
free.' Let your mighty hand cast him out of your servant, Heinrich, so he may no longer hold captive this
person whom it pleased you to make in your image,
and to redeem through your Son; who lives and reigns
with you, in unity of the Holy Spirit, God, forever and
ever."

"Amen," said the other priests in following Father
Cavanagh.

"*Christ be defiled!*" screamed the demon. "*You sinners
have no power over the servant of Lucifer—*"

"I command you, unclean spirit, whoever you are,
along with all your minions now attacking this servant
of God, by the mysteries of the incarnation, passion,
resurrection, and ascension of our Lord Jesus Christ,
by the descent of the Holy Spirit, by the coming of
our Lord for judgment, that you tell me by some sign
your name, and the day and hour of your departure. I
command you, moreover, to obey me to the letter, I
who am a minister of God despite my unworthiness;
nor shall you be emboldened to harm in any way this
creature of God, or the bystanders, or any of their
possessions."

"*You do not believe that, you of little faith!*" the demon
mocked Father Cavanagh. "*We will never be defeated; this
soul swore with an eternal, unbreakable oath to the devil that no
mortals, like you three shivering souls, have the power, capacity,*

or audacity to challenge!"

"Silence, demon!" shouted Father Cavanagh. "I command you, give some sign of your name, and the day and hour of your departure!"

"We are Legion, for we are many!" screamed the demon before taking control of Heinrich's body and breaking the ropes that the priests had bound and set upon him. It startled the priests who took a defensive step backward.

"Brethren!" Father Cavanagh called to the others. "Restrain the anguished soul!"

They leaped into action and seized hold of him. They thrust him back into the chair and re-tied the bonds.

Father Cavanagh laid his hand upon the head of Heinrich, "They shall lay their hands upon the sick, and all will be well with them. May Jesus, Son of Mary, Lord and Savior of the world, through the merits and intercession of His holy apostles Peter and Paul and all His saints, show you favor and mercy!"

The demon shrieked and kicked at the priest, knocking Father Cavanagh over. He got back up and out of danger. *"Fuck the Virgin! Fuck her Son! Fuck the Father, the Holy Spirit and their Malignant Offspring!"*

"Silence, unclean spirit!" Father Cavanagh called upon Legion, as he signed the cross over himself and Heinrich. It was terrifying doing so over Heinrich's brow, lips, and breast as the demon caused Heinrich to snap at Father Cavanagh. "When time began, the Word was there, and the Word was face to face with God, and the Word was God. This Word, when time began, was face to face with God. All things came into being though Him, and without Him there came to be not one thing that has come to be. In Him was life, and the life was the light of men. The light shines in the darkness, and the darkness did not lay hold of it. There came upon the scene a man, a messenger of God, whose name was John. This man came to give testimony to testify on behalf of the light. Meanwhile, the true light which illuminates every man, was making its entrance into the world. He was in the world, and the world came to be through Him, and the world did not acknowledge Him. He came into His home, and His own people did not welcome Him. But to as many as welcomed Him, He gave the power to become children of God to those who believed in His name; who were born not of blood, or of carnal desire, or of man's will; no, they were born of God. And the Word became man and lived among us; and we have looked upon His glory such a glory as befits the Father's only begotten Son full of grace and truth!"

"Thanks be to God," recited Father McNally and Father Flanagan.

"*The God-man be damned!*" Legion howled in a damnable voice.

"May the blessing of Almighty God, Father, Son, and Holy Spirit, come upon you and remain with you forever!" Father Cavanagh beckoned.

"Amen!" the other priests said before Father Cavanagh sprinkled Heinrich with holy water. Again, the water burned on Heinrich's skin; hot and producing perspiration. The demon that pilfered control of Heinrich's body felt every ounce of pain from the burning. Heinrich tried to regain control of his body, but Legion overpowered him.

"Almighty Lord, Word of God the Father, Jesus Christ, God and Lord of all creation; who gave to your holy apostles the power to tramp underfoot serpents and scorpions; who along with the other mandates to work miracles was pleased to grant them the authority to say: 'Depart, you devils!' and by whose might Satan was made to fall from heaven like lightning; I humbly call on your holy name in fear and trembling, asking that you grant me, your unworthy servant, pardon for all my sins, steadfast faith, and the power—supported by your mighty arm—to confront with confidence and resolution this cruel demon. I ask this through you, Jesus Christ, our Lord and God, who are coming to judge both the living and the dead and the world by fire."

"Amen," the priests replied.

Father Cavanagh again signed the cross over himself, and Heinrich. Legion recoiled and knocked Heinrich's chair from underneath him. The demon contorted Heinrich's neck to such a degree that the priests worried for the structural integrity of his neck.

Father Cavanagh stayed right on course, not to be dissuaded. He placed the end of the stole on Heinrich's neck and cast his right hand upon Heinrich's head. The demon again snapped at Father Cavanagh with hasty intent.

"See the cross of the Lord; begone, you hostile powers!" Father Cavanagh shouted at Legion.

"The stem of David, the lion of Judah's tribe has conquered," Father McNally and Father Flanagan uttered in support.

"Lord, heed my prayer," cried Father Cavanagh.

"And let my cry be heard by you," said the other priests.

"*The Lord does not hear your foul, filthy, and excremental prayers!*" the demon mocked the priests.

"The Lord be with you," Father Cavanagh said.

"May He also be with you!" the other priests echoed.

"God and Father of our Lord Jesus Christ, I appeal to your holy name, humbly begging your kindness, that you graciously grant me help against this and every unclean spirit now tormenting this creature of yours; through Christ our Lord," said Father Cavanagh.

"Amen!"

From Heinrich's body came a scream like the roar of a herd of hyenas. The demon threw Heinrich's body to the ground. An apparition manifested to the right of Heinrich, which caused Father Flanagan to step back in fear. Father Cavanagh stumbled to the ground in surprise.

"I am Lucifer!" bellowed the apparition, "and I alone possess authority over this soul. The Almighty One has no claim to this sinner's soul, for by the powers of free will, this soul is owed to me, and me alone, and I am not one to be denied the justice afforded to me."

"Brethren!" shouted Father Cavanagh. "Take hold of the tormented soul!"

The priests grasped Heinrich's arms to return him to the chair, but Legion beat them away. The demon gave Heinrich such strength he knocked them to the ground with one blow each.

Father Cavanagh rose again and thrust his cross forward. He presented it toward Lucifer, "The gates of

Hell shall not prevail against the authority and power of our Lord Jesus Christ. Begone, demon!" Father Cavanagh shouted as he forced himself closer, "You, Lucifer have received your payment and justice in full." The priest thrust the cross even closer toward Lucifer.

The hands of Lucifer's apparition were thrown to the ground, elevating objects in the room like Heinrich's chair, desk, and papers. Lucifer had them drop to the ground with a heavy thud. Lucifer scowled at Father Cavanagh and with a swirl of Lucifer's hands, the same objects lifted again and spun around the room. The other two priests took cover, but it was no use as the objects hit them and afflicted them. "No man shall have domain or power over me," screamed Lucifer in a fury.

Father Cavanagh struggled to stand up from his knees as a chair was launched into his head though it failed to knock him unconscious. Blood spilled from the side of his skull. Father Cavanagh screamed in righteous anger, "It is not the power of man that compels you to leave this place, but the power of Christ! Begone from this place, you father of lies!"

Lucifer stretched its arms out toward the two assisting priests. They levitated against their will. They screamed in sheer terror. Lucifer screamed in a soul-wrenching voice that sounded like that of a bear speaking, though screeching to the point that it was almost impossible to understand, "*You are not master over me, you are but a little lower than the angels. You come before me with sticks that I were a dog. I will feed you to the birds who will feast upon your flesh.*"

Lucifer threw the body of Father McNally against

the far wall, leaving an imprint on the wall. Father McNally dropped to the ground unconscious. Father Flanagan, Lucifer threw the opposite direction toward the window that overlooked New York City. Though the window was super-reinforced, it shattered as Father Cavanagh watched Father Flanagan fly through the window to fall to the street below.

Father Cavanagh stared in horror as his brother was gone from their sight.

"This residence is my abode, and the will of Lucifer shall abide, and I shall have domain over all who enter!" bellowed Lucifer. Painful boils covered Father Cavanagh's body. He screamed in pain. *"You shall fear me, servant of the Almighty God, and you shall leave this place or suffer my wrath!"*

Heinrich rose. He regained partial control of his body and looked upon Father Cavanagh, who never looked so terrified. Father Cavanagh picked up his boil-ridden body. He defied Lucifer and stood with the cross held in front of him. "You have no mastery over the flock of the Great Shepherd, you devil!" the priest shouted.

"Have you not seen the end of your brethren? You shall be my next victim, but you shall suffer greatly first!" Lucifer screamed. Lucifer seized possession of the cross in Father Cavanagh's hands, and in return, Lucifer used the cross to slash at Father Cavanagh. Lucifer drew blood from parts of Father Cavanagh's body. With each slash, Father Cavanagh screamed in pain.

Heinrich was moved with compassion for the priest, but his thoughts turned to personal condemnation toward himself. He had wrought this upon yet another innocent person, and as he focused on these thoughts, Legion retook control of Heinrich's body. The demon made Heinrich approach the down-trodden priest, as Father Cavanagh lay on the ground shielding himself from the attacks of the devil. Legion placed Heinrich's foot upon the priest's neck, which caused him to gasp for air. Heinrich pushed his foot firmer on the poor priest's airway. Heinrich screamed at Legion inside of his soul to resist and spare the priest, but Legion couldn't be overcome.

In one last pained gasp, Father Cavanagh cried out: "Saint Michael the Archangel, defend us in battle. Be our defense against the wickedness and snares of the devil!"

A blistering light shone through the broken glass of the window to the outside and instantaneously, Michael the Archangel appeared. The force of Michael's arrival thrust Heinrich and Legion off of the body of Father Cavanagh. Lucifer turned to Michael with indignation.

"You have no place here, Michael!" shouted the father of lies.

"Silence! The Almighty One has heard the cries of his flock!" Michael replied, taking steps toward Lucifer. Legion picked up Heinrich's body from the ground and ran at Michael the Archangel.

"Fitting we are to meet again, Michael!" screamed Lucifer. *"It has been too long since you turned your back on me!"*

"Speak not, lest you further impale yourself upon the Almighty One's sword of judgment," Michael commanded Lucifer. "You were well condemned. You know your end, and you know it is all you may look forward to now."

Legion leaped at Michael, knocking the Archangel to the ground. The two wrestled as Legion fed Heinrich's body with adrenaline to fuel greater strength. Father Cavanagh gasped and fed air into his oxygen-starved lungs. He watched in horror as Legion subdued his rescuer to the ground under the watchful eye of Lucifer.

"I shall enjoy seeing you suffer, Michael! You were far too great of a coward to ever realize your potential!" snapped Lucifer.

Father Cavanagh approached Father McNally and stirred him from his unconsciousness while Lucifer was distracted. When the latter priest awoke, the priests charged at Legion to restrain the demon from attacking Michael the Archangel further, but were knocked away.

"You cannot harm me, you wicked demon!" said Michael in between blows from Legion's fist.

The priests charged at Lucifer, but the devil threw the desk in their way causing them to stumble and fall on their heads. It knocked both of the priests into a daze. Lucifer directed Legion to step back and restrain the two priests while Lucifer cast its rage and anger on Michael.

Lucifer grabbed the neck of Michael and strangled the angel, but Michael made no fear of losing breath. The devil cast Michael from the chamber and out the window, but Michael didn't stay outside the building for long. Instead, the Archangel flew back into the chamber in a defiant posture. Lucifer spun to the restrained priests, *"Watch as you will see the demise of my hated enemy!"*

Michael and Lucifer became entangled in combat with each delivering painful blows. Lucifer's strategy was to destroy the angelic body of Michael and render the angel helpless. The priests' minds were alarmed as they sought to understand the powers of Michael and Lucifer in this spiritual battle.

"Go back to the Abyss, you demonic terror!" Michael shouted as the two wrestled.

"*I have no home to roam but the Earth and Hell while I await my final judgment,*" the Master of Hell said. "*Until then, I shall feast upon the souls of the Almighty One's creation. You have no power over me here on Earth, for I am the master of this world. The Almighty One allows it, and you know that you are powerless to stand in between me and my revenge against the Almighty One. You shall be destroyed before my end, and you will see your failure come before you, and the Almighty One will look upon you with shame and condemnation. You who rejected me in my quest that we might be gods above the creation made after the Almighty One's own likeness. Die now, Michael the Archangel!*"

At Lucifer's last word, Legion threw the priests to the ground. The demon bound the priests' hands in knots they couldn't break. Legion approached Lucifer to assist with the final dispatch of Michael the Archangel. The two demons beat upon Michael with such a fury that the priests wondered if it might be possible that Michael be dispatched from their presence. The two lords of the fallen realm so beat upon Michael the Archangel that Michael struggled to defend against the attacks. The priests cried out for Gabriel and Raphael, but they didn't appear. The priests cried out to the Almighty One for their salvation, that Michael might be saved, and the whole earth with the angel.

Through the barricade of the chamber came a familiar blue glow, which gave way to the blue apparition of Mephistopheles. The demon's apparition threw itself at Legion, which drew an angry glare from Heinrich's body. Legion threw Mephistopheles away, but Mephistopheles wasn't dissuaded and regrouped for another attack. Mephistopheles yanked Legion off of the Archangel, while Lucifer struggled with the commander of the Almighty One's Heavenly Army.

"Lucifer, cease your attacks, for you are defeated!" Mephistopheles shouted.

"Curse you, unloyal slave!" Lucifer shouted back. *"You who know no faithfulness!"*

Mephistopheles cast Legion and Heinrich's body across the chamber and rushed to the priests to free them from their bonds. The priests didn't understand what was going on. Legion rushed Mephistopheles and threw the apparition away from the priests. Legion attempted to restrain the priests again, but Mephistopheles intervened and tormented the body of Heinrich. Legion felt every blow from Mephistopheles. Lucifer was unaided by Legion, which enabled the Archangel, Michael, to regain its footing and thrust the demonic lord off.

Father Cavanagh stood over Heinrich's body as Mephistopheles and Legion battled against each other. The priest bled, but stood sure of his salvation despite his blood loss. He spoke with power against Lucifer and Legion, "Therefore, I adjourn you every unclean spirit, every specter from hell, every satanic power, in the name of Jesus—" the priest made the sign of the cross against Legion, "—Christ of Nazareth, who was led into the desert after His baptism by John to vanquish you in your citadel, to cease your assaults against the creature whom He has, formed from the slime of the Earth for His own honor and glory; to quail before wretched man, seeing in him the image of Almighty God, rather than his state of human frailty. Yield then to God!"

"Your day of reckoning is here, Lucifer!" shouted Michael the Archangel.

Lucifer retched where it stood while Legion threw Heinrich's body to the ground.

"Who by His servant, Moses, cast you and your malice, in the person of Pharaoh and his army, into the depths of the sea. Yield to God, who by the singing of holy canticles on the part of David, His faithful servant, banished you from the heart of King Saul!" commanded Father Cavanagh.

Mephistopheles had Heinrich and Legion restrained to the ground, though Legion fought to be freed from Mephistopheles, the weaker demon.

"Yield to God, who condemned you in the person of Judas Iscariot, the traitor. For He now flails you with His divine scourges, He in whose sight you and your legions once cried out: 'What have we to do with you, Jesus, Son of the Most High God? Have you come to torture us before the time?' Now He is driving you back into the everlasting fire, He who at the end of time will say to the wicked: 'Depart from me, you accursed, into everlasting fire, which has been prepared for the devil and his angels.' For you, O evil one, and for your followers there will be worms that never die. An unquenchable fire stands ready for you and for your minions, you prince of accursed murders, father of lechery, instigator of sacrileges, model of vileness, promoter of heresies, inventory of every obscenity!"

Heinrich's body contorted in such a manner it seemed as though Legion was intent on trying its hardest to bring Heinrich within an inch of his death.

"Remove the accursed ring from the sinner's finger!" Michael commanded the priests. "He bears the symbol of the devil's wickedness and must be ridden of it."

Lucifer howled in fury at Michael's command, *"Dare you not commit such an obscenity upon the domain of Lucifer! You shall not touch the cursed one, for you have no domain over him! He is mine!"*

Father Cavanagh spoke, while Father McNally reached for the ring as Michael instructed, "Depart, then, impious one, depart accursed one, depart with all your deceits, for God has willed that man should be His temple. Why do you still linger here? Give honor to God the Father, Almighty, before whom every knee must bow. Give place to the Lord Jesus Christ, who shed his most precious blood for man. Give place to the Holy Spirit, who by His blessed apostle Peter openly struck you down in the person of Simon Magus; who cursed your lies in Annas and Sapphire; who smote you in King Herod because he had not given honor to God; who by His apostle Paul afflicted you with the night of blindness in the magician Elyma, and by the mouth of the same apostle bade you to go out of Pythonissa, the soothsayer. Begone, now! Begone, seducer!"

Father McNally struggled to grab hold of Heinrich's hand to remove the ring, as Legion flailed Heinrich's hand in such a violent manner. When Father McNally grabbed a firm grip of Heinrich's hand, Lucifer unleashed a demonic scream, "*I shall destroy this soul before you take his soul from me! You will not free him; he shall be obliterated!*"

Lucifer sprang to attack Heinrich's body, but Mephistopheles pushed the devil off from approaching Heinrich's body. Michael also intervened and dragged the dark lord away, which allowed Mephistopheles to restrain Legion from resisting the priests' intervention. Lucifer broke free from Michael's grip and spoke a curse upon Mephistopheles, "*Cursed are you, Mephistopheles! Your service is rendered complete! Go forth unto the judgment of the Almighty One for your treachery!*"

The priests watched as Mephistopheles's apparition trembled and shook with fear. Mephistopheles attempted to resist enough that Michael might stop Lucifer, but lesser spirit screamed in horror. The demon knew that it was over. Mephistopheles spoke with a trembling voice, "*Dead are you, Lucifer, among all demons! Your punishment shall not be less than mine, but yours will bear the full weight and wrath of the Almighty One's fury against your sin!*"

Father McNally extracted the ring of Mr. Condannato off Heinrich's hand, which threw the possessed body into a satanic rage. Heinrich's body spun in circles on the ground, knocking the priests from their feet and to the ground.

"*Begone, demon! Take your place in the Abyss, and barred are you from ever returning to the Earth!*" shouted Lucifer at Mephistopheles, which caused the apparition of Mephistopheles to disappear into a blue cloud that was sucked into an invisible vacuum.

Heinrich's torso lifted from the ground as a stream of air passed from his chest. Blood poured from Heinrich's chest cavity. Heinrich screamed in pain, though this time it was his own voice, albeit raspy from the tormented sounds that Legion had made through him. Michael struck the head of Lucifer from behind and knocked the Commander of Hell to the ground. "I call upon the judgment of the Almighty One against this malignant spirit!"

"*Show yourself, Almighty One!*" shouted Lucifer from the ground. The spirit of Legion was extinguished from Heinrich's body and passed out from the broken window and out of the Earth. "*Show your face, you who rule in Heaven! Send not your servant, but show your face before me!*"

"The Lord owes you nothing, Lucifer!" Michael responded on the Almighty One's behalf. "You were served your judgment!"

"Send not my equal, who has no power over me—"

"I come with the power of the Almighty One and His blessing," said Michael as the angel wrenched Lucifer's neck.

"Your place is in solitude; your abode is in the nests of serpents; get down and crawl with them!" screamed Father Cavanagh at Lucifer, which resulted in the dark lord being thrown again to the ground by Michael. "This matter brooks no delay; for see, the Lord, the ruler comes quickly, kindling fire before Him, and it will run ahead of Him and encompass His enemies in flames. You might delude man, but God you cannot mock! It is He who casts you out, from whose sight nothing is hidden. It is He who repels you, to whose might all things are subject. It is He who expels you, He who has prepared everlasting hellfire for you and your angels, from whose mouth shall come a sharp sword who is coming to judge both the living and the dead and the world by fire!"

"You are condemned, oh wicked one!" shouted Michael as the angel constrained Lucifer's throat tighter. "Begone!"

A loud rushing of wind arrived in the room, shaking the entire building. The still hanging broken window shattered before the priests and crashed to the ground. Heinrich in a near unconscious state attempted to get up, but he was knocked to the ground. He grabbed hold of his chest as he screamed in pain from something happening inside of him. Lucifer also screamed as if in pain, but also in anger. Its loud screams sounded like that of a whirling wind as if the earlier howling bear drowned as it screamed.

In the hands of Michael, Lucifer's physical presence split apart with light shining through the apparition that Lucifer dominated. The priests covered their ears in terror and lay low to the ground. They covered their eyes as Michael constricted Lucifer more.

Heinrich screamed in torment as he realized his chest cavity was torn open. Though Legion was ridden from him, something else still needed to be drawn from his soul. His torso levitated again as his ribs broke with the last remnants of Lucifer's control being taken from him. Heinrich almost cried out that it was too much, but even this, he couldn't speak out over the torturous pain. It stopped, and his torso fell to the ground.

Michael departed from the chamber with the fractured physical presence of Lucifer over the angel's shoulder. As Michael fled with the devil, Lucifer screamed in terror at being dragged away by its archenemy, Michael the Archangel.

It fell silent, but not before the entire room crumbled around Heinrich and the priests. Father Cavanagh protected Heinrich from the walls falling to the floor. They feared the whole building might collapse, but it let up. The room was a rubble filled wasteland. Father Cavanagh covered Heinrich's chest with his hands but withdrew them to see that the scar had disappeared. His chest cavity was open, exposing his ribcage and his heart, but no satanic symbol was visible. It had been cut through.

"Father McNally!" shouted Father Cavanagh. "Come quickly!"

Father McNally crawled through the rubble and applied pressure to Heinrich's chest. The priest wondered if it might be futile. Father Cavanagh removed his robe and laid it upon Heinrich's chest and took over from the other priest. Heinrich winced from the pressure but was too weak to protest. Father Cavanagh attempted to gage the strength of Heinrich's pulse; it was weak. Heinrich drifted in and out of consciousness. Everything sounded like a muffle. He perceived from the streets below a distant wail of a siren before passing out.

XLVI

Heinrich awoke in a dazed state; his vision was not what it used to be. He struggled to make out anything with his eyes. Heinrich tried to focus, but everything moved as if he were underwater; he was weakened. He perceived Father Cavanagh in front of him, but he couldn't be certain.

A cold liquid was placed upon Heinrich's head. "Through this holy anointing, may the Lord in His love and mercy help you with the grace of the Holy Spirit," said the priest in a muffled sound.

An oily substance anointed Heinrich's hands. "May the Lord who frees you from sin save you and raise you up, and may you be reunited with your sister, Greta, in Heaven, Heinrich Falk," said Father Cavanagh. "Lord Jesus Christ, Redeemer of the world, you have shouldered the burden of our weakness and borne our sufferings in your passion and death. Hear this prayer for our sick brother whom you have redeemed. Strengthen his hope of salvation and sustain him in body and soul, for you live and reign for ever and ever."

Heinrich tried to say amen, but he was much too weak. Father Cavanagh led Heinrich in the Lord's Prayer. As the priest continued with the Viaticum, Heinrich realized that for the first time since returning to Earth, his mind rested in peace. The demons were no longer a part of him. It drew a weak smile from him, and afterward, his heart monitor went flat. Heinrich fell into the deep sleep that awaits us all.

About the Author

Joel Bain makes his home in Vancouver, Canada. His first novel, A BULLET FOR THE BRIDE, debuted in 2009, while his latest novel, EACH OUR OWN DEVIL, hit bookshelves in 2017.

He started Dumple Meadows Publishing in 2008, delving into a variety of platforms including fiction and digital magazines in the pursuit of developing and encouraging aspiring writers. He formerly held the role of Editor-in-Chief of Sour Grapes Winery from 2010-2014.

He is a graduate of the University of British Columbia (2009) with a B.A. in International Relations and English Literature. In 2016, he completed his Certificate of Editing from Simon Fraser University.

Among his writing interests are storytelling, social commentary, and film.

Follow and connect with him on Twitter: @joelbain

Visit his website: http://www.joelbain.com

Acknowledgments

My wife, Michelle, who pushes me without question to pursue this dream of writing. Your support and encouragement is what fuels me.

My precious son, Austin, who without him knowing pushes me to do this right. You in my life are my inspiration.

The #ameditingcrew, who have been a source of encouragement throughout this process. Thanks especially to Jessica Calla for reminding me to not martyr myself in the process of getting this book finished.

My readers, who kept pestering me for when my next novel would arrive. It's a relief I'm not writing these stories just for me, myself, and I.

Also by Joel Bain

A Bullet for the Bride
Previously released as Teardrops in the Rain

Each Our Own Devil